A DEADLY AFFAIR

A HOPGOOD HALL MYSTERY

E.V. HUNTER

Boldwood

First published in Great Britain in 2024 by Boldwood Books Ltd.

Cover Design by Rachel Lawston

Cover Illustration by Rachel Lawston

A CIP catalogue record for this book is available from the British Library.

Paperback ISBN 978-1-83561-329-0

Large Print ISBN 978-1-83561-330-6

Hardback ISBN 978-1-83561-328-3

Ebook ISBN 978-1-83561-331-3

Kindle ISBN 978-1-83561-332-0

Audio CD ISBN 978-1-83561-323-8

MP3 CD ISBN 978-1-83561-324-5

Digital audio download ISBN 978-1-83561-327-6

Boldwood Books Ltd
23 Bowerdean Street
London SW6 3TN
www.boldwoodbooks.com

1

'I thought the winter would never end.' Alexi Ellis leaned back in her chair and smiled as spring sunshine broke through a heavy bank of cloud, peppering the side of her upturned face with its warmth.

'Easter's coming up so don't hold your breath,' her oldest friend, Cheryl Hopgood, warned. 'The English weather seems to think it has a duty to rain on everyone's parade come bank holidays.'

Alexi waved a hand in casual dismissal of Cheryl's assertion. 'Not this year,' she decreed firmly. 'It wouldn't dare. We've had a quiet six months since that fiasco over Halloween and no lasting damage has been done to the hotel's reputation. We're overdue a break from drama, and that includes the weather.'

She was referring to Hopgood Hall, the boutique hotel in Lambourn in which she was an investor. The house had been in Cheryl's husband's family for decades but had been on the point of going out of business at the same time as Alexi had lost her position as an investigative journalist on the *Sunday Sentinel*. She had run off to Lambourn with her feral cat Cosmo to stay with Cheryl and Drew and lick her wounds. She hadn't reckoned on settling in the sticks, though. She was a city girl through and through with a nose for a story but had surprised herself by finding the peace she'd been unaware she was searching for here in the valley of the racehorse.

Unfortunately, since her arrival, not one but four murders had occurred in this sleepy backwater where horses outnumbered people and many locals now considered her to be a jinx. Some had gone so far as to try and drive her out of the village and at her lowest ebb, Alexi had been at the point of leaving, afraid that local superstition would have an adverse effect upon her friends' business. She was no quitter though and hadn't been responsible for any of the killings, so she'd allowed Cheryl to talk her out of leaving. Besides, with the help of Jack Maddox, an ex-Met police inspector turned private eye, she'd managed to find the culprits in all four of the murders. She and Jack were now an item and country life, she had good reason to know, definitely had its advantages. In any event, it most certainly hadn't proven to be the dreary existence she'd feared.

'Drew kept telling you that the publicity created by the murders and your fair reporting of the facts could only enhance the hotel's reputation,' Cheryl pointed out, leaping from her chair to pick up Verity, her eighteen-month-old daughter, when she took a tumble on the grass. She had been attempting to chase Cosmo. Alexi's cat was decidedly anti-social but knew better than to harm a hair on the precious baby's head. Instead, he glanced at Verity through piercing green eyes, as though checking to make sure that she was unharmed, and then twitched his rigid tail before stalking off. He was, as always, pursued by Toby, Cheryl's terrier who was half the cat's size but devoted to the taciturn feline. 'And you know my husband is always right about these things.'

'Well, of course he is. He's a man, isn't he?'

They both laughed. 'Not that we would still have a hotel if it weren't for your investment and innovative ideas to enhance our reputation,' Cheryl pointed out. 'Drew and I wouldn't have done anything half so daring, left to our own devices.'

'My innovative ideas, as you call them, almost finished you off,' Alexi replied, shuddering, 'but let's not go there.'

The ladies fell momentarily silent, watching Cosmo's black tail swishing as he crept through the undergrowth, presumably on the hunt for rodents that didn't have the sense to get out of his way. Toby spoiled the party by charging after him with enthusiasm and a distinct lack of stealth.

'Well anyway, we're full over Easter, regardless of the weather, and have an encouraging number of bookings coming in for the summer. Of course, half of them only want to meet his highness,' Cheryl said, nodding towards Cosmo. 'All the publicity over the murders has made him quite the celebrity.'

'Don't tell him that! He's already quite insufferable enough.'

Cheryl laughed. 'I suppose one thing that Rat Face did for you was to feature Cosmo in his Sunday rag and enhance his reputation, which worked in the hotel's favour, especially now that Cosmo has his own Instagram profile. He has more followers than either of us.'

'He only did it to curry favour.'

Alexi folded her arms and huffed. Any reference to Patrick Vaughan, the editor of the *Sunday Sentinel* who had been her significant other at the time the paper had downsized, still rankled. Patrick had known her position was under threat but hadn't warned her. Nor had he fought her corner. She knew that he regretted that stance now, having assumed that she would hide away in Lambourn, get bored and then return to the paper to take up the demotion that was on offer.

How little he understood her!

He'd been a perpetual thorn in her side since then, but all communication between them had finally come to an end when he and Cassie, Jack's business partner, had joined forces in an effort to have Alexi ostracised in Lambourn. Patrick had hoped that her unpopularity would force her to return to what she knew best. Their plan had almost worked too, thanks in no small part to Polly Pearson, a local B&B owner and famous gossip, who had led the campaign to drive Alexi away. What Alexi had done to set Polly against her remained a mystery.

But all of that was now water under the bridge. The *Sentinel* no longer benefited from her insight. Its competitors on the other hand lapped up everything she submitted, which hopefully embarrassed Patrick and made him realise the error of his ways.

'Well anyway,' Alexi said, smiling and tugging at one of Verity's pigtails when she tottered up to her and offered her a flower that she had plucked without bothering to include the stem. 'Thank you, darling. Is that for me?'

'She's a budding conservationist,' Cheryl said, beaming with pride.

'Might be a good idea to teach her about stems, in that case.'

Cheryl adopted an expression of mock censure. 'Rome wasn't built in a day.'

'I take your point. But as I was saying, everything's settled down now and no one is having the bad manners to get killed on our patch, so hopefully we can look forward to a calm and profitable summer.'

'I'd drink to that or would...' Cheryl words trailed off, but she grinned as she placed a hand protectively over her stomach.

'Cheryl?' Alexi eyed her friend with the dawning of awareness. 'What is it that you're not telling me?'

'Well...' Cheryl's smile widened. 'We didn't want to say anything until we knew everything was okay but...'

Alexi squealed, jumped from her chair and threw her arms round Cheryl. 'Verity is going to have a sibling. Wow! Congratulations! When?'

'Christmas.'

'That's fabulous.' Alexi resumed her chair. 'No wonder Drew has been grinning like the proverbial these past few weeks. I've been busy with the book,' she added, referring to a commission she'd accepted to write a collection of in-depth exposés about cases of abuse, corruption and violent crime in which the perpetrators had evaded justice. Stories that she had written for the *Sentinel* but which had not seen the light of publication because the paper's legal team weren't willing to risk being sued. An opportunity to lay out the facts and highlight the loopholes in the legal system pounced upon by expensive defence barristers was too good to resist. There was a lot to be said for going freelance, Alexi had long since discovered.

'The first draft is finished, but never mind all that. Your news is much more important and I want to know everything.'

'Not much to tell, other than I feel as sick as a dog every morning. So come on, give me more about the book. I want to know.'

'Well, I'm happy with it and now my editor is doing his thing. Time will tell if the publishers have the courage of their convictions, no pun intended. I've given them what they asked for and hopefully they won't be as lily-livered as the paper was. Besides, I don't think I've said anything libellous.' She grinned. 'Provocative perhaps but that's a different beast. Provocation equates to soundbites which equate to sales. Anyway, I shall be on hand to be the best aunt in the world when your time comes. Is Drew hoping for a boy this time?'

'He says he doesn't mind but I think he secretly would prefer a son.'

Alexi nodded. 'Might be best. He's so besotted with Verity that I can't see him having enough love to spare for another daughter.'

'Hey, I'm a big guy.' Huge arms wrapped their way around the back of Alexi and Cheryl's necks. For a large man, Drew moved with surprising stealth and had obviously overheard their conversation. 'And I have more than enough love to satisfy all the women in my life.'

Alexi jumped up again and hugged him. 'Congratulations!'

'Ah, so she has told you, not left you to guess. I suggested holding off for a bit longer, just until we're sure everything's definitely okay, but I knew she wouldn't be able to resist sharing.'

'And why should she?' Alexi asked, watching Verity as she ran up to Drew and he crouched down to catch her between his large hands, swinging her in the air and making her giggle. 'You've played your part. It's Cheryl's turn to enjoy herself.'

Drew pulled a disapproving face. 'I hope you're not implying that she didn't enjoy making the brat.' He waggled his brows at her. 'It takes two, you know.'

'So I've been told. Never been tempted to embrace motherhood myself. The mere thought of all that responsibility terrifies me.'

'You'd never met the right man before Jack came along,' Drew replied, taking the chair next to his wife and watching Verity as she tottered after Cosmo and Toby.

'We were just speculating upon a profitable summer for Hopgood Hall,' Alexi remarked.

'And it will be too, thanks to you. Lots of conference jollies booked for the annexe.' Drew paused to rub his chin. 'And organised tours of training yards, which was also your suggestion.'

'Well, trainers always seem to be short of dosh, despite the outrageous fees they charge, so it made sense to ask a few of them if they wanted to participate.'

'We tried it a few years back, before the pandemic, and they all turned their noses up.' Drew shrugged. 'Seems they're now as broke as the rest of us and no longer quite so elitist.'

Alexi smiled. 'How the mighty have been brought back to earth.'

'When's Jack back?' Drew asked. 'He's been away on his latest assignment for ages. I've forgotten what he looks like.'

'It's all done. He's reporting to his client in person today, clearing up some paperwork and then he'll be home.'

'To make babies,' Drew suggested, waggling his brows again.

Alexi laughed. 'We're not all set on procreation,' she pointed out. 'The world is quite over-populated enough.'

'Seems to me he's too busy to spare the time to make babies, even if you wanted to,' Cheryl said. 'We barely see him.'

'Oh, he prioritises,' Alexi assured her friends.

Drew grinned. 'I'll just bet he does!'

'Anyway, he and Cassie have decided still to work together.'

'After the way she tried to get you out of Jack's life?' Cheryl pulled an affronted face. 'How will that work? The trust must be gone. And more to the point, how do you feel about it? The last time we broached the subject, you said they were considering their future. I just assumed that he'd either go out on his own or find someone else to take over Cassie's position.'

'It's more complicated than that.' Alexi waggled a hand from side to side. 'Nowadays, a lot of investigation is done online. Jack hates that and prefers to be out and about, sticking his nose in and acting on instinct. Cassie, on the other hand, can make computers sing for her.'

'Point taken.'

'Besides, they're equal partners. If they split then they'd have to value the business, somehow, and one would have to buy the other out. Not sure either of them can afford to do that. Anyway, it was me who persuaded him to think carefully and not to act in anger.

Cassie is not my favourite person, but she was manipulated into doing what she did by the hand of a master.'

'Patrick,' Cheryl said, grimacing.

'Patrick,' Alexi agreed. 'He picked up on Cassie's partiality for Jack and her resentment of me and once he had, she'd have been putty in his hands. They've had a good heart to heart, and Jack is as sure as he can be that Cassie won't step out of line again. Patrick had convinced her that I would tire of life in the country, and run back to London. Cassie believed it because she wanted to.'

'She thought she was protecting Jack from getting his heart broken,' Drew said. 'I can see how she would have bought that because I know just how convincing Patrick can be.'

'Well anyway, business is booming and they're going to hire another investigator to take the load off Jack.'

'Good news,' Drew said, leaping from his chair and catching Verity moments before she took another tumble.

As though aware that he was being talked about, Jack chose that moment to wander into the gardens.

'Hard at work, I see.'

Alexi's heart lifted at the sound of his voice. She turned slowly to smile at him, appreciating the sight of him in jeans and his signature leather jacket that had definitely seen better days. His hair was a little too long and flopped over eyes hidden behind dark glasses. He had absolutely no idea just how sexy he looked without putting any effort into it and Alexi wondered, not for the first time, what she'd done to deserve him.

'Always,' she replied, lifting her face to receive his kiss.

Jack dragged up another chair and placed it beside Alexi's.

'There are police cars all over the village with lights flashing and sirens sounding,' he said. 'Glad to see they weren't headed in this direction for once.' He grimaced. 'I did worry, just for a moment.'

'Don't even joke about such things,' Cheryl scolded. 'Alexi and I were just contemplating the murder-free summer that's in front of us.'

'Too right,' Jack agreed, leaning back in his chair and crossing one foot casually over his opposite thigh.

'The police are probably on the trail of horse thieves,' Drew said. 'I hear a couple have gone missing from a trainer's yard.'

'I thought they were better protected than the country's gold reserves,' Alexi said. 'Alarms, cameras, electronic gates... the works.'

'Where there's a will,' Drew said, shrugging.

'Aren't the horses chipped, like dogs are?' Cheryl asked. 'I mean, how could they be sold on?'

'Stallions could be used to do what they do best and a decent mare with a track record could be used as a baby machine, I'm guessing,' Jack replied. 'No idea. I'm definitely off duty.' He linked his hands together behind his head. 'And I'm taking a long overdue week off to give some attention to my girlfriend.'

'Talking of baby machines,' Drew said, grinning.

'Drew, I am not the maternal type. How many more times? We don't all want little people running around causing mayhem,' Alexi said, smiling in spite of herself.

'Keep telling yourself that,' Cheryl said.

'Alexi and Drew are expanding their family,' Alexi told Jack. 'Verity will have a sibling come Christmas.'

'Congratulations!' Jack righted himself in his chair, stood up and shook Drew's hand, then gave Cheryl a hug and kiss. Cosmo stalked up to Jack and pushed his head under his hand, as though not wanting to be left out. Jack laughed as he made a fuss of him.

'Do you fancy going away somewhere for a few days?' Jack asked Alexi once the subject of the new arrival had been exhausted. 'I was thinking the Lakes. I'm sure they must have cat-friendly hotels up there.'

'There's cat friendly and then there's Cosmo,' Drew pointed out. 'He's not for the fainthearted. You know what he's like if he takes against a person.'

'He's mellowing with age,' Alexi said defensively, making them all smile. 'And yes, a few days away would be lovely. We've both got relatively clear desks at present, so the time is right.'

'Yep, and we have a new investigator, so anything that comes in over the next week or so will be his problem.'

'Who did you go for in the end?' Alexi asked, aware that there had been a number of applicants for the position.

'Danny Fisher.'

Alexi nodded. 'I thought you would. Better the devil you know.'

'Precisely. We worked together at the Met,' Jack explained to Cheryl and Drew. 'He had my back when the press tried to stitch me up and the head honchos hung me out to dry. He's disillusioned himself with the direction the police service has taken and has opted for early retirement. But at forty-five, he's too young to sit about twiddling his fingers. He's not married any more. Like a lot of serving officers, his marriage didn't survive the anti-social hours. His kids are grown and he's a free agent, happy to move to Newbury.'

'Does Cassie like him?' Alexi asked.

'She seems to. Anyway, we're agreed that he fits the bill and so he starts on Monday.'

'Does he need temporary accommodation, while he gets himself sorted?' Cheryl asked. 'We can arrange something.'

'Thanks, Cheryl.' Jack nodded at her. 'I'll mention it to him. Not sure what he's got sorted.'

'Probably hasn't even thought about it,' Alexi said, rolling her eyes.

'It will ease the tension between you and Cassie with someone else on the team, mate,' Drew said.

'Amen to that,' Jack replied with feeling.

A commotion had them all turning in the direction of the hotel's back door. A woman who Alexi recognised but had never expected to see setting foot on Hopgood Hall's property flew through the open door, waving her arms in the air, tears streaming down her face.

'You have to help me!' Polly Pearson, Alexi's main detractor cried. 'I'm being accused of murder.'

2

Jack was the first to recover from the shock of Polly's arrival, to say nothing of her dramatic announcement, which explained the police presence he'd noticed as he'd driven through the village earlier. They were in the part of the garden reserved for the family, but a couple of the hotel's guests were strolling about in the formal gardens on the other side of the privacy hedge. Polly's arrival had drawn their attention and sensing an unfolding drama, they'd instinctively wandered closer.

'Let's talk in the kitchen,' Jack said, placing a hand on the small of Polly's back and steering her in that direction.

He glanced at Alexi, nodded towards the lingering guests and could see that she'd caught on. He could also sense her resentment at Polly's intrusion. That was hardly surprising, given the way she'd bad-mouthed Alexi so openly. Jack had no idea whether he'd agree to help her and would hear her out before deciding.

Polly was a tall, slim woman and Jack estimated her to be in her mid-forties. With her tear-stained, ravaged face, she looked more like sixty at that precise moment. Her shoulder-length, blonde hair showed signs of greying roots and mascara followed a line of wrinkles down her cheeks.

Once in the kitchen, into which Cosmo, always alert to a drama, had preceded them with Toby in his wake, Jack ushered Polly towards a chair at the scrubbed, pine table. Cosmo stalked up to Polly, regarded her for a prolonged moment, twitched his rigid tail in a gesture of disapproval and let out a warning hiss before retreating to Toby's basket and taking up the majority of the space. Toby wagged his stubby tail as he occupied the small corner that Cosmo graciously left for him.

'Sit down before you fall down,' Jack told Polly.

Polly did so, snuffling into a handkerchief and dabbing at her eyes. Drew poured a healthy measure of the brandy he kept to hand for cooking purposes and passed it to Polly.

'Drink this for your nerves,' he said, his voice neutral. Like Jack, he was well aware of the angst that the spiteful woman's tongue had caused for Alexi and was clearly also reserving judgement now that she'd had the nerve to run to them for help in her hour of need. She definitely didn't warrant the expensive brandy kept behind the hotel's bar in Drew's estimation and Jack couldn't argue with that.

Jack glanced at Alexi, who stood just inside the door with arms folded defensively across her chest, her expression set in stone. Jack offered her a questioning look. He would send Polly packing without hearing her out if Alexi gave him the nod. She clearly understood and shook her head, which didn't altogether surprise Jack. Alexi had a big heart, understood the meaning of compassion, and was undoubtedly curious to know who'd been murdered and why Polly appeared to be the main suspect.

'Why did you come to us?' Alexi asked, her tone neutral, giving nothing away about her inner feelings.

Polly slurped the brandy too quickly. It made her cough. Alexi remained silent until she recovered, but Jack knew she wouldn't allow the woman to evade a question that she must have been expecting. A question that would help to decide whether or not she and Jack *would* help Alexi's nemesis.

'I... I didn't know where else to go,' she eventually replied, sounding both pathetic and desperate.

'And you assumed we would help you because...'

Polly had kept her gaze focused on Jack but now finally turned to look directly at Alexi. 'I'm sorry,' she said. 'I've been a bitch.'

'And then some,' Alexi replied. 'I have yet to figure out is what I did to you to deserve your spite.'

Instead of responding, Polly returned her attention to Jack. 'You have no idea who I am, do you?'

'Nope,' Jack replied without hesitation. 'Should I?'

'I've had the B&B in Lambourn for five years.' She paused, took another sip of brandy and swallowed it more cautiously. 'Before that, I worked at Holby's.'

'The headquarters of the countrywide logistics firm,' Cheryl explained. 'You see their trucks everywhere.'

Jack could see that Alexi had now caught on, as had he. 'You worked with my ex-wife, Grace, I take it?' he said caustically.

'And assumed I'd taken Jack away from her,' Alexi added, shaking her head in disgust when the penny dropped. 'Why the hell would you think that? You know nothing about me, or my relationship with Jack.' She threw up her hands.

'It's not that.' Polly spread her hands, attempting to explain the inexplicable. 'Grace and I were good friends. Surely you heard her mention my name?' She again glanced at Jack.

'I vaguely recall a mention of Polly, but I had no idea that person is you. I'm absolutely sure that we've never met.'

'You were still in the force, always working whenever there was a company do.' There was accusation in her tone, which Jack thought remarkable, given that she required his help and that his domestic arrangements were none of her business anyway.

'Not that it's any of your concern,' he said in an acerbic tone, 'but Grace and I were divorced long before I met Alexi.'

'You kept in touch with your friend,' Alexi said. 'Told her about Jack and me and decided to bad-mouth me out of a sense of misguided loyalty. Or did she ask you to do it? Anyway, why should I help you now that you find yourself in the middle of a murder?'

'I'm sorry.' Polly bowed her head and tears dripped onto the table's surface. 'Really I am.'

'I'll just bet that you are,' Alexi muttered.

Jack had never seen Alexi half so angry before. She was always more than ready to help anyone who genuinely needed it, but this woman's audacity had even taken his breath away and he thought he'd seen everything.

'Grace really regrets your breakup and was hoping you'd get back together once you left the force,' Polly said into the ensuing silence.

'I'm aware of that and she knows it will never happen.' Jack threw back his head and closed his eyes.

'Okay.' Alexi pulled out a chair across from Polly. 'There's no point dragging all that up. Let's get back to your reason for coming to us and establish the facts. Tell us who died and why you're a suspect.'

'My partner, Gerry Dawlish. He didn't come to breakfast this morning but that's nothing unusual. He's a driver for Holby's. That's where I originally met him, when I still worked there. We kept in touch and whenever his schedule brought him down this way, he'd stay with me. Our relationship grew from there.'

'Not so much a partner then,' Drew said. 'More a friend with benefits.'

Polly shrugged. 'I suppose. Anyway, he got in late last night.

Had probably driven for longer than he should have to keep up with his schedule, so I left him to sleep in. When he still didn't appear for lunch though, I went to wake him. I knew he had to be on the road again later today and that's...' She choked on a sob. 'That's when I found him on our bed with a knife through his chest.'

'Dear God!' Cheryl muttered.

'The blood. There was blood everywhere and the smell.' She started to cry again. 'I'll never forget the smell.'

'Did you check to see if he was still alive?' Jack prompted.

'I did, even though it was obvious from his staring eyes that he wasn't. Then I called the police and that's all I know.'

'Who came?'

'A patrol car at first and then a whole circus. Forensics, detectives...'

'Can you remember the name of the senior detective?' Alexi asked, glancing at Jack. They both wanted to know if it was DI Vickery. He was a personal friend of Jack's, had investigated the last three murders in Lambourn and was fair and methodical. Jack couldn't decide if he wanted him to be involved or not. If he wasn't then it would be easier for him to walk away and leave Polly to her fate.

'Vickery,' Polly said. 'I saw him here that last time at Hopgood Hall when that man was killed. Do you know him?'

'Tell us what initial conclusions he drew?' Jack said, avoiding giving a direct answer.

'He asked if anyone else had access to our room. I told him I have three rooms taken right now, our door to the street is never locked and nor is the one to my personal rooms so anyone could have got in there. DI Vickery didn't seem to take that onboard. He asked a lot of questions, like did anyone staying with me at present know Gerry or have any issues with him? He wanted to know if

Gerry and I had fought, which unfortunately we had the night before. He was drunk and loud and I suspect some of the guests would have heard him, which doesn't look good for me.'

'He drove his truck drunk?' Alexi asked, disapproval radiating through her voice.

'No. He'd parked up and been to the pub, I think.'

'Did they say how long he'd been dead?' Jack asked.

'Well, I told them he was alive and well when I got up at seven this morning but if they think I killed him then they won't take my word for that, I suppose.' She dashed at fresh tears with the back of her hand. 'Anyway, he was alive when I left the room, snoring loud enough to wake the dead, and I'll swear to that on a stack of bibles. Perhaps some of my guests heard the snoring through the walls,' she added, sounding as though she was desperately clutching at straws.

'The police want to talk to you again, I imagine,' Alexi said.

'I have to go to the station at eleven tomorrow to be interviewed under caution. I'm terrified.'

'Do you have legal representation?' Jack asked.

She blinked at him. 'Do I need it?'

Jack shook his head, surprised by her stupidity, which he put down to shock. 'You'd be an idiot if you didn't have someone there to protect your interests.'

'But I'm innocent!' she wailed. 'For all his faults, I loved Gerry. I thought we'd be together forever. I was sure he was building up to popping the question, then we could have run the B&B together. I could have got rid of my other part-time staff and turned a proper profit. We talked about it.'

'I'll give someone a call. A friend who might be able to help you,' Jack said, extracting his phone from his back pocket and pulling up Ben Avery's number. The gangly solicitor with a mop of unruly, red hair was often underestimated because he always looked so scruffy, so unprofessional, but Jack knew that he possessed a fierce intelligence. More to the point, he'd helped to exonerate suspects in the last two murders that had taken place in Lambourn when the odds had been heavily stacked against them.

'This is getting to be a habit,' Ben said, taking Jack's call.

He listened without interrupting as Jack explained the situation and agreed to meet Polly at the station at eleven the following morning.

'Tell her to say nothing until I get there and not to talk to anyone else about this,' was Ben's parting advice before ending the call.

'Ben Avery will meet you at the station tomorrow,' Jack told her. 'Don't say anything to anyone, especially not the police, unless he's there.'

Polly looked completely dazed but managed a feeble nod. 'Who would I talk to?'

'All your friends in Lambourn will want to know what happened,' Alexi pointed out.

'But they're my friends!' Polly wailed.

'You came to us for help and advice and if you don't take it then there's nothing we can do to help you.' Jack's voice was harsh.

'*If* we decide to help,' Alexi added.

Polly glanced at her. She looked shocked and ready to argue her corner. Presumably, she then recalled just how vindictively she'd vilified Alexi's name when she'd been in a similar position to the one that Polly now found herself in and closed her mouth again without speaking. Only Cosmo's occasional growls broke the uneasy silence.

'Alexi, I'm sorry,' Polly said, meeting Alexi's gaze and holding it.

Alexi let out a long breath. 'Apology accepted,' she said. 'I understand now that you thought you were protecting your friend's interests but it's worth bearing in mind that there are always two sides to every story.'

Polly lowered her head. 'I hear you.'

Jack and Alexi exchanged a glance. Alexi nodded and Jack knew she was prepared to help Polly, just as he'd suspected she would be now that they'd cleared the air, after a fashion. What malicious lies his ex-wife had been spreading to cause Polly to take Alexi in such extreme dislike was another matter entirely and one that bothered Jack more than he was prepared to let on.

'What happens now?' Polly asked.

'You could leave it to the police,' Drew said, clearly not nearly so ready to forgive and forget the harm that Polly had done to Alexi.

Polly shook her head. 'They think I did it and won't look too hard for anyone else. I could tell that from the look on that woman detective's face.'

'DC Hogan?' Alexi asked.

'That would be her.' Polly wrinkled her nose. 'She looked at me like something she'd scraped off the bottom of her shoe.'

Jack nodded, aware that Vickery was fairer than some coppers but even so, at face value, this case did look pretty open and shut.

'If you want our help, you have to be completely transparent. Are we clear?' Jack drilled her with a look. 'If you lie, or hold anything back, then you're on your own.'

Polly nodded.

Drew, with Verity still in his arms, nodded to Cheryl. 'We'll leave you to it, in that case,' he said.

'What do you need to know?' Polly asked when the door closed behind Drew, meeting Jack's gaze and holding it.

'Everything. To start with, the victim, Gerry: how long have you known him?'

'Seven or eight years. Like I say, we met at Holby's. He was popular with everyone. The life and soul. A handsome brute all the ladies adored but he was a man's man too, if that makes sense. Never seemed to fall out with anyone. He said bearing grudges was too much like hard work.'

Jack nodded. 'Go on.'

'Six years ago, my mum died and left me an inheritance. I'd always wanted to be in the hospitality trade, and I love horses so when the B&B came up for sale in Lambourn at that precise time, it seemed like providence. My offer was accepted but then I got cold feet. I mean, wanting to do something but not having any experience, leaving behind everything that was familiar. I wasn't sure I could do it, but Gerry talked me into it. Said he loved a woman who knew her own mind, that he'd make a point of stopping by on his runs up north, and that kinda made my mind up for me.'

'You were in love with him?' Alexi suggested, her tone softening.

Polly threw up her hands. 'Ridiculous as it sounds, but yes, I was. So why would I kill him?'

'Did he stop by often and how long for?' Jack asked. 'I don't recall seeing you about the town with him.'

'I'd see him once or twice a month but never for more than a night or two. I started to think that he was playing me, that I wasn't the only one. I was a useful free place to stop when he broke his trips, if you like. That's what we were arguing about. I'd had enough and gave him an ultimatum. He either committed to me, gave up travelling the country and linking up with God knows who, and helped me run the B&B, or we were done.'

'What did he say?'

'He agreed. Said it was time we settled down.' Fresh tears dripped down her face. 'So why would I kill the man I loved? A man who had agreed to give up everything for me?'

'If he did agree,' Alexi pointed out, raising a hand to cut off Polly's protest. 'Sorry, but we only have your word for the fact that he did. The police might take a very different view.'

'He'd been sponging off you for years but when you demanded a commitment, he laughed in your face,' Jack added.

'No!' Polly half rose from her chair. 'That isn't what happened. I thought you were on my side.'

'You will need to explain everything you just told us to Ben Avery before the police speak with you.'

'I can't tell the police the truth about our argument!' Polly protested.

'I would strongly advise against holding vital information back,' Jack shot back at her. 'They weren't born yesterday.' He paused. 'Besides, if you were shouting then you were probably overheard. Where are your private rooms?'

'At the back on the ground floor. I have a bedroom, sitting room and bathroom.'

'And that's where the argument took place?'

Polly nodded.

'And your paying guests, where are their rooms?'

Polly swallowed. 'Immediately above mine,' she admitted.

'So if you were yelling at each other, they would have heard you clearly.'

Polly looked glum but suddenly brightened considerably. 'We did argue,' she said. 'I screeched at him like a fishwife. I'd had enough, you see. He'd left his phone in the sitting room and when he was in the bathroom, it rang and a woman's name flashed up on the screen. And… well, I lost it, which is what made me give him an ultimatum. I'd been thinking about it for a long time. Grace encouraged me to force his hand.'

Jack grimaced, well able to imagine his ex-wife doing precisely that.

'Go on,' he said.

'I demanded to know who this Melanie was, but he became evasive. His voice was loud because, like I've already said, he'd hit the whisky before he got to me, and carried on drinking once he arrived. Said he'd had a rough week but looking back on it, I'd swear he had something playing on his mind. He was subdued, definitely not his normal self. However long he worked and believe me, Holby's get their pound of flesh, he was always upbeat and positive.'

'There are rules about how long truck drivers can be behind the wheel,' Alexi said.

Polly blew air through her lips. 'Are there?'

'Go on,' Jack said. 'You were telling us about your argument.'

'Well, when I asked about Melanie, he basically told me to mind my own business. His voice was loud but it was me who did the screaming. When he refused to tell me anything, that's when I lost it and started pummelling his chest with my fists. After all the meals I'd cooked for him, all the nights he'd spent beneath my roof for nothing, all the side benefits, all the socks I'd washed for him, all the occasions when he made excuses not to go out... well, I saw red.'

Gerry sounded like a real piece of work, Jack decided, who had Polly just where he wanted her.

'I started to think he was ashamed to be seen with me, had a secret life that he didn't want to risk or something. My imagination got the better of me, and that name on his phone changed everything. So I told him it was her or me. If he didn't give up the life of a truck driver and move it to help me with the business then we were through, and I meant it. I think he must have realised that because he agreed.' She shared an earnest look between Jack and Alexi. 'And that's the God's honest truth.'

'Okay,' Jack said, raising a placating hand. 'Take a breath and let's look into things in greater detail. First things first. Has Gerry ever been married?'

'Yes, but it ended in divorce ten years ago. His ex, Pauline, is happily remarried. He sees her occasionally because they have two kids in common. They're teenagers and the family lives in Southampton. Gerry has always paid full child maintenance, above the going rate in fact, and there have never been any issues that I'm aware of between him and his family.'

'What about close friends?' Alexi asked.

Polly lifted one shoulder. 'He gets along with everyone but he's driving five days a week. It doesn't make for close friendships.'

In other words, Jack thought, she had no idea what else he got up to when he wasn't with her.

'What can you tell me about the guests you have staying?' Jack asked. 'Are they regulars?'

'One couple are. Jane and Derek Grant have a half share in a horse here in the valley. Their trainer has an open day on Sunday and they decided to come down a few days early. They just love being anywhere near the horses and watching them in training. They'd met Gerry several times and shared a few drinks with us. They are almost friends rather than paying guests.'

'And the others?' Alexi asked.

'Paul and Michelle Sears are first timers. Booked in for the weekend as well. Not sure why they're here early or what their purpose is. They didn't say. And I also have a single gent. James Alton. He's a newbie too. I think he's an ex-jockey and has something to do with a bookmaker. We often get scouts down here watching the horses on the gallops.'

Jack nodded. 'The police have spoken to them all, I assume.'

'And they told them that they'd heard us arguing, I imagine.' Polly shrugged. 'Well, what else could they do?'

'What about local people?' Alexi asked. 'You're a well-known figure about town with a lot of friends. Have you had a falling out with any of them?'

Polly shook her head. 'No, but if I had, I don't think any of them would go to such extreme lengths to have the final word.'

It *did* seem extreme, Jack accepted, but stranger things had been known to happen. If Gerry was half as attractive and as flirtatious as Polly had implied, then perhaps he'd tried it on with one of Polly's friends. And when he wouldn't commit to her... well, if Polly was to be believed then Gerry seemed capable of stirring extremes of passion and exciting jealousies, so anything was possible.

'Did your close friends socialise with you and Gerry?' he asked.

'Yeah, sometimes, but always in our house or theirs. Like I say, Gerry wasn't big on being seen out and I understood that. Or thought I did.'

'I've seen you a lot with Linda Beauchamp. She runs the convenience store,' Alexi said. 'She refused to serve me once, presumably because she was in your corner.'

'Sorry about that. I didn't know.'

'She's on her own, I think.'

'Yes, she and her husband split a few years back and she's sworn off men as being more trouble than they're worth.'

'And Maggie Ambrose is the third member of your coven.'

Polly blinked, but Alexi's expression remained implacable.

'Yes, Maggie runs the yoga studio. Very spiritual, she is.'

But not averse to taking Polly's side in a vendetta against Alexi, Jack thought.

'I wish I could point you in the direction of a viable alternative suspect,' Polly said, spreading her hands, 'but I absolutely can't think of anyone who bore Gerry a grudge sufficient to result in such a violent death. I really do wish I could think of someone, but it seems that I didn't know nearly as much about him as I thought I did.'

'The police will have taken his phone,' Jack said, rubbing his chin as he thought about his next move. 'His contacts might have given us a starting point.'

Fresh tears spilled down Polly's face. 'It's hopeless, isn't it?' she said. 'I have to grieve for the man I loved *and* try to prove that I didn't kill him when all the evidence seems to imply otherwise.'

'It's early days,' Jack said, realising how inadequate that must sound. 'Have your paying guests upped sticks?'

'No. The police have said that they can stay. I didn't think that they'd want to, but they are either being loyal, enjoying being at the centre of a murder investigation or have pressing personal reasons to hang out. It's hard to know which. I can go back but my private rooms are a crime scene, and I can't enter them on pain of being arrested. Not that I'd want to, but still.'

'Well, as long as you're not alone. It's at times like this that we find out who our friends really are,' Alexi said pointedly.

'Go home, leave it to us and keep your appointment with the police tomorrow,' Jack said. 'Call me when it's over and I might have found something out by then.'

'Thank you.' Polly stood. 'I know I don't deserve your help and believe me, I'm more grateful than you could ever know.'

Cosmo sent her an imperious look and hissed at her.

3

Alexi waited for the door to close behind Polly before letting out a long breath. As though sensing her emotional turmoil, Cosmo unfurled himself, stalked across the floor and leapt onto her lap. She absently stroked his sleek back, taking comfort from his solid presence as she tried to formulate her feelings.

'You okay with this?' Jack asked, standing to move behind her and place a placating hand on her shoulders. 'We don't owe her anything. Quite the reverse, in fact. She must either be exceedingly presumptuous or very desperate even to ask us to help her.'

'Not sure what I feel right now,' Alexi replied. 'But I agree, she has some nerve. The very last thing we need is to get embroiled with another murder, even though it didn't happen on these premises and has no possible connection to us. Even so, we're trying to enhance our reputation, not terminally damage it.'

'But…'

'But annoyingly, I want to know what happened.'

'Yeah, I figured you would.'

Jack reached for the coffee pot and poured for them both.

'Want some brandy in it?' he asked, placing a mug in front of her. 'The good stuff, obviously.'

She smiled. 'Don't tempt me.'

Jack resumed his seat beside her and caught the hand not stroking Cosmo. 'So,' he said. 'Initial thoughts. Did she do it?'

Alexi took her time responding. 'Actually, I don't think she did. She clearly loved the guy and let him use her. No one can pretend that degree of anguish.'

'You'd be surprised. They were arguing, remember, and feelings were running high. Plus, Gerry had been drinking and Polly chose the wrong time to push him for commitment. Perhaps he did tell her who Melanie was and she lost it.'

'Possibly, but if she took a knife with her into their bedroom it implies premeditation, and I somehow can't see that.'

'Wouldn't have taken her a moment to slip into the kitchen and grab said knife,' Jack pointed out. 'She loved the guy, you got that much right, and had been trying to convince herself for years that her feelings were reciprocated. You would be very surprised to learn what a woman scorned is capable of doing. A spur-of-the-moment crime of passion, if you like. It happens more often than you'd think. Only afterwards would she have come to her senses, realise what she'd done, fall into a state of shock and then claim innocence.'

'Hmm. It's possible.'

'She probably half believes she's innocent too because she couldn't possibly harm a single hair on the head of the man she adored, even though he sometimes drove her to distraction.'

Alexi nodded. 'She called the police, which implies innocence.'

'No choice in the matter,' Jack replied. 'She had to think on her feet. She wouldn't have been capable of moving a dead body alone and even her closest friends would likely have balked if she asked them to aid and abet.'

'So she fronted it out.'

'Or she's innocent and someone slipped into their room after Polly got up this morning and before she went back to wake him for his lunch. Given that access was freely available to all and sundry, it can't be discounted.'

'That's one possible explanation.' Alexi felt as dubious as she sounded and blinked up at Jack. 'I have every reason in the world to dislike Polly after the vicious whispering campaign orchestrated by her that almost drove me out of Lambourn so why do I feel inclined to believe she's innocent?'

'Because, unlike her, you're fair-minded and logical. Me, I'm sitting on the fence until we know more.'

Alexi chuckled. 'Once a policeman...'

'Absolutely. I was trained to have a suspicious mind.'

'Jack, about Grace.' She swallowed. 'What's going on there?'

'Your guess is as good as mine.' He spread his hands, met her gaze and held it. 'I had absolutely no idea that she and Polly are tight.'

'Did you know that she'd split from the guy she was seeing after she separated from you?'

'Yes,' he replied without hesitation. 'Just after you and I met on the Natalie Parker case, she contacted me.'

'You never said.'

Jack shrugged. 'It didn't seem relevant. Anyway, she got in touch, and we met for a drink. Still not sure why I went. She said there was something important that she needed to tell me in person. Her big news turned out to be that she'd split from Jason. She said that she'd made a terrible mistake, had never stopped loving me, blah blah, and now that I was no longer a serving policeman, perhaps we could give it another go.' Jack threw back his head and sighed. 'Like I was supposed to forget all about her playing away with Jason, and others for all I know, whilst we were still married. Anyway, I told her that ship had sailed and that was that.'

'First Cassie and then Grace.' Alexi forced a smile. 'You're in demand.'

'The only feminine demands I respond to, darling, are the ones that you make. I hope you realise at least that much. I'm committed to you and don't look at other women that way. Why would I?'

'Right answer, Mr Maddox.'

'Phew!' Jack wiped imaginary perspiration from his brow, making them both smile.

Alexi wanted to pursue the subject of Grace but held back for fear of appearing too possessive or unsure of Jack's affection. She knew what he'd just told her was the truth and she'd leave it at that. For now.

'In the spirit of full disclosure, I've received a few texts from Grace since then, but I've deleted them unread and not responded. There is absolutely no reason for us to remain in contact and I have no intention of giving her false hope.'

'Thanks for telling me.'

Alexi didn't add *now*. She was in a similar position with Patrick who, until recently, had plagued her with unwanted attention, half of which she hadn't mentioned to Jack because... well, because it hadn't seemed important.

However, the fact remained that Jack's ex-wife still had the hots for him, as did Cassie, his business partner. Grace had even given her friend Polly a biased account of Alexi's relationship with Jack, making it seem as though Alexi had broken up their marriage. She wondered if Grace realised how much damage she'd done, deliberately or otherwise. She also blamed Polly for not checking her facts before turning half the town against Alexi, which made her desire to look into Gerry's murder in an effort to prove Polly's innocence harder still to fathom.

'What does it feel like to be in such demand?' she quipped.

'Just so long as you demand my attention, then all is right with my world.'

'Soooo, I assume we're going to delve a little deeper.'

'Only if you're good with that.'

Alexi smiled and leaned across to give Jack a peck on the cheek. 'I'll try to be the bigger person. And you're relishing the challenge, I can see that, so don't try and tell me you don't miss your old career. You can take the man out of the police force but...'

'Yeah, guilty as charged.' Jack flashed that lazy smile of his that still possessed the ability to make Alexi feel weak at the knees.

'I guess this means our few days break is on hold.'

'Your call.'

'You know I can't walk away from this either. There might be a story in it, which will equate to a decent payday. What?' Alexi bridled when Jack raised a brow. 'Don't look at me like that. I'd be less than human if I didn't want to profit from Polly's downfall, even if she's innocent. After what she put me through, she's getting off lightly. I'm reckoning that half the town think I'm responsible for breaking up your marriage, thanks to Polly's tattle, which would explain why I've been cold-shouldered by so many.'

'I will make it a personal mission to ensure that they know differently,' Jack replied, frowning at a possibility that clearly hadn't occurred to him before now. 'I didn't know you were still getting hassle.'

'Don't worry about it. I'm a big girl.'

'Even so.'

'Shall you speak with Vickery?'

Jack shook his head. 'Not yet. I'll wait to get feedback from Ben following Polly's interview with him tomorrow, just so I know which way they're leaning. Although I could make an educated guess right now.'

'Based on what you know, you reckon they'll think it's an open and shut case? A crime of passion committed in the heat of the moment.'

'I wouldn't bet against it. With no other obvious suspects and with the victim and Polly having been heard arguing violently... Can't see the search for alternative suspects featuring high on Vickery's agenda myself.'

'We didn't ask Polly if there's anyone significant in her background who might have objected to Gerry's presence in her life.'

'Good point. We will do that when we next see her, but in the meantime, let's try and track down Polly's paying guests and see what they have to say for themselves.' He glanced at his watch. 'It's gone five o'clock. I'm betting we'll find one or more of them having an early dinner in one of the locals, talking up a storm. It's probably the most exciting thing that's ever happened to them. My guess is that we'll find them at the Malt Shovel.'

'Come on then.'

Cosmo leapt from her lap and was the first to reach the door.

'He hasn't lost his touch, I see,' Jack said, grinning.

'I keep telling you, he's highly intuitive and recognises a crisis when it arises. He wants to help and will be offended if we leave him behind.'

Cosmo gave an indignant mewl, making them both smile.

'Okay then, big guy,' Jack said, leaning down to run a hand along Cosmo's back. 'It looks like I'm outnumbered.'

They headed for the front door, but Alexi paused when passing the hotel bar. Two couples she'd never seen before were huddled round a table with drinks in front of them, conducting a subdued conversation. There was something about them that made Alexi think they might be Polly's guests.

'What do you think?' she asked Jack, nodding towards them.

'Could be,' he said, leading the way into the bar with Cosmo and Alexi close behind.

He stopped at their table, his presence halting their conversation.

'We're looking for Mr and Mrs Grant and the Sears,' he said. 'Would that happen to be you? We were told we'd find you here.'

Had they been? That was news to Alexi.

One of the men glanced at his friends and then nodded. 'That's us,' he said. 'Who are you? Are you the police?'

'Nope,' Jack replied with an easy smile that Alexi could see had resonated with both ladies. She suppressed a sigh. Whatever it took, she supposed. 'We're helping Polly and wondered if you could spare us a few minutes. I'm Jack Maddox, this is Alexi Ellis, co-owner of this hotel, and this,' he finished, waving a hand towards their feline companion, 'is Cosmo.'

'Everyone knows Cosmo,' one of the ladies said, risking life and limb by offering the cat her hand. Cosmo sniffed at it, found nothing to object to and kept his claws furled. 'He's famous. We came in here in the hope of seeing him. I'm Jane Grant. Pull up chairs, both of you. We've been hoping to meet Cosmo for a while actually, but Polly advised against frequenting your bar. Said the prices were prohibitive but that's not what we've found.'

Ah, Alexi thought, so she'd not only tried to drive her out but also attempted to kill off custom at Cheryl and Drew's hotel. She glanced at Jack, who gave a grim nod.

'We asked Polly about you, Alexi. I mean, we all read and enjoyed your articles in the *Sentinel* and hoped to run into you, but she expressed very frank views to your detriment,' Jane said. 'Anyway, she seems to have rushed to you quickly enough in her hour of need.'

'She'll need all the help she can get,' the man who was presumably her husband replied. 'I'm Derek Grant and this is Paul and Michelle Sears.'

Alexi and Jack shook hands with them all and then sat down. 'Refills anyone?' Jack asked.

Everyone accepted and Jack went to the bar to place the order, returning quickly with a trayful of drinks. Once everyone had their beverage of choice in front of them, he gradually eased the conversation in the direction that he wanted it to take. Not that it took much engineering. All four of Polly's guests were more than willing to express their views and looked enthralled to be in the middle of a murder investigation.

'You know Polly well?' Alexi asked.

'We've been staying with her regularly for years,' Derek replied. 'We're devotees of the turf and Polly is... well, cheap. We couldn't afford this place and the upkeep of an expensive equine.'

His wife nodded her vigorous agreement.

'We're first-timers,' Paul said. 'We're considering investing in horseflesh and Derek and Jane have been giving us a tutorial, pointing out the highs and lows. Stuff that trainers don't tell you when you look at prospective horses. The lows mostly come in the form of severe damage to the old bank balance, but still, what can one do? Can't take it with us when we pop our clogs, don't believe in letting the kids expect too much by way of inheritance, and so we might as well have some fun.'

All four of them nodded their agreement.

'Never expected to land up in the middle of a murder, though,' Michelle said. 'That did catch us unawares.'

'Nice bloke, Gerry. A bit fond of the old sauce,' Derek said, lifting his glass to emphasise his point. 'But then, aren't we all.'

'He was a real charmer,' Jane added, glancing at Jack as she spoke. 'I'm sure you know the type.'

'You heard them arguing, I gather,' Alexi said.

'Nothing new there,' Derek replied. 'They were always going at it hammer and tongs. Fierce arguments and from what we couldn't help overhearing, equally boisterous reconciliations.'

'The argument last night,' Jack said. 'Was there anything out of the ordinary about it?'

'I couldn't say. No idea what they fell out about this time, but I do know that Gerry definitely wasn't his normal, cheerful self,' Jane responded. 'I remarked upon it, and he said he had a lot on his mind.'

'I overheard him on his phone,' Michelle said. 'He was outside at the back, having a smoke and talking to someone. I had our window open and couldn't help overhearing. The conversation was heated, and he told whoever he was talking to that he would get things sorted. To give him time. I got the impression that he was in debt to someone nasty, but that was just my interpretation. I didn't actually hear anything said to back up that supposition. His tone was meek though, pleading almost.' She lifted one shoulder in a negligent shrug. 'I didn't think anything more of it until just now.'

'You didn't tell the police?' Alexi asked.

Michelle shook her head. 'What with the shock and everything, it only just came back to me. Should I, do you think? They said if we thought of anything...'

'Probably best to,' Jack replied. 'It goes a little way to casting doubt upon Polly's guilt.'

'I only just met the lady,' Paul said, joining the conversation for the first time. 'But I just can't see her thrusting a knife into a man's chest, I don't care how worked up she was. By all accounts, their arguing was nothing out of the ordinary and it was obvious to anyone with eyes in their head that she adored the man.'

'Was that adoration reciprocated?' Alexi asked.

Paul glanced at the others, none of whom seemed certain.

'He showed her affection,' Jane replied, 'but also flirted quite outrageously with anything in a skirt. He did it with me, in front of her.'

'Did he try it on with you in private?' Jack asked.

'No.' Jane shook her head emphatically. 'I think he just enjoyed being the centre of attention, but I did feel sorry for Polly when he did stuff like that. I asked her about it once and she laughed it off. Said it was his way and didn't mean anything, but in view of what's happened, it does make you wonder, doesn't it?'

'You never really know what's going on inside people's heads,' Paul agreed.

'There's someone else lodging at Polly's right now,' Jack said. 'Do any of you know anything about him?'

All four shook their heads. 'James Alton. About forty, I'd say,' Derek replied. 'Saw him at breakfast and exchanged pleasantries but I don't know anything about his background. He didn't seem that keen on talking to any of us and buggered off as soon as he'd had his breakfast, now that I think about it.'

'You can ask him yourself,' Jane said, nodding toward a short, overweight man who'd just walked through the door.

Alexi assessed him as Jane waved him over. He looked as though he wanted to turn and run but changed his mind at the last minute. Derek made the introductions and Jack offered to buy the man a drink.

'All a bit of a kerfuffle,' he remarked when Jack placed a pint in front of him and he nodded his thanks. 'Didn't sign up for murder.'

Alexi smiled, despite having taken an instinctive dislike to the man. 'What did bring you this way, if you don't mind me asking?'

'*You* can ask me anything you like,' he replied, leering at Alexi. 'The police already did, and I'll tell you what I told them. I'm a scout for a leading bookie and there's a particular horse that created quite a stir at the end of the last flat racing season. My boss wants my expert opinion on its chances of qualifying for the Oaks. And believe it or not, I *am* an expert. I know it's hard to fathom, what with the way I look now,' he added, patting his bulging belly with obvious affection, 'but I used to be a leading jockey myself back in the day.'

'Of course!' Derek slapped his thigh. 'I should have recognised the name.'

'Yeah well, if I was still seven stone nothing, you probably would have but people tend to see only what's in front of their eyes.'

Alexi wondered how successful he could actually have been if he was now a humble bookie's scout. She had absolutely no idea how much top jockeys earned but would make it a priority to find out. She'd also take a look at James Alton's track record – quite literally – to see how well he'd done as a rider. Her journalistic nose told her there was something off about the little man who had an inflated opinion of his own self-worth. That didn't mean he had anything to do with Gerry's death. As far as she was aware, the two men had never met. But even so...

'Your work must bring you to this neck of the woods quite often,' Jack said, assessing the man over the rim of his glass. His expression gave nothing away, but Alexi would bet her bank balance on Jack finding the ex-jockey's appearance at Polly's as suspicious as she herself did. 'Yet I gather it's your first visit to Polly's B&B. Where do you usually stay, if you don't mind my asking?'

James sniffed and looked at first if he would tell Jack to take a hike. Then he glanced down at his half-drunk pint, appeared to recall that Jack had paid for it, and had a change of heart.

'Don't see what it has to do with anything,' he said, a defensive edge to his voice as he drained his drink and banged his now empty glass down on the table with unnecessary force, 'but I usually stay with my old guvnor at Baxter's yard. We go way back.'

'Not this time?' Alexi asked, aware that Baxter was a local trainer. She picked up on all sorts of horsy gossip, she couldn't have avoided it if she'd wanted to, and knew that Baxter's reputation was suspect. Why, she couldn't have said, but did know that the gossip was ordinarily not far off the mark.

'Nope. They've got a shindig on. No room at the inn.'

Or, Alexi thought, maybe James had abused the trainer's hospitality once too often. Either that or it was one of Baxter's horses he'd come to check out.

'What made you decide to stay at Polly's?' Alexi asked.

'Cheap and convenient.' He glanced around the half-full bar and nodded at an acquaintance. 'Certainly couldn't afford this place, more's the pity.'

Alexi smiled her sympathy. 'What did you make of Gerry and Polly, as a couple, I mean?' she asked.

'Didn't see much of them. I had a quick chat with Gerry, man to man like. He was fond of the turf and remembered me from my riding days. He seemed like a decent enough bloke. Shame about what happened to him. But still, it's true what they say about a woman scorned. There's no telling what she'll do.'

Jack probed him with a look. 'You think Polly did it then?'

'Who else could it have been?' James looked pointedly down at his empty glass. When no one offered to refill it, he showed no sign of putting his hand in his pocket. Presumably because he would have had to offer everyone at the table a drink. The man, Alexi decided, was not flush with cash. 'We all heard them having a right old barny.'

He looked towards the others for confirmation, and they all nodded with varying degrees of reluctance.

'You all think it was Polly then?' Alexi asked.

'I hope it wasn't,' Michelle said, and her assertion produced mumbled agreement from her husband and the Grants. 'We all liked her but as James says, it's hard to see who else it could have been.'

'Were you all in at lunchtime, when he was found?' Jack asked.

Alexi thought it was a good question and one she ought to have asked herself before now. They all shook their heads.

'We'd gone to the yard to see our trainer,' Derek said. 'We left straight after breakfast.'

'And we'd been exploring the area,' Paul said. 'Arrived back to police activity and all hell had broken loose.'

'I was out and about too,' James said, declining to elaborate.

'So, none of you would know if anyone else entered the place during the course of the morning,' Alexi said. 'I gather the door is never locked during the daytime.'

'True,' Jane admitted. 'Even so, it doesn't look good for Polly, does it?'

'Innocent until proven guilty,' Jack said. 'She might need your support over the coming days. I gather you're all staying on.'

Jane nodded. 'Is it wrong to say it's exciting to be in the middle of a murder investigation?'

'It's honest, at least,' Alexi said, smiling at her.

'Might be worth talking to the local rag,' James said, rubbing his hands together. 'My night of terror in a murder lair.'

The others all glowered at him.

'It was just a joke,' he protested. 'I wouldn't actually do it.' He stood up. 'Excuse me, there's someone I need to talk to.'

They watched him saunter across to the bar on bandy legs and join a crowd of horsy types, none of whom seemed particularly pleased to see him.

'What a charmer,' Alexi muttered as she too stood up. 'Thanks for your time,' she said to the others. 'We're trying to help Polly get to the bottom of things so if you think of anything that might have a bearing, please give me a ring.' She handed her card to both ladies.

'We will,' Jane replied, returning her smile. 'Despite everything, I really don't want Polly to be the guilty party.'

Cosmo appeared from beneath the table on cue and walked from the bar between them, tail swishing.

'That James Alton is a piece of work,' Alexi said, as they reached the entrance hall. 'I swear if he'd undressed me with his eyes one more time, I'd have clocked him one.'

'You'd have had to beat me to it,' Jack replied, taking her hand in his and giving it a squeeze.

'What now?' she asked.

'Now we go home, have something to eat and think about our next move.'

'Good plan.'

4

————

Jack drove them back to their cottage and volunteered for kitchen duty.

'You won't get any arguments from me on that one,' Alexi replied, kissing his cheek before heading for the stairs. 'A soak in the bath is calling to me. Resistance would be futile.'

Jack laughed. 'Take your time. Dinner will be an hour.'

'No wonder so many women lust after you,' she said, coming back down forty-five minutes later wrapped in a towelling robe and with wet hair hanging round her shoulders. 'The smells lured me from the bath and made my mouth water. You are a man of many talents, Mr Maddox.'

'I live to serve, my lady,' he said with a flourishing bow, placing a steaming plate of fish stew in front of her and pouring her a glass of wine.

'Has his lordship been fed?' she asked, glancing at Cosmo, who was curled up in his basket, his eyes wide open and fixed on their food.

'You think he'd be so placid if he hadn't been?'

Alexi smiled. 'Good point.' She took a forkful of fish, savoured it and closed her eyes in appreciation. 'Delicious! I might keep you around for a bit longer... and not just in the kitchen,' she said, grinning.

They ate mostly in silence after that, enjoying one another's company without the need for words. Jack worried that this latest murder investigation would take a toll on Alexi and warp her judgement. That would hardly be surprising, given who it was that they'd been asked to help and the trouble that she'd caused for Alexi in the past. So far, she seemed energised by the prospect but Jack knew she'd be disturbed by Grace's antics, as Jack himself was. He had no idea that his ex could be quite so vindictive and hadn't yet decided what if anything he intended to do about her spiteful meddling.

He hadn't told Alexi that Grace had quizzed him about his association with her that one time they'd met. At that point, he and Alexi had been colleagues, working together on the Natalie Parker murder. They both had compelling reasons to solve it and it had made sense to pool their resources, even though Jack had equally good reasons for despising the press, who had hounded him out of the Met by printing a plethora of unfounded allegations about his conduct.

But there were exceptions to every rule, he now had good reason to know, and one was sitting across the table from him at that precise moment, hair now half dry, her towelling robe falling open and failing to conceal her enticing body. Jack had thought himself in love with Grace when they married but knew now that hadn't been the case. But Alexi... well, he'd walk over hot coals for her and commit a murder or two of his own if anyone tried to harm her. That, he now knew without a shadow of doubt, was the true meaning of love.

Grace had obviously gotten her information about his relation-ship with Alexi from her obliging friend, Polly. He and Alexi had been constantly in one another's company during the course of that first investigation. Polly had added two and two, come up with seventeen and clearly decided that Grace needed to know all about Jack's latest conquest.

Now that same interfering woman needed their help.

'I'll clear up,' Alexi said, pushing her empty plate aside and sighing with satisfaction. 'It's the least I can do. Your turn to hit the bathroom.'

Jack grinned at her. 'Won't be long,' he promised as he ran up the stairs. 'I know you're anxious to get to grips with this case.'

Half an hour later, they settled in the lounge with another bottle of wine. Alexi had a pad in front of her and had already made concise notes, Jack could see.

'Right,' she said, all business. 'Let's lay out what we know and what areas we need to investigate.'

'Polly Pearson's partner, and I use the term loosely, was murdered in the bedroom they share in Polly's B&B,' Jack said, stating the obvious. 'We don't know if the knife used came from Polly's kitchen. We need to find out. We also need to know if there were prints on the knife and blood on Polly's clothing.'

Alexi nodded and made a note on her pad.

'Polly is the obvious suspect,' she said. 'Her guests were all out for the morning, but the door isn't locked and anyone could have slipped in. That is one point in her favour and might well be the only reason why Vickery didn't take her in last night.'

'We need to know more about what Gerry got up to in Lambourn,' Jack pointed out. 'Did he make any enemies? Why was he so reluctant to be seen in public with Polly? Who was the Melanie woman who called him?'

Alexi sent Jack a look. 'I assumed he had a woman in every port, to bastardise a phrase, and didn't want to rock the boat if he was seen with Polly too often.'

'Who would see him? I doubt whether he had anyone else in this part of the world. My guess is that he had places to stay on his regular routes all over the country. It would help if we knew what routes he drove. Vickery will likely know because if he's done his job right, and he's usually thorough, he will have asked Holby's. I'll ask him if we decide to remain involved.'

'We know Gerry was a flirt, but did it go further than that?' Alexi mused. 'Had he committed himself elsewhere and 'fessed up when Polly pushed him?'

'It's possible.' Jack's expression turned grim. 'That *would* be a motive for murder. She'd waited all this time, only to discover that she was a bit player, not the leading lady.'

'We need to speak to his ex-wife,' Alexi said, making a note on her pad and under lining it heavily. 'We know Polly and Gerry argued, and her regular punters say that's nothing out of the ordinary. She was pushing him to give up his job as a long-distance driver for Holby's and settle down with her to run the B&B. If he enjoyed playing the field, that would have clipped his wings.'

'The ex Mrs Dawlish might be persuaded to tell us why their marriage broke up,' Jack agreed. 'I guess long-distance driving rates up there with being a copper in many respects. The hours, I mean, and the amount of time spent away from family commitments.'

'We also need to speak with Polly again. Find out about her past, just in case someone crawled out of the woodwork if they knew she was serious about settling for someone else. We know she finds it hard to keep her mouth shut and likes to gossip. Gerry was a good-looking bloke apparently and she was probably proud to have pinned him down. *If* she did.' Alexi put her pen aside and looked at Jack. 'What did you make of our ex-jockey?' she asked.

'Not sure I bought his story about not knowing Gerry.' Jack

shrugged. 'Can't say why. Call it instinct but he definitely held something back.'

'I agree with you.' She picked up her pen again. 'That's certainly worth Googling.'

'Since we're speculating, I'd very much like to know if Gerry did more than just drive a lorry.'

Alexi raised a brow. 'You think he had some racket going on the side?'

'Wouldn't surprise me. And we know from that overheard phone conversation that he was in trouble of some sort. We're thinking unpaid debts.'

'Don't forget the call from Melanie that seemed to promote the latest fight between victim and suspect.'

'Yeah, I've got that in mind. I'll have a word with Vickery tomorrow after we've had an account of Polly's interview from Ben. I'll see if I can persuade him to let me see Gerry's contact list.'

Alexi looked dubious. 'Do you suppose he will?'

'All depends whether he thinks he has his woman. But like I say, if he has personal doubts but nothing to back them up, he might let us do a bit of private sleuthing. He won't be able to justify putting many man hours in if the case is as open and shut as it appears to be at first glance.'

'Right, well we have enough to be going on with.'

Alexi reached for her laptop and Googled James Alton's name.

'Hello,' she said when she got a load of hits, 'seems our instincts aren't too far off. Our friendly jockey forgot to mention that he got a lifetime ban for race fixing.'

'Did he indeed.' Jack peered over her shoulder and read the first of the articles she'd pulled up. 'It happened twenty years ago. I wonder how he's kept the wolf from the door since then.'

'Whichever bookie he was in bed with has probably employed

his services in some capacity or other in return for Alton keeping his name out of the frame.'

'Doesn't mean he knew Gerry or had anything to do with his death,' Jack said. 'It does definitely make him a person of interest though, as they say.'

'We need to ask Polly if she heard any exchanges between the two men that indicated a connection. We need to ask as well whether Gerry recommended the B&B to him.'

'She advertises online. It would have been easy enough to find if he was looking for a cheap deal. Besides, he's a regular visitor to Lambourn so would have known about it.'

'I think we've done all we can for today,' Alexi said, hiding a yawn behind her hand as she shut her computer down. 'Let's call it a night.'

'Yes, ma'am.'

Cosmo, as attuned to their habits as always, removed himself from a bookshelf where he'd taken up residence and preceded them up the stairs.

Jack found it hard to sleep, his mind alive with suspicions and possibilities but mostly filled with annoyance. Annoyance with Grace, not to mention Polly and her meddling. Why couldn't he and Alexi be left alone by people from their past and allowed to get on with their lives?

By the time that dawn came around, he was no closer to deciding whether Polly was as innocent as she claimed to be or desperately attempting to cover up a serious crime. If she was innocent, then someone had done a very effective job of framing her. Jack had doubts about getting involved but knew that Alexi had got the bit between her teeth. She wanted to prove something by helping the woman who had tried to break her, and Jack loved her all the more for her sense of fair play.

He slid from between the sheets without disturbing Alexi.

Cosmo, asleep on Alexi's feet, sprang lightly to the floor and waited outside the bathroom until Jack had showered and dressed. He then preceded him down the stairs and waited beside his empty dish, sending Jack an imperious look through piercing green eyes as he swished his tail impatiently.

'Okay, okay, big guy, I get the message,' Jack said, opening a tin of cat food and decanting it into Cosmo's bowl.

Jack made tea and took a cup up to Alexi, who was just stirring. She sat up and pushed a tangle of hair away from her eyes, smiling sleepily at Jack.

'Hey.'

'Hey yourself,' he said, depositing her tea on the bedside table and leaning over to kiss her.

'Have you been up for long?'

'A while. You were dead to the world. It seemed a shame to wake you.'

'Hmm well, I'm awake now.' She picked up her tea, blew on it and took a sip. 'Just what I need.'

'I'll make us some breakfast while you shower.'

She kissed the end of his nose. 'Definitely a keeper,' she said, pushing back the covers and padding barefoot in the direction of the bathroom.

'I'm assuming that we'll run our investigation from the hotel,' Jack said later across the breakfast table.

Alexi nodded round a mouthful of toast. 'Seems like the best plan,' she said, once she'd swallowed. 'Besides, Drew and Cheryl will want to know what's happening. We didn't have a chance to update them before we left yesterday.'

'They won't be best pleased to learn that Polly warned her customers away from Hopgood Hall's bar and I can't say as I blame them. Our client, for want of a better word, is a malicious woman.'

'Can't argue with that.'

Cosmo was the first one at the door the moment they'd cleared breakfast away. Jack rolled his eyes but refrained from comment. Instead, he unlocked his car and opened the rear door for Cosmo, who leapt athletically onto the seat and settled down.

'I wonder if the press has latched on to another murder here in Lambourn yet,' Alexi said, anxiously tapping her fingers against her thigh as Jack took up his place behind the wheel.

'You're worried that it will bring Patrick scurrying down here, I imagine,' Jack replied, pausing at the junction of their lane to allow a string of leggy racehorses to cross it on their way to the gallops.

'I doubt whether even he would have the nerve, but you can bet your life that the local press will cover it and no doubt an ambitious journalist will get in on the act, attempting to sell the story to the big boys. Since it has nothing to do with Hopgood Hall this time, hopefully they'll not bother to descend upon us.'

'The coast is clear,' Jack said when he approached the hotel and there were no gaggles of press stationed outside. 'At least for now. Sorry,' he added over his shoulder to Cosmo when he growled. There was nothing he enjoyed more than attacking the ankles of interfering newsmen.

They made their way into the private kitchen. Cheryl and Drew were there, with baby Verity rolling about on a rug with Toby. The terrier abandoned their game the moment Cosmo stalked into the kitchen and rubbed his head against the cat's belly. Verity squealed and rushed in Cosmo's direction too.

'He likes being the centre of attention,' Alexi explained unnecessarily as she hugged Cheryl and then kissed Drew's cheek.

'Right then, you two, give,' Drew said, plonking mugs of coffee in front of them both when they sat at the table. 'We want to know what's happening and whether you think Polly is a murderer. Murderess. Whatever.'

'The jury's still out on that one,' Jack replied, taking a sip of his coffee. 'But it's not looking good for Ms Pearson, that much I can say.'

He continued to outline what they had learned so far, and what they suspected. Drew and Cheryl alternately nodded and asked pertinent questions.

'Not that we have anything to back our suspicions up with,' Alexi added when Jack ran out of words. 'A lesser woman would rejoice in her nemesis's downfall but annoyingly, I just think it's all too neat. Too convenient.'

'Well, I hope you don't try too hard to get her off,' Cheryl said, sniffing. 'She is not a nice person. Think of the way she persecuted you, Alexi, *and* warned her clients off patronising our bar. Talk about spiteful, and all because she believed your ex-wife, Jack. I hope they throw the book at her, and I also think you are good people for even trying to help her.'

'She doesn't deserve it,' Drew said, nodding in agreement with his wife.

'Well, our involvement might be short lived,' Jack said, stretching his arms above his head. 'If Ben thinks she did it and more to the point, if Vickery decides he has enough to charge her then there isn't much more we can do. And even if there was, I'm not too sure that I'd make the effort. We can't be all things to all people.'

'I am concerned about Lambourn's reputation, though,' Alexi said. 'I know my ex-colleagues will latch onto yet another murder in this comparative backwater. The gutter press will have a field day and get carried away with speculation about an evil jinx, or some such nonsense. The reading public lap that sort of thing up. We all love a conspiracy theory.'

'Well, it's worked in our favour so far,' Drew said. 'We've never been so busy.'

Alexi acknowledged the point with a tilt of her head. 'True enough but even so, you have to admit that it seems a bit odd.'

'What's your first line of attack then?' Drew asked.

'Not much we can do until Ben reports back,' Jack replied, 'but I would like to get hold of Gerry's ex-wife, if at all possible. Trouble is, she's remarried and we've no idea what her new married name is.'

'Give Polly a call,' Alexi said. 'She won't have left for the station yet and there's a chance she might have her number.'

Jack placed the call and put it on speaker.

'How you holding up?' he asked when Polly's wan voice was barely audible on the line.

'My friends rallied round. So did my guests. They filled me with wine, but I didn't sleep much and now I have the hangover from hell. Not the best look when confronting a police interview but there's not much I can do about it.' Her voice had gained in strength. 'Was there anything in particular that you wanted?'

'We'd like to speak to Gerry's ex-wife and wondered if you have a name and number for her.'

'What on earth for? They've been amicably divorced for a decade now.'

'Even so.'

Jack's silence worked in his favour. Polly wouldn't risk losing his help by being obstructive, even though it was clear that she would prefer not to give him the lady's name. Jack wondered if Gerry had remained on better terms with his ex than Polly had implied. Polly was clearly possessive and that would have rankled. Enough to make her murder her lover? Jack honestly didn't know.

'Her name is Pauline Turner,' Polly eventually said. 'She lives in Southampton, but I've never had anything to do with her. I don't suppose she even knows I exist.'

She will now, Jack thought but didn't say. The police would have

informed her of her late husband's demise and likely told her
where his murder had taken place too. They would not have
mentioned Polly's name but if Pauline knew the name of the B&B,
it would be easy enough to find out. And put two and two together.

'Do you know her number?' Jack asked.

'Sorry, the police took Gerry's phone and all his personal stuff.
Anyway, I'm not allowed into our rooms. Not that I would want to
set foot in them again, but still...'

'Not to worry.' Jack paused. 'Did you ever meet Pauline?'

'No. There was no reason to. Gerry kept in touch because of his
kids, nothing more.'

'Are you sure she didn't know about you?'

'Right now, I'm not sure of my own name,' she replied evasively.
'Gerry might have mentioned me. I never asked.'

Liar, Alexi mouthed.

'Okay,' Jack said. 'We'll take it from here. Good luck this morning. Remember to think before you speak. Listen to Ben's advice
before you go into the interview and call me when you're through.'

'If they don't lock me up.'

Jack could hear the terror in her voice but had no words of
reassurance to offer since it was likely that they would keep her in
custody, at least for twenty-four hours whilst their enquiries
continued.

He cut the connection and glanced at Alexi.

'Of course she would have wanted to know if Gerry had told
Pauline about her,' Cheryl said. 'It would have made her feel more
established in Gerry's life.'

'I agree.' Alexi nodded decisively. 'And the chances are that he
didn't tell her, otherwise Polly would have used that knowledge to
support her claim that Gerry had agreed to settle down with her.
Pauline would be able to say that they were an established
couple.'

Jack sighed, wondering if he should do what he knew had to be done.

'Go ahead,' Alexi said, anticipating his dilemma. 'Cassie will find out sooner or later and we both know she'll tell her friend Grace all about it. Stands to reason given that Grace was Polly's friend too. She might already know. Anyway, Cassie's the only person who'll be able to find Pauline's number quickly.'

Jack nodded and placed the call.

'I thought you were on holiday,' Cassie said when Jack explained what he needed.

'The best laid plans and all that.'

'Okay, leave it with me. I had heard about Gerry...' she added after a pause.

'Get back to me with that number as soon as you can,' Jack said, not bothering to ask how she'd heard. He already knew.

'Bad news travels fast,' Alexi said as Jack cut the call. 'The gossip machine is clearly in good working order.'

The wait for the call back from Cassie was a short one. She was still trying to re-establish herself in Jack's eyes following her clumsy attempt to oust Alexi from his life. She reeled off a mobile number for the only Pauline Turner she could find in the Southampton area.

'If that's not her then I can't help you,' she said.

'Thanks, Cas. I'll give it a try.'

'You could do worse than speak with Polly's coven,' Cheryl said after Jack hung up. 'Find out just how well Polly and Gerry actually got on. Women tend to talk to one another about that sort of thing.'

'But they're her friends,' Drew pointed out. 'They'd hardly say anything to her detriment. Would they?'

Cheryl and Alexi exchanged a glance. 'How little men understand our sex,' Cheryl said, widening her eyes.

Jack laughed as he dialled the number for Pauline that he hoped would connect him with the right person.

'Hello.'

'Hi,' Jack replied. 'Am I talking to Pauline Turner. Formerly Pauline Dawlish?'

'Who is this?' The voice at the end of the line had turned suspicious.

'My name's Jack Maddox. I'm a private detective.'

'Is this about Gerry's murder?' she asked. 'If so, I know nothing about it.' She sniffed and sounded genuinely upset. 'I'm on my way to Lambourn now to talk to the police and try and find out more.'

'Do you have anywhere to stay?' Jack asked, glancing at Cheryl, who nodded.

'No. I haven't thought that far ahead.'

'Come to Hopgood Hall. There's a room for you there. We'd like to talk to you about your ex-husband, if you're willing.'

Pauline said that she needed to talk to someone who knew what was going on and would see them in half an hour.

'Right,' Jack said. 'We'll wait for her and then seek out Polly's friends. See what they have to say for themselves.'

5

Once Cheryl and Drew had left them to get on with their day, Alexi glanced at Jack and raised a questioning brow.

'I know that look,' Jack said. 'You're wondering why Gerry's ex felt the need to come down so quickly, if at all.'

'The thought crossed my mind. I know Gerry was her children's father but still...'

'The kids are teenagers. They will want to know what happened to their dad, one assumes.'

'So talk to the police. Why come here?'

'You're wondering if she still had feelings for the guy.' Jack shrugged. 'I'm thinking along the same lines. He seems to have roused strong passions in Polly but I'm getting a feel for the guy's *modus operandi* and reckon that he knew how to play the ladies.'

A tap at the kitchen door caused them both to turn in that direction.

'She made good time,' Alexi remarked.

But it wasn't Pauline. Instead, Linda Beauchamp put her head round the door.

'Can I have a word?' she asked, strolling into the room without waiting for a reply. 'There was no one out front but I heard your voices so thought I'd intrude, given the circumstances.'

Alexi bridled at the woman's audacity. She knew things had changed drastically since Gerry's murder and that Polly would have told her friend that she and Jack were investigating. Even so, Linda's bald assumption that her past behaviour would be over-looked still rankled. Cosmo clearly shared Alexi's view. He unfurled himself from Toby's basket, arched his back and hissed aggressively. Alexi failed to conceal a smile when Linda hastily backed up towards the door.

'How can we help you?' Jack asked tersely.

'Well, about Polly.' She glanced at Alexi but quickly looked away again, finally appearing to be embarrassed. 'I know we haven't always seen eye to eye, but things have changed, and I hoped we could at least compare notes in an effort to help Polly. She might have her faults, but she's no murderer. I'll stake my life on that.'

'I have never had a problem with you.' Alexi's tone was dismissive. 'All the aggression has been one-sided, to the extent that my custom isn't welcome in your shop. What I've done to offend you remains a mystery.'

'Sorry. It's just that...'

'If you have something worth telling us about Polly's relation-ship with Gerry then sit down and get it off your chest,' Jack said. 'Otherwise, we have stuff to do.'

Linda pulled out a chair.

'You knew Gerry well?' Alexi asked her.

'Better than I ever wanted to.' Linda shuddered. 'The man was a complete jerk and treated Polly appallingly.'

'Polly didn't think so,' Jack pointed out.

'He worked a number on her. Used her for free board and lodging and... well, use your imagination. She was the only one who couldn't see it. I tried to tell her that she was being played but she was having none of it.'

Jack and Alexi exchanged a prolonged look. Linda's take on the relationship between Gerry and her friend was very different to Polly's version, and highly inflammatory.

'I hear Gerry was popular with the ladies in general,' Jack remarked.

Linda snorted. 'He thought he was God's gift and that no female on the planet could resist his legendary charm.'

'Did he try it on with you?' Alexi asked. Linda was reasonably attractive and single, and Gerry didn't seem to respect boundaries.

Linda waved the suggestion aside. 'No way,' she replied a little too quickly. 'Even if he had, I wouldn't have given him the time of day. He was my friend's partner, or so she liked to think, and I would never do that to her.'

From which Alexi deduced that she'd tried to attract him, but he hadn't made a move on her, and her feelings were hurt as a consequence.

'Polly told us that he'd agreed to give up long-distance driving and move in with her. Do you think that's true?'

'She told me the same thing last night when I went to see her.' Linda paused. 'I think they had the discussion and I also think that he offered her platitudes that she chose to interpret positively. She is so needy. So damned gullible.' She leaned across the table, bringing her face closer to Alexi and Jack. 'But I'll tell you one thing with absolute certainty: Gerry wouldn't have given up the freedom of the road.'

'How can you be so sure?' Alexi asked.

'Because he would never settle down with one woman in a million years. He has previous in that regard. Ask his ex-wife.'

'People get older. They change,' Jack said.

Linda shook her head emphatically. 'Not Gerry. He was still

very much in the game. Besides,' she added, 'all those long trips to Europe, I'm pretty sure he had a lucrative sideline going and he wouldn't have given that up in favour of making beds and cleaning toilets for a living.'

'What sideline?' Alexi and Jack asked together.

'I have absolutely no idea, or any proof. It's just an impression I got. He'd come back from Holland or wherever flush with cash and shower Polly with expensive gifts to keep her sweet. I know those drivers cut corners, so to speak, put in more hours behind the wheel than they should, sleep in the cab and claim for a hotel, stuff like that. But they don't earn the sort of dosh that Gerry used to flash about without being into something decidedly dodgy. Fags, booze, even people smuggling... He'd have been unable to resist the thrill, if you like. He'd have looked upon it as a game.'

'We've been told the opposite with regard to his financial situation and that recently, he'd been boxed into some sort of corner,' Jack said, playing a hunch based on the overheard phone conversation.

'Yeah, Polly said he was pretty down, angry about something, when he arrived this time. He was distant with her too, which made her worry that he'd gone off her. And that, I think, was what forced her to confront him. She'd dealt with his moods in the past, weathered the storm and mollycoddled him into a better frame of mind. He could do no wrong in her eyes, unless she even suspected him of cheating on her. Then... well, I have no idea how she'd respond.'

'But you said when you came in that she was incapable of murder?' Alexi pointed out. 'You were emphatic.'

'She's possessive, highly strung and emotional. If Gerry gave her the heave-ho, she'd be devastated. She'd rant and rave and throw things but murder...' Linda shook her head. 'No. I just can't see it. She'd fight tooth and nail to keep him but if she murdered anyone, it would be the rival for Gerry's affections, always assuming there was such a person.'

'Okay,' Jack said, turning sideways on his chair and giving Linda his full attention. 'I know Polly's your friend, but you've made it clear that she was also besotted with Gerry. So, if he *did* reject her, do you stand by your assertion that she's incapable of murder? Because, here's the thing: Alexi and I remain to be convinced.'

'She shouldn't have come to you.' Two spots of colour appeared high on Linda's cheeks. 'How could she expect you to remain impartial after the way that she… that we all treated you, Alexi?'

'But Polly did come to us and we're struggling to figure out what precisely went on, so help us out here,' Jack said. 'Hand on heart, do you think she *could* have snapped on the spur of the moment and taken the ultimate form of revenge?'

'Anything's possible, I suppose.' Linda shook her head. 'But no, I don't,' she said emphatically. 'They've had bust ups before, but he always came back. Not because he's in love with Polly, which is what she believed, but because she's a soft touch and Gerry enjoyed his creature comforts.'

'What if he actually told her there was someone else?' Alexi asked.

Linda hesitated. 'She would have been distraught, but I honestly don't believe she would have killed him over it.'

Alexi didn't share that belief, but then she hardly knew the woman. Besides, given the vendetta that she'd conducted against Alexi, she had every reason in the world to imagine her capable of just about anything. 'Then who do you think did do it?' she asked.

Linda spread her hands. 'I don't have the foggiest. Unless he took up with another woman nearby who got wind of Polly. Gerry roused strong passions in the opposite sex; that much could never be in doubt. It's hard to explain why to someone who never met

him.' She paused, clearly struggling for words. 'He was charis-
matic, one of those people who lit up a room the moment he
walked into it. Everyone's best friend, if you like. The men were
drawn to him as well as the women. He was always joking and flirting, and never seemed to take life too seriously.'

'I gather that he didn't like being seen in public with Polly,' Jack
said.

Linda snorted. 'Another indication if any is necessary that he
liked to keep his life compartmentalised. He didn't have any other
contacts in this part of the world, as far as I know, but I guess he'd
learned to be cautious and didn't want to be seen out and about
with her. Anyway, why go out when he had everything he needed
on tap twenty-four seven at Polly's?'

'You really didn't like him much, did you?' Alexi asked.

'I didn't like the way he used Polly. I'm not telling you anything
that I haven't said to her face, but her emotions were engaged and
she wasn't listening to anything she didn't want to hear. Polly's
been on her own for a long time, or had been before Gerry swept
her off her feet.'

'She's been married?' Jack asked.

'She married straight from school. It was a disaster, but she
stuck it for ten years, then had a breakdown.' Linda paused. 'She
was sectioned.'

Jack and Alexi shared a glance. 'He was as big a shit as Gerry,
from what I can gather. Polly has lousy taste in men. Anyway, he
led her a merry dance. Out all hours, flirting with the letter of the
law as well as with anything in a skirt. And Polly meanwhile was
stuck at home with three kids under five.'

Alexi's mouth fell open. 'She has children?'

'Yes, but they were taken into care when her mental health
deteriorated, and she never got them back once she'd recovered.'

'Did she try?'

Linda shook her head. 'She never says. She doesn't talk about that horrible period in her life very much but the long and short of it is that her ex knocked her about. She was a frequent visitor at the local A&E with broken bones and what have you, but she always made excuses for the bastard and now I see... or saw history repeating itself with Gerry.' She sighed. 'It made me so damned mad to have to sit on the sidelines and watch him manipulate her.'

'Her ex didn't look after the kids when she was sectioned?' Alexi felt a glimmer of sympathy for the woman who'd made her life difficult in so many annoying ways since her move to Lambourn.

'No. Her husband got caught robbing a jewellery shop. It wasn't a first offence and he got sent down. It was that rather than all the beatings that pushed Polly over the edge, and she tried to kill herself.'

'Blimey!'

'I'm telling you all this because I know she won't. She doesn't like to revisit that period in her life, and I guess you can see why.'

'Where are her children now?' Alexi asked. 'Does she see them?'

'They're all grown with families of their own. She was only seventeen when the first was born. She tried to get in touch once she came out of hospital, but they didn't want to see her. As far as I'm aware, there has never been any contact between them.'

'And the husband?' Jack asked.

'Got killed in a gang fight six years ago. The only decent thing he did for Polly was not to divorce her and so she got a healthy life insurance payout.'

'Which financed the B&B,' Alexi said, almost to herself. She'd been wondering about that.

Jack nodded. 'Do you know his name?'

'Charlie. Charlie Pearson, but like I say, he's history.'

'Phew!' Alexi blew air through her lips. 'That's quite a story.'

'Is there anything else we need to know?' Jack asked.

'Not that I can think of.' Linda gathered up her bag and stood. 'You know where to find me if you need more background. And again, I'm sorry we were such bitches, Alexi. It was ridiculous to get dragged into Polly's vendetta but she's the sort of person who, when she gets obsessed, is impossible to stop. You get caught in the slipstream before you know what you're actually protesting about.'

Alexi nodded. 'I hear you,' she said.

And she did understand a lot better now that she was aware of Polly's mental health issues. Did one ever completely recover from such frailties, she wondered? She'd once done an in-depth exposé on the growing awareness of mental instability. The illness still carried a stigma, people were reluctant to talk about it, but what she'd discovered had torn at her heartstrings. The pace of modern competitive life placed a toll on an increasing number of young people's emotions, some of whom became as desperate as Polly and attempted to take their own lives. But an overloaded system struggled to cope and the care on offer was at best spasmodic.

Charlie Pearson had run around on Polly, treating her like his personal punchbag when he got frustrated or if she questioned his activities, it seemed. Perhaps it had been the thought of Jack treating Grace the same way that had caused her vendetta against Alexi? It would have been helpful though if she'd established the facts first.

'Well,' Alexi said, flapping a hand in front of her face once Linda had left them to the accompaniment of feral hisses from Cosmo, 'that opens up a whole new can of worms.'

'Just a little,' Jack agreed, taking Alexi's hand and giving it a soft squeeze. As always, he was attuned to her anguish. 'Okay, let's assess what we just heard. Basically, do we believe Linda's account?'

'I'm not sure I believe that Gerry didn't come on to her.' Alexi waved her free hand. 'No, scrub that. I think she was jealous and that *she* tried it on with him, but he didn't want to know. If we're right and he had other women scattered about, he wouldn't risk what he had going with Polly by playing in her backyard. But whatever his reasons, he rejected Linda and hurt her feelings.'

'Yeah.' Jack nodded. 'I wasn't taken in by what she told us. There's something else going on there. She came to us, pretending to fight for her friend. But all that stuff she revealed only succeeded in making Polly look unstable, capable of anything when roused. Linda continued to defend her, insisting she couldn't possibly kill anyone, but left us with the precise opposite impression.'

'Yeah, I agree, but going back to Linda's feelings of rejection, would that be enough for her to take a knife to Gerry?'

Jack waggled a hand from side to side. 'I wouldn't rule it out. Like you just pointed out, she was very willing to tell us about Polly's chequered history and her mental illness, all the while pretending that she was doing so out of friendship.'

'Will Vickery find out about her being sectioned?'

Jack shook his head. 'She didn't commit any crime so her records won't necessarily come to light. Vickery will find out about the abusive ex but that's old news. Ben will need to know. I will emphasise to Polly that she needs to tell him everything and that it needs to come from her. Apart from anything else, if she is charged, her mental instability would be a good form of defence.' He leaned back in his chair and let out a slow breath. 'If she isn't forthcoming with Ben then we walk away from this.'

'Agreed.'

'Is this hard for you?' Jack slipped an arm around her shoulders. 'We don't have to do it. They don't deserve our help after the way they've behaved.'

'Even so. I intend to be the bigger person.'

'Well, if it gets too much, we can bail at any time.'

'I wonder who benefits in the event of Polly dying?' Alexi mused after a short pause. 'I don't know if the B&B is mortgaged but even if it is, there must be a fair bit of equity in it as a going concern.'

'You're thinking about the estranged kids, I guess.' Jack nodded as though answering his own question. 'Perhaps they thought their dad's life insurance payout should have gone to them. Perhaps it should have, given what they went through. Perhaps Polly tried to cut them out. It's all speculation and we'll have to ask her. For all we know, she could be in daily contact with those kids, they saw a chancer muscling in on their inheritance and took action to prevent it.'

'It's possible. In any event, it'll give Vickery another avenue to explore. As will Gerry's trips to Europe and whatever sideline he had going.'

'We need to find those kids, but we'll talk to Polly about them first. See if she was in touch with them.'

'She might not tell us.'

'In which case, I'll remind her that she's on her own.'

'Well anyway, Gerry sounds like a real piece of work.'

Jack smiled as he stood to refill their coffee cups. 'The ex-wife should be here any time. It will be interesting to see what she has to say about him.'

No sooner had they sipped at their coffee than the door opened again, and Cheryl ushered a woman through it.

'Pauline Dawlish,' Cheryl said. 'This is Alexi Ellis and Jack Maddox. I'll leave you with them to talk in private.'

Cheryl disappeared again as quickly as she'd arrived, flashing a *what-the-hell* look at Alexi over her shoulder as she went. Alexi smiled at her friend and then transferred her full attention to

Pauline. She was a middle-aged blonde, much the same as Polly, and carried a few extra pounds that her height helped to disguise. Her ravaged face was a clear indication of her grief, as was the scrunched-up tissue clutched in one hand. Alexi felt sympathy for her. She appeared to pass Cosmo's test too since he made do with sniffing the air and then settling back down to sleep again.

'Let me get you some coffee,' Jack offered, as Alexi helped Pauline to a chair. 'I am sorry we have to meet under such circumstances.'

'As am I,' she replied in a low, melodic voice, 'although I suppose I shouldn't be surprised.' She nodded her thanks when Jack placed a mug in front of her, along with a jug of cream, sugar and a plate of Cheryl's homemade biscuits. 'He always did enjoy sailing close to the wind. He said that routine bored him.' She paused with her cup raised to her lips. 'Can I ask why you called me? What your interest is in the affair?'

'I'm a private investigator,' Jack said, 'and Alexi is an investor in this hotel as well as being a respected journalist. We're simply trying to discover what happened to your late husband.'

'We know what happened. He was murdered.' She looked hesitant suddenly. 'Are you helping the woman who...'

'We're simply trying to establish the facts,' Jack said easily. 'If Polly's the guilty party, then we will allow the law to take its course.'

'I see.' She looked unhappy with Jack's explanation but didn't show any indication of leaving.

'Gerry drove long distances alone for a living,' Alexi remarked. 'That seems a bit at odds with his life and soul of the party persona. It's a solitary occupation.'

'I don't suppose for one moment that he was always alone,' Pauline replied, rolling her eyes. 'That's one of the reasons why we divorced. The moment he got behind the wheel, he looked upon himself as a free agent rather than a married man and a father with responsibilities.'

Alexi smiled at her. 'Is that the only reason why you divorced, if you don't mind my asking?'

'Basically, yes.' Pauline added cream and sugar to her coffee and stirred it more vigorously than Alexi thought necessary. She was clearly struggling to contain her emotions and dragging up the past only added to her grief. 'I was left at home with two small kids whilst he was swanning off all over the place, usually coming back stinking of cheap perfume and taking sod all interest in family life.'

'But you still love him?' Alexi touched the older lady's hand. 'It shows.'

Pauline let out a long breath. 'Yes and no. He's the father of my children and we did have some good times in the early days.' She smiled through fresh tears. 'He could be the life and soul and possessed the capacity to charm the birds out of the trees. I gave him so many ultimatums that I lost count, but he knew he could talk me out of walking away with just a bit of attention and that damned smile of his.'

'So we've been told.'

'The thing about Gerry was that he always stirred something in me. Sometimes love, often exasperation, regularly anger, but never *nothing*, if that makes any sense. There's a line from an old song that always makes me think of him. "I'd rather hurt than feel nothing at all".'

'I hear you,' Alexi said softly.

'Why did you finally throw him out?' Jack asked.

'I'd been away looking after my mum, who had dementia. We were trying to find a suitable care facility for her. The kids were with his mum. Anyway, I got home earlier than planned and caught him literally with his trousers down, in *our* bedroom with some slut. Well, that was it. He'd crossed a line. The kids were due back that day too. If they'd been early, they would have caught him at it. So, I threw him out and that was that.'

'But he continued to look after you... financially?'

'To his credit, yes he did. He paid over the odds when it came to child maintenance and until I met my new husband, he paid the mortgage as well. Actually, we got on better when we were divorced. He called in frequently to see the kids in the early days, before I met Bill, and it was like we were courting again. He flirted outrageously, made me feel young and appreciated and it was great fun.'

'But he wasn't good at monogamy,' Jack said.

'To put it mildly.' She sighed. 'I gather the woman he was shacked up with here finally had enough and snapped. God alone knows, that could have been me.'

'Where did the money come from?' Jack asked after a pause in the conversation.

'Sorry?' Pauline blinked at him. 'What do you mean?'

'Well, he was a long-distance driver. How did he find the dosh to support you so well and live himself? They don't get paid that well, do they?'

Pauline lifted one shoulder. 'I have absolutely no idea. It didn't cross my mind to ask.' She frowned. 'You think he was into something dodgy that got him killed? Well,' she added, not waiting for a response, 'I suppose you would be looking to besmirch his reputation, given that you're fighting for the woman who likely murdered him.'

'That's the last thing we're doing,' Alexi assured her. 'As Jack already explained, we're simply gathering facts. As things stand, it does look as though the lady he was with is the guilty party, but we like to be thorough.'

'Okay.' Pauline drained her mug. 'I hear you. The police have asked to talk to me. They said they'd come to Southampton, but I wanted to be here, close to where it happened. God knows why.'

'That's understandable,' Alexi said, standing, aware that they'd got everything from the lady that they were likely to. 'We have a room prepared for you upstairs. Let me show you to it.'

'Thank you.' Pauline stood and collected up her belongings. 'I didn't sleep a wink last night after I got the news. I must look a wreck so a shower and a doze would go down well.'

6

Jack mulled over what they'd learned that morning as he waited for Alexi to return. They had leads to chase down, enquiries to make, and that prospect brought him alive. He didn't like Polly Pearson very much but now that he knew more about her history, he did have some sympathy for her situation. If she'd been consistently abused and had mental health issues, then it helped to explain some of her bizarre behaviour.

'Battered women are victims... until they're not,' Alexi said as she walked back through the door.

'Yeah, my thoughts precisely. The worm eventually turns, which implies that she could well be our killer but is in denial and actually believes she didn't do it. Perhaps she doesn't even remember because her mind has blocked it out.' Jack shrugged. 'It happens.'

'How do you get over losing your kids?' Alexi asked, her eyes filling. 'I can't begin to imagine.'

'You must have seen it in your line of work. Kids having kids when they're still kids themselves. We haven't heard any mention of a mother, so I guess Polly came from a deprived background herself and had no one to help her cope with the little ones.'

'And her husband was obviously a waste of space. Knocked her up at regular intervals and then took no responsibility.' Alexi sighed. 'It's so sad but you're right, a familiar story.'

'She tried to rebuild her life here in Lambourn and must have thought all her Christmases had come at once when she met Gerry and he worked a charm offensive on her. She was punching above her weight though, attempting to clip the wings of a free spirit. He didn't take it well when she tried to force him into a life of domesticity and rejected her. Given her history, I can see why she would have struck out in anger.'

'If he did fob her off then something might well have snapped.' Alexi perched her backside against the edge of the table as she articulated her thoughts. 'History was in danger of repeating itself. Her husband ran around on her, she finished up sectioned and estranged from her children, but managed to build a life for herself again.'

'Yeah. Then made the mistake of putting her trust in another terrible man.'

'Or,' Alexi said, resuming her chair, 'someone who Gerry crossed in his dodgy dealings, always supposing there were any, got pissed off and topped him. Or else Linda's the epitome of a woman scorned, or...' she threw up her hands. 'There have to be more ors. You're the one with the suspicious mind. Help me out here.'

'Or one of Polly's kids took action to protect his or her inheritance.'

'Leaving their mother with her name in the frame for murder?' Alexi shook her head. 'Is that likely?'

'Wouldn't surprise me. They were rejected and wouldn't have felt much love for a mother who neglected them and tried to kill herself. Not sure how old they were but I'm betting the eldest remembers his mum and resents what happened to him. Or her, of course.'

'But if she had made contact with one or more of them and that child saw a man muscling in,' Alexi reasoned, 'then yeah, I don't suppose they'd have felt much compunction about removing the threat and seeing their mother banged up for murder. Revenge and all that. They could then move in and take over the business.'

'Harsh, but I've seen worse in my time. I've seen murder committed with less provocation too.'

'Then again, perhaps Polly did it and has no recollection, as you suggested just now. If her mental health is fragile, that's entirely possible. She always seemed like a perfectly rational adult to me, albeit one with a nasty attitude, but then you seldom know what goes on inside people's heads, do you? Anyway, Polly is still my prime suspect.'

'Mine too,' Jack agreed.

'You don't think Pauline, Gerry's divorced wife, is involved?'

Jack shook his head. 'No. Vickery will check on her whereabouts at the time of the killing, but I don't see it myself. She seems happy enough with her life now and even if Gerry *did* plan to shack up with Polly, I don't suppose it would have lasted. Pauline knew him well enough to have reached the same conclusion. Besides, if they had agreed to live happily ever after just before he died, he wouldn't have had time to impart the glad tidings to Pauline.'

'True.' Alexi nodded her agreement. 'Men are too macho to pick up the phone and talk about that sort of stuff.' She bent to scratch Toby's ears when Cosmo stretched himself out in their shared basket, almost forcing Toby out of it. 'Don't let him bully you, baby,' she said, blowing the dog a kiss. 'Anyway,' she added, straightening up again, 'there's James Alton, don't forget. There's something about that cheating jockey that doesn't sit right with me.'

'But unless we can tie him to Gerry in some way, we can't prove motive.'

'Stop thinking like a policeman, Mr Maddox, and go with your instincts.'

'Sorry, darling. Old habits...'

Alexi glanced at the clock. 'It's gone one. Time flies when you're having fun.' She folded her arms and tapped the fingers of one hand restlessly against her opposite forearm. 'Shouldn't we have heard from Ben by now?'

Before Jack could respond, Drew came through the door with a platter of overfilled sandwiches.

'Marcel says you can't sleuth on empty stomachs,' he said, referring to their temperamental chef. Jack and Alexi had once cleared him of suspicion in a murder that had occurred at Hopgood Hall, and he'd been devoted to them ever since, showing his appreciation by feeding them his culinary masterpieces at regular intervals.

'Tell him we appreciate it,' Jack said, sitting down and tucking into avocado and smoked salmon.

Alexi shook her head as she sat opposite him. 'Where do you put it all?' she asked accusingly. 'You eat for England and never seem to put on a pound.'

'It's all in the metabolism,' he replied, grinning at her.

Alexi helped herself to prawn and bacon, sighing with pleasure as Marcel's spicy creation slipped down her throat. 'The man's a genius with food, even if he does say so himself.'

Jack laughed. 'He has his uses.'

'So, what now?' Alexi asked, wiping her fingers on a napkin

and watching Jack as he continued to make inroads into the sandwiches.

'We wait to hear from Ben, and if Polly hasn't been detained then we need to talk to her again. She has questions to answer and we need her to be honest if she expects us to continue helping her. For a start, I want to know more about her estranged family. After that, we'd best go and enrol in yoga classes.'

Alexi chortled. 'Can't see you doing sun salutations,' she said.

'You'd be surprised. I have hidden talents.'

'Very well hidden.'

'Grace tried to get me to go to yoga in the early days of our marriage. Said it would help me to find myself, or some such crap. I told her that I knew exactly where I was and didn't need to look but she was having none of it.'

'How many classes did you manage?'

'Two.'

'Ah.' Alexi grinned. 'Perhaps that was an early sign of your incompatibility.'

'Absolutely. If you asked me to attend classes, then I'd sign on the dotted without hesitation. No question.'

Alexi wagged a finger at him. 'You're only saying that because you know I won't ask.'

'Damn, you're good!'

'Save some for the impecunious workers,' Ben said, striding through the door on his long, gangly legs, his gaze zeroing in on the depleted platter.

'Knock yourself out,' Jack replied, pulling out a chair for the solicitor whilst Alexi got up and poured him coffee. 'How did it go with Polly? Should we read anything into the fact that your client isn't with you?'

Ben chewed for a moment before clearing his throat and

responding. 'Probably, but she hasn't been detained.' He allowed a significant pause. 'Not yet, but it isn't looking too good for her.'

'Vickery thinks he has his woman?' Jack asked.

'Wouldn't you? If the front door wasn't permanently left open, as I was at pains to remind him, implying that anyone could have walked in, then I think she would have been charged. As it is, everything he has is circumstantial. Polly insists that Gerry had agreed to move in with her and that whoever overheard their argument would also have overheard their reconciliation when they sealed the deal, so to speak.'

'Fair point,' Alexi said, nodding. 'Her regular guests told us that they were frequently treated to both scenarios whether they wanted to hear them or not.'

'Right. So she maintains that she had no reason to kill the love of her life and every reason to keep him alive.'

Jack leaned back and stretched his legs further beneath the table. 'Vickery knows we're in her corner? Kinda.'

'Yeah. He rolled his eyes when I told him it was you who had engaged my services, but I think he was pleased. It's a tough one for him. He'll be under pressure from above to put this one to bed quickly, but I got the impression that he's not entirely sure about Polly's guilt.'

'We've found out a few things about her past. And about the victim.'

Jack went on to give Ben a succinct account of the findings in question. Ben carried on munching and didn't bother to take notes but Jack knew he would absorb all the salient facts, process them mentally and probably draw the same conclusions that he and Alexi had reached.

'The plot thickens,' Ben said when Jack ran out of words.

'Did she tell you anything about her past?' Alexi asked. 'About her kids? About her mental health?'

'Nope, but then I didn't ask.'

'She didn't volunteer the information to us either,' Jack said. 'It was her *friend* who enlightened us out of a sense of concern for Polly's wellbeing, or so she'd have us believe, but I'm not sure I buy that.'

'You have your doubts about her?'

'You know me, Ben. Doubt is programmed into my DNA. All those years of being a copper and constantly being lied to affects a man. Some might say it makes him cynical.'

Alexi laughed. 'Never!'

She and Ben shared a high-five.

'We're wondering,' Alexi said, when the laughter died down, 'if Polly has been in contact with any of her kids. We know she tried to find them.'

'Right.' Ben had cleared the last of the sandwiches. 'If she was planning to settle down with another guy, I can see that they might have objections. But murdering the man to prevent her mother from committing...' Ben looked dubious. 'Seems like a stretch.'

'You need to talk to Polly. Get her to open up about her past. It could be relevant, or at the very least a plausible defence.'

'She's gone back to the B&B to shower. Said the police station made her feel dirty. I told her to meet us here. That we needed to talk about the next step. But Vickery is likely to call you as well. He won't want to talk to you, even on the phone, in front of her. He has to play this one by the book and be seen to be obeying the rules.'

'I hear you,' Jack said, stretching his arms above his head and yawning.

'Do we know if the murder weapon came from Polly's kitchen?' Alexi asked.

Ben shook his head. 'She uses the same brand of knives but one the same size as the weapon was found in a drawer, along with the rest of the set.'

'Doesn't mean she didn't have two of her favourite size,' Jack said.

'Doesn't mean that she did,' Ben replied.

Jack chuckled. 'Glad to see you haven't lost your edge.'

'I can't help thinking that if she stabbed him whilst of sound mind, she'd still have had enough sense to remove the weapon and dispose of it, if it could be traced back to her,' Alexi said.

Ben inclined his head. 'Fair point. I gather there were no prints on the weapon. So, if it was a crime of passion or a spur-of-the-moment job, it shows a clear head at the time the deed was committed.'

Jack nodded. 'Because the murderer either wore gloves or wiped the knife handle down while it was still stuck in Gerry's chest.'

Alexi and Jack exchanged a dubious look. For his part, Jack simply couldn't decide if Polly *was* actually the guilty party. So much of the evidence pointed her way but niggling doubts lingered in the back of his mind, and he had long since learned to depend upon his instincts. Besides, Gerry led a complex, compart-mentalised life and until they'd delved deeper into it, Jack would never feel satisfied that Polly was the killer.

'And reduces the effect of a diminished responsibility plea, should it come to it,' Ben added.

'Yeah, it would,' Jack agreed. 'I've dealt with spontaneous murders in my time but can't think of a case where the killer was *that* meticulous. I blame all the bloody TV crime procedural shows. They had no consideration for the hard-working cop.'

'I hear you,' Ben said, yawning behind his hand.

'The inability to find any physical evidence of Polly's guilt is one of the reasons, I suspect, why she isn't locked up.' Jack grimaced. 'Yet.'

'What about her clothing?' Alexi asked. 'Wouldn't there be blood splatter?'

'If she'd removed the knife while his heart was still beating, then yeah,' Jack replied.

'Some traces of blood were found on her hands, even though she'd washed them, and on the cuff of her sweatshirt. But she explained that away by having checked the body for a pulse, which is plausible.'

Alexi shuddered. 'Well, presumably the police have her clothes and will do further tests. I hear about arterial spray from the shows you detest, Jack, which is often invisible to the human eye.'

'They do have them.' Ben nodded round a mouthful of biscuit. 'And will subject them to microscopic examination. Vickery's probably hanging on for the results, hoping for the smoking gun to make his case rock solid, if you like.'

'It seems to me,' Jack said, leaning his elbows on the table and resting his chin in his cupped hands as he articulated his earlier doubts, 'that there are a lot of imponderables. In other words, it's not quite as open and shut as Vickery would like. And a good defence brief could cast all sorts of doubt over Polly's guilt.'

'That sounds like the man himself,' Alexi said, cocking her head to one side when a familiar voice echoed from the entrance hall.

'If he's here that soon,' Ben said, 'it can only be a good sign for Polly.'

'Yeah, he wouldn't come looking for our help if he was sure of himself,' Jack agreed.

Vickery tapped at the kitchen door and then strolled through it. 'No quips about this becoming a habit, please,' he said.

Alexi smiled and got up to pour coffee. 'Help yourself to Cheryl's biscuits, Mark, before Ben scoffs the lot.'

'Hey, I'm the brains of this operation and brains need to be fed and watered!' Ben protested.

Vickery shook his head at Ben, then shook hands with Jack before taking a seat at the table and getting stuck into the biscuits.

'No DC Hogan?' Alexi asked, resuming her chair.

'She's pursuing other enquiries. We do have more than one case on the go, you know.'

'I do know.' Jack nodded his sympathy. 'But you're not absolutely convinced that Polly did it, are you?'

'Not up to me to decide innocence or guilt, thank God.'

'But you don't like sloppy policework and want to get it right.' Jack pressed home his point, watching his friend in the hope of picking up indications of his thought process.

'At the moment, I don't have any other suspects and only Ms Pearson's word for the fact that she and the victim were about to ride off into the sunset together. So, I wondered if...'

'If we'd done any digging for you,' Jack said, grinning.

'I have to say I was surprised when Ben mentioned that you'd gone into bat for Polly. Especially after the way she picked on you, Alexi.'

'I've risen above her pettiness.' Alexi grinned. 'For now. Anyway, you can blame Jack for that. We've found out that she's friendly with his ex-wife, Grace and thinks I'm a maneater.'

'Ah, I see.'

'Anyway,' Alexi said, 'you know me, Mark; when I get my teeth into a story, I can be more tenacious than a mule.'

'Ah, a story. That would be it.' Mark Vickery grinned but didn't look convinced. 'You're a good person, Alexi Ellis, even if you do make my life difficult sometimes by producing alternative theories for open and shut cases.'

Jack grinned. 'If you thought this was open and shut, you wouldn't be here.'

Vickery inclined his head but said nothing.

'As it happens,' Alexi remarked into the ensuing silence, 'we have found out a few things about Polly's life, and that of the victim, that suggest other avenues of investigation.'

'I'm all ears,' Vickery said, picking up his coffee and taking a sip.

'Are you aware that Polly was married and had three kids?' Jack asked.

'We're not complete amateurs, you know. She came out of an abusive marriage, tried to top herself and was sectioned. She'd neglected the kids and they were taken into care.' He shrugged. 'Don't see the relevance myself.'

Alexi repeated their theory that one of the kids might have been in contact with Polly and taken drastic action to prevent their inheritance from being frittered away on an undeserving cause.

Vickery twitched his lips. 'Unlikely. And I don't have the resources or any plausible reason to delve.'

'Nothing to stop us asking Polly if any of her kids have been in contact,' Jack said casually, aware that Vickery wanted him to do the legwork.

'Then there's Gerry's trips abroad,' Alexi said. 'He returned flush with cash, we're told, but was recently overheard on the phone pleading with someone for more time... Might that have been linked to a debt he was in?'

Vickery jerked upright in his chair. 'First I've heard of it.'

'One of the regular guests, Jane Grant, overheard him on his phone. She said she only remembered about it after making her statement but would tell you about it.'

'And you can find out from Holby's what runs he regularly made,' Jack pointed out. 'That might throw up something.'

'Tenuous.' Vickery lifted a shoulder, but Jack knew he had his attention. 'We'll check his call log but if he was talking to someone who's into dodgy dealings, you can bet your pension on him using a burner phone.'

'Someone called Melanie rang Gerry on the day he died. Polly saw the name on his phone and challenged him. She's told us that much,' Alexi said, 'and it's what instigated their argument. But she's adamant that Gerry agreed to commit, and it all ended happily.'

'Well, she would say that, wouldn't she?'

Jack and Alexi shared a look and both nodded.

Vickery shook his head. 'I find it easier to believe that a woman with a previously disturbed mind and a lousy choice in men lost her rag. There's probably nothing more sinister than that about this case. Abusees do sometimes turn into abusers, you know.' Vickery drained his mug and stood up. 'Anyway, I came to tell you that I'm under pressure from above to charge her and let the CPS decide if they have enough to proceed.'

'Yeah, I thought that would be the case,' Jack replied. 'So why didn't you? Charge her, that is?'

'You know me, Jack. Never was one to be told what to do, but unless something else comes to light in the very near future then I will have to. It can wait a day or two, but no longer than that.'

'Until we've done your sleuthing for you,' Alexi said, grinning, 'you are not absolutely convinced that you've got your woman, are you, Mark?'

'Perhaps I'm giving her the benefit of the doubt right now because you two got involved,' Vickery said.

Jack laughed and stood as well. 'I'll walk you out,' he said, shaking his head when Cosmo gave a desultory hiss as Vickery passed the basket he shared with Toby.

'He's warming to me,' he said.

'What is it that you're not telling me, Mark?' Jack asked as soon as he and Vickery reached the entrance hall.

But before Vickery could respond, the door opened and Polly walked through it. She was not alone. Jack stopped dead in his tracks and glowered at her companion.

'Sorry,' Vickery said. 'Didn't want to mention in front of Alexi that Ms Pearson had a Rottweiler waiting for her interview to end.'

'Grace,' he said, barely hearing Vickery's words. 'What the hell are you doing here?'

7

'Hello, darling. It's been a while.'

Grace stretched out a hand to touch Jack's arm, but he moved deftly away, leaving her stroking thin air and looking rather ridiculous. She wore tight jeans that showed off her slim figure and a top that sculpted her body. Her hair and makeup were immaculate, giving a lie to the casual approach. Grace had taken a lot of trouble over her appearance whilst supposedly rushing to support her friend in her hour of need.

Sorry, Vickery mouthed as he headed for the door.

'What's going on?'

Jack ignored Grace and addressed the question to Polly. He was furious with Grace and more than ready to cut Polly loose. Grace had definitely leapt on Gerry's murder as an excuse to come to Lambourn and inflict herself upon Jack, but he had yet to decide what she hoped to gain by her behaviour. His relationship with Alexi had been plastered all over the news during the recent murder cases. Did she seriously imagine that turning up in person and reminding Jack of what they'd once had would change his feelings for Alexi.

Get real, woman!

Grace's inflated opinion of her own self-worth defied belief. Worse, she was using Polly's dilemma for her own ends and that was inexcusable. He had yet to decide whether Polly was an innocent victim or vindictive killer but either way, she didn't deserve to be manipulated.

'The moment I heard about Polly's plight, naturally I took time off work and came down to see if there was anything I could do to help.'

Again it was Grace who spoke and Jack turned to her with a snarl. 'I wasn't talking to you,' he said.

'I'm sorry,' Polly said, clearly taken aback by Jack's violent reaction. 'Grace heard and wants to be here for me. I think Linda called her.' Jack suspected that the news had reached Holby's and Grace had seized the opportunity even before Linda involved herself. 'I need my friends. I'm scared, Jack. I'm sure I'm going to be charged with killing the man I loved, and I didn't do it!'

Her voice had risen, drawing the attention of some of the customers in the bar. Aware that one or more of them might be a local journalist, Jack thought on his feet. He glanced at Polly properly for the first time. She looked dreadful, on the verge of collapse if he was any judge as she leaned heavily on Grace's arm. Her complexion was pale and drawn and her eyes were red-rimmed. Her hair was tangled, her clothing rumpled, and remnants of mascara made black trails down her face. Now that he was aware of her fragile mental state, he was very worried about her ability to withstand the pressure of a murder investigation and wondered if perhaps she should be in hospital, getting proper medical care.

More expediently, he absolutely didn't want to inflict Grace upon Alexi, at least not without warning her first, but he also couldn't see how to separate Polly from her in her present near-hysterical state. The problem was taken out of his hands when, presumably alerted by Polly's shouting, Alexi opened the kitchen door.

'Jack?' she said, taking in the scene and frowning. He had no idea if she realised who Grace was.

'Polly, as you can see, hasn't come alone,' he said through gritted teeth. 'This is Grace, my former wife, without whom it seems Polly can't function.'

Alexi glanced at Jack, who sent her a *what-the-hell* look.

'I see,' she said, making no effort to introduce herself. Grace would be well aware of her identity and was frowning now, clearly not liking the quality of the opposition.

'Do you want to carry on helping Polly, darling?' Jack asked, smiling at Alexi and completely ignoring Polly and Grace. 'Given this latest provocation.'

Polly's eyes darted between Jack and Alexi, putting Jack in mind of a rabbit caught in headlights and freezing on the spot. She clearly realised the mistake she had made in bringing Grace here, but it was also equally obvious that she was unaware of Grace's real agenda. At least Jack thought that was the case and would give her the benefit of the doubt until proven otherwise.

'Polly needs her friends,' Alexi replied after a prolonged pause. 'As to helping her, we still haven't committed but do have more questions before we decide.'

Grace's frown intensified at Alexi's total disregard for her presence. She'd played it exactly right, Jack thought. Grace had probably expected some sort of verbal sparring, expressions of territorial rights or whatever, but Alexi was too secure to indulge in such infantile pursuits. She turned back towards the kitchen without another word. Ben, alerted to the drama, stood in the doorway. Predictably, Cosmo picked up on the tension too. He stalked up to Grace, hissed, unfurled his claws and looked ready to strike.

'Cosmo!' Alexi's harsh voice caused her cat to back off, still hissing. He looked accusingly up at Alexi as though wondering why he hadn't been permitted to strike out at this presumptuous person. 'Sit down,' she said curtly to Grace when she followed Alexi and Jack into the kitchen, still supporting Polly.

'You're here as a courtesy,' Jack told Grace as he took the seat beside Alexi, across from Ben, Polly and Grace, and pointedly also took her hand in his. Alexi gently disentangled their fingers, making it clear that she could fight this particular battle without his physical support.

Grace looked crestfallen. What the hell else had she expected, Jack wondered. Grace patted the back of Polly's hand almost aggressively as she focused her attention upon the friend whom she'd manipulated into causing problems for Jack and Alexi. It was now very obvious to Jack that Polly was easily influenced by strong-willed people of either sex and that this murder and Polly's potential guilt had played straight into Grace's conniving hands.

All that remained to be explained was why? What the hell did Grace expect to achieve by thrusting herself into the heart of the investigation?

'We need to know more about your family life, Polly,' Ben said. 'About your children especially.'

Polly jerked out of a reverie. 'Why?' she asked.

'Do you see any of them?' Ben persisted, sharing a resigned look with Jack that implied this would be like pulling teeth.

'She tried to find them,' Grace said when Polly appeared to have been struck dumb.

'I need you to speak for yourself, Polly,' Ben said.

'What Grace said. Actually, Grace helped me to trace them. They were split up and adopted by different families. My middle one, a daughter, is living in Australia and never answered my letters. The youngest works in London and doesn't want to know me either. He was only two when... when things fell apart and won't remember me.' She sighed. 'Probably better that way. Michael, my eldest, was seven and does remember. He's a landscape gardener working on the south coast and doing very well for himself. He lives with his male partner,' she added, a defensive edge to her voice. 'I've seen him once or twice, but he blames me for ruining his childhood, which I did, I suppose. He says he remembers the constant shouting and me always having bruises and never standing up for myself.'

After a long rush of words, Polly felt silent again. Now that Jack was aware of her mental frailties, it seemed obvious that she was still struggling and he wondered if she was getting professional help.

'Did he ever meet Gerry?' Alexi asked.

'Yes.' Grace answered because Polly had again fallen into a catatonic state. Her gaze was focused on the hands folded in her lap and Jack knew that she'd retreated somewhere in her mind where she couldn't be reached. He was aware that abuse victims often created safe havens for themselves within their heads that only they had access to and that she wouldn't re-emerge until it felt safe to do so. 'Why? Does it matter?' Grace added, aggression in her tone.

'Grace, I am on the point of walking away from this investigation now that you've intruded into it,' Jack said, his voice hard and uncompromising. 'So why don't you keep quiet and let Polly speak for herself.'

Grace lowered her gaze. She had yet to meet Alexi's eye and Alexi seemed perfectly happy with that situation. 'I'm just trying to support my friend,' she muttered.

'Michael and I have met just three times.' Polly spoke softly and seemed rational again. 'Like I said already, Grace encouraged me to make contact with all my children. She thought it would help me to move on and perhaps atone for being such an atrocious mother. My younger son and daughter both ignored my efforts, but Michael called me. I went down to Portsmouth to meet him the first time, about a year ago now. He looks so much like his father did at that age that it knocked me back a bit. But he's gentle and considerate as a man – nothing like Charlie.'

'How did he feel about meeting you?' Alexi asked.

'How do you think?' Grace snapped but at a look from Jack, she closed her mouth again and fell into a sullen silence.

'He has anger issues, which is hardly surprising,' Polly replied. 'He says he had nightmares for a long time after… after he was taken into care. He remembers all the fights, loud voices, the beatings.' She lowered her head. 'It seems Charlie took a belt to him as well as me and I didn't even know. I was so wrapped up in my own misery that it didn't occur to me that a bully and misogynist would take his hostility out on his own kids. Michael never said but I should have noticed. I failed to protect them.' She glanced at Alexi through tear-filled eyes. 'What sort of mother does that make me?'

'You feared for your life.' Unsurprisingly, it was Grace who responded, patting Polly's hand as she did so, but Jack wasn't fooled by her performance. She was using Polly's friendship as an excuse to intrude into Jack's life.

Why was still a question that Jack had failed to come up with an answer to.

Their marriage hadn't been a bed of roses, but Jack had been fully invested in it in the early days and Grace had always been able to manipulate him into doing whatever it was that she wanted. Those days were long gone but for reasons that escaped Jack, she appeared to want him back and incredibly, also appeared to think that she'd manage to entice him. She was an attractive woman and knew it, but her charm had long since lost its appeal and Jack felt absolutely nothing for her.

She obviously looked upon Alexi as a mild inconvenience that could be overcome. Jack almost laughed aloud at a possibility that proved beyond doubt his ex's highly inflated opinion of her own self-worth. Alexi was the love of Jack's life and nothing and no one would come between them.

Not ever.

'Grace!' Jack snapped.

Cosmo lifted his head, growled and then stalked across to Jack, leaping athletically onto his lap and purring loud enough to wake the dead. Jack struggled not to smile as he stroked Cosmo's silky coat, always astonished by his intuitiveness. Still purring, he occasionally turned a piercing green glower towards Grace and let the purring slip for just long enough to let out a warning growl. Cosmo had made his feelings about Grace crystal clear and was supporting Jack with a display of feline intimidation.

'Polly's very vulnerable right now,' Grace replied weakly, clearly terrified of Cosmo, as well she should be. If he took a dislike to a person, he had been known to draw blood.

Was Polly vulnerable? Jack was unable to decide whether that was the case or whether she was putting in an Oscar-winning performance. He'd had enough experience of interviewing suspects to get a feel for their guilt or otherwise, but Polly's reactions had got him stumped. Especially now that he understood more about her earlier life and her mental issues.

'Since you're here,' Jack said curtly, addressing Grace, 'perhaps you can tell us what routes Gerry regularly drove.'

She stared at Jack. 'Why? What has that got to do with anything?'

Jack inhaled and counted to ten inside his head before responding. 'Just answer the question,' he said wearily.

'I don't know off the top of my head, but I can make a few calls and find out.'

'Do that.'

'Did he have any issues with the people he worked with?' Alexi asked. 'Any serious disputes?'

'Truck drivers mostly work alone,' Grace replied without looking at Alexi. 'It's the nature of the job.'

'He went to Holland regularly,' Polly said. 'He liked that run.'

'Holby's moves components for various manufacturing firms. Something to do with the car business, I think. It's more cost effective to transport these things by road rather than air freight,' Grace said.

'Do you know where he stayed?' Jack asked, thinking it was likely a dead end but asking the question anyway.

'No,' Grace said, shaking her head.

'There was a man, a few weeks ago, came to the B&B,' Polly said, her eyes widening as she recalled the event. 'Looking for Gerry. He had a foreign accent. He told me his name, but I can remember... Hank? Henry? Something like that. He said he knew Gerry from his trips into Holland and called by on the off chance of linking up with him. He said Gerry had told him all about me,' she added, preening. 'But Gerry was on the road, and I wasn't sure when I'd see him again.'

'Did the guy leave contact details?' Alexi asked, leaning forward. Jack could tell that like him, she believed they might be onto something.

'He did actually.' Polly snapped her fingers. 'Gerry got quite angry when I told him about the guy. Said not to talk to him if he called again. I asked why and he fobbed me off with a story about a debt that he'd already repaid. The guy was disputing the amount.'

Jack, Alexi and Ben looked at one another. It sounded implausible but Jack could see that Polly, far too trusting because she adored Gerry, had believed every word that spilled from his mouth. She would, Jack knew, have learned never to question anything the man in her life said during the course of her abusive marriage. One wrong word in such situations could result in a beating.

'Did you keep his details?' Alexi asked.

Polly looked uncertain. 'Probably. I wrote them down on a scrap of paper and stuck them to the pinboard in my office. If Gerry didn't take them, they'll still be there.'

'We'll look when we go back,' Grace said, appearing to think that it would be okay for her to contribute again. Jack knew she was attempting to exert control over Polly, but hell would freeze over before she did the same thing to him. 'I've taken time off and I'm going to stay with Polly until this mess is sorted out. She needs someone she's comfortable with looking out for her.'

Ben hadn't said anything for a while but had listened intently and watched Polly closely.

'We will need to speak with Michael,' he said now. 'Can you give us his contact details?'

Polly nodded, pulled her phone from her bag and reeled off a number. Jack and Ben both noted it down.

'He won't know anything,' Polly said weakly.

'Even so.' Jack glanced at Alexi and Ben who both shook their heads. 'Okay, Polly, go home and get some rest.'

'Just one more thing,' Alexi said. 'Did you get the impression that Gerry knew James Alton, Polly?'

'The jockey?' She seemed surprised by the question. 'No. They chatted when Gerry first got back. I heard them. I was in the kitchen at the time. But Gerry had never met a stranger. He'd talk to anyone about anything. Besides, he liked the horses, so was probably asking for tips.'

'Okay, don't talk about the murder to anyone,' Ben said. 'Local journalists will sniff round, perhaps the nationals too given Lambourn's recent track record when it comes to unexplained deaths, but do not say a word. I mean it. Things get taken out of context, twisted, and you'll be doing yourself no favours.'

'I'll make sure she isn't harassed,' Grace said.

Which is more than Polly did for Alexi, Jack thought, grinding his teeth.

'Okay, I'm out of here,' Ben said, standing. 'I'll be in touch,' he added vaguely.

Polly stood too but Grace hesitated.

'Can I have a word in private, Jack?' Grace asked hesitantly.

Still with Cosmo on his lap, Jack shook his head. 'We have nothing to say that needs to be said in private,' he replied.

Grace glanced at Alexi and looked set to argue. But she changed her mind at the last minute, stood up and left the room with Polly without saying another word.

'That went well,' Alexi said into the ensuring silence.

'I'm sorry, darling. I wish I knew what the hell she thinks she can achieve by pitching up here.'

'I'd say that's pretty self-evident, given the way she was all tarted up and couldn't keep her eyes off you.' Alexi's chuckle owed little to humour. 'For reasons that escape me, she didn't seem to like me very much.'

'Well, who gives a toss about her feelings? I like you… more than like you and have absolutely no interest in Grace.'

'Makes you wonder why she wants to get her claws into you again after all this time.' Alexi smiled but Jack could see that the gesture was strained. 'After all,' she added, sweeping his body with her gaze, 'there's nothing special about you.'

Jack leaned over and kissed her. 'At least she'll be able to find out which routes Gerry regularly drove. Save us jumping through hoops to get that information and I doubt whether Vickery will bother.'

Alexi nodded. 'We need to speak with Michael.'

'Yeah, we do, but in person. I want to gauge his reaction when he talks about Polly. And Gerry.'

'In which case, we'll need his home address. I doubt whether Polly has it.'

Jack winked at her. 'Not a problem. Cassie'll find it.'

Alexi rolled her eyes. 'Of course she will.'

'We'll go down to Portsmouth this evening and try to catch him unawares.'

'A long way to go if he isn't home.'

'It's a weeknight, he works for a living. He'll be home.'

'And in the meantime?'

'There's one person in Polly's life who's been conspicuous by her absence up until now.'

'Yeah. Maggie Ambrose.' Alexi frowned. 'The same thought had occurred to me. Ordinarily, her, Polly and Linda are joined at the hip. They're always together. Mind you, she has her yoga studio to run. Perhaps she's backed up with classes.'

'Or she might have been to see and support Polly but doesn't feel the need to involve herself with us.'

Jack knew from his old profession that not everyone wanted to be the focus of attention during an investigation. Not necessarily because they had something to hide. Often, as most likely in Maggie's case, they had a local business that they didn't want damaged by association. It didn't do to jump to conclusions.

'You've got that sun salutation look in your eye.' Alexi chuckled. 'No point in denying it.'

Jack tipped Cosmo off his lap and stood up, holding out a hand to Alexi. 'Come on then,' he said. 'Let's see what the third member of Polly's coven thought of Gerry the womaniser.'

8

Alexi felt increasingly unconvinced of Polly's innocence given what they now knew about her background and Gerry's disinclination to stick to one woman, and had been inclined to withdraw her offer of help even before Grace had descended upon them. The woman's appearance had been the final straw. What was it about their previous partners, hers and Jack's, that made them so intransigent, so determined to reclaim what they themselves had destroyed, she wondered. What purpose could there be in striving to recreate a past that was beyond life support?

When she'd heard screeching and stepped out of the kitchen to see what was going on, she'd seen the glamorous woman with Polly and realised who she must be immediately, mainly due to Jack's reaction. She also knew that her appearance was a declaration of war. Their gazes had clashed, and she'd seen the malicious challenge in Grace's eye. The woman had total confidence in her ability to beguile. Self-doubt had not, Alexi suspected, ever kept Grace awake at night.

Alexi's heart had stood still and just for a moment, and her confidence had taken a nosedive. She had seen the way that Grace looked at Jack, as though she wanted to eat him whole, and couldn't think how to fight back. She had felt like a junior reporter again, good only for making the tea and doing the photocopying; excluded from the grown-ups' games.

She had only wallowed in self-doubt for nano seconds before reminding herself of what she'd achieved. Of how she'd played the big boys at their own game in the media world and come out on top. Of how she'd tracked down four murderers and withstood Polly's vicious whispering campaign. She had total faith in Jack's feelings for her and wasn't about to step aside now, graciously or otherwise.

'What does she want?' she asked, as she and Jack made their way on foot to Maggie's studio a short distance away. Cosmo had been left in the kitchen with Toby and would be sulking, Alexi knew. He hated being excluded from their investigations but sometimes, his intimidating presence was more of a hinderance than a help.

Jack shrugged. 'Whatever it is, she's out of luck.' He grasped Alexi's hand. 'Don't let her get to you.'

'She won't, but it's annoying. Why can't people leave us alone? The intrusions are never ending. It's like we're jinxed. Cassie, Patrick and now Grace.'

'What it is to be in demand.'

'I'm serious, Jack.' She swatted his arm with her free hand. 'She worries me. There's obviously something she wants from you.'

'Grace is high maintenance. My income as a policeman was never enough for her, which is why she traded me in for a more successful model. Now he's had enough of her and given her the heave-ho—'

Alexi frowned. 'You know this how?'

'Cassie mentioned something. They're friends, remember.'

'Right.' Alexi inhaled sharply. 'That would explain it.'

'Grace is probably looking back through rose-tinted glasses and has decided I was the love of her life.' Jack grunted. 'She'll know from Cassie that the agency is doing very nicely thank you and probably thinks that I'll make a decent meal ticket after all.'

'Is she aware that Cassie has the hots for you, too?'

'How would I know?' Jack shrugged and looked uncomfortable by the direction their conversation had taken. He was the only person who didn't seem to realise just how attractive he was to the opposite sex. Alexi found his modesty mostly endearing but occasionally irritating. 'Perhaps. Probably.'

'Well, if she does know then she'll also be aware that Cassie and Patrick tried to split us up.'

'Which ought to tell her all she needs to know about the strength of our commitment to each other.'

'Either that or she enjoys a challenge.'

Jack sighed. 'I have no idea what her agenda is, Alexi, but I'm sure we'll find out before too long.' He paused. 'The question we should be asking ourselves now concerns Polly's situation. Do you want to carry on trying to help her? If not, we can walk away, and Grace will eventually go back to her job.'

'Let's give it another day,' Alexi said, wondering why she felt the need to be so generous. Perhaps Polly's mental health issues had softened her attitude towards her nemesis. Or then again, perhaps the journalist in her sensed a story. That, she decided, was the more likely explanation. 'We'll talk to all the people we've identified and then reassess.'

Jack squeezed the hand that he still held in his. 'Good plan.'

'The studio's down this lane, at the back of Maggie's house,' Alexi said, steering them in that direction.

'Blimey!' They stopped in their tracks when confronted with a shuttered studio. A notice on the door stated that classes had been cancelled until further notice. 'What's that all about?' Jack mused.

'I thought she was popular and ran either yoga or Pilates classes every morning.'

'Something isn't right,' Jack said.

'Yeah, that's my impression. We know she hasn't run to Polly's side so why jeopardise her business now of all times?'

Jack turned towards the house. A short, covered walkway led from the studio to the back door. They both peered through the window and could see into an immaculate kitchen that looked as though it had never been used for its intended purpose. He glanced at Alexi, then tapped at the glass.

'She isn't in,' Alexi said, when there was no response.

'I dunno.' Jack tapped again, harder this time.

Eventually, a sound came from deep within the house.

'Classes are cancelled this week,' a wan voice called out. 'I'm not well and its infectious. I sent a WhatsApp round.'

Jack knocked again. And kept on knocking.

'She won't come,' Alexi said.

'She'll come.'

Sure enough, a few minutes later, Maggie appeared, wrapped in a robe, her hair a tangled mess, her face pale and drawn. She peered through the glass door panel and glowered at them. Jack merely smiled and they were eventually rewarded with the sound of a lock turning.

'I told you, I'm not well. Don't come too close,' she said in a passive-aggressive manner.

'Mind if we come in and talk about your friend?' Jack asked at the same time, barging past Maggie into the kitchen. Alexi shrugged and followed in his wake.

'Hey, just a minute! You can't...'

Alexi knew very well that Jack could. In fact, he already had.

'I assume you'd like to help Polly,' Jack said, fixing Maggie with a penetrating look. 'Or have I got that wrong? Are you going to turn on her the way you did on Alexi? Do you get off on bullying people?'

'What the... How dare you barge into my house. I know you two think you're God's gift, but this is *my* house and I want you out of it. Now. Before I call the police.'

'Go right ahead.' Jack folded his arms. 'I'll give you their number if it helps.'

Maggie looked furious when neither of them budged. She tried to pull closed a door to the adjoining lounge, but Jack was too quick and put a foot out to prevent her. Alexi gasped when she looked to see what it was that Maggie was so anxious to hide. There were screwed up tissues all over the floor and a large photograph propped up on a table.

Suddenly, things became a whole lot clearer.

'You,' she said, pointing a finger at Maggie. 'You were carrying on with Gerry behind your friend's back.'

Alexi shared a glance with Jack and could see that he'd been way ahead of her. How the hell had he known, or ever suspected? Either way, it was nice of him to share. She expected a volley of denials from Maggie but instead, she sank into the nearest chair, buried her face in her hands and sobbed fit to break her heart. Alexi was unsure how she felt to see one of the women who'd caused her so much upset having a meltdown. What she did know was that she didn't take any pleasure from Maggie's crippling grief. She and Jack stood watching her, saying nothing, waiting for the flow of tears to abate.

'I suppose it'll all come out now,' Maggie said, blowing her nose and glaring accusingly at Alexi. 'Why couldn't you have kept your nose out?'

She walked into the lounge and fell into the seat she'd obviously occupied before she'd been disturbed: the one with a direct view of the enlarged picture of Gerry. Jack and Alexi seated themselves on a couch opposite Maggie, who now appeared to be fighting mad as opposed to falling apart.

'Care to tell us how it happened?' Jack asked.

She shrugged. 'How do these things ever happen? It wasn't planned. Believe it or not, Polly's my friend.'

Alexi screwed up her features, struggling to refrain from remarking about friends of her calibre and speculating about Polly's need for them.

'I know what you're thinking.' Maggie blew her nose again and sat a little straighter, 'and you'd be right. I don't like myself very much. Polly was nuts about Gerry and he was all she could talk about when she came to one of my yoga classes. She, Linda and I became friends, and we were happy for her.'

'What made Polly decide to set up shop in Lambourn?' Jack asked. 'She has no connections to the area as far as I know.'

'It was Gerry's suggestion. He said there were opportunities here. Owners coming down and needing somewhere on the cheaper side to stay overnight. Mind you, he could have suggested the bowels of hell and she'd have gone there. She'd do anything he asked of her without hesitation.'

Jack and Alexi glanced at one another. Lambourn was clearly pivotal in whatever scam Gerry had been running, always assuming there was one. Jack's copper's nose was twitching enough to make him pretty damned sure of it.

'Polly's not a strong person, despite the public image she displayed. She gradually opened up about her past to Linda and me when we got to know her better. You know how it is,' she added, glancing at Alexi, 'women get together and chat about their lives and loves. I don't know how much you know about her younger years...'

'Enough,' Jack said.

'Well then, you'll also know that she was overdue a little happiness and we were really pleased for her because she had Gerry. He was a charmer but about as constant as a ram in the mating season. Only she couldn't see it and all the time he kept his dalliances away from her, we figured there was no harm in them. He'd never change but he did care about Polly, in his way.'

'He used her,' Alexi said softly.

'Don't tell me you feel sorry for her,' Maggie replied accusingly. 'Not after the way she treated you.'

'We just want to get to the facts,' Jack replied.

'Well, one undeniable fact you need to take on board is that Gerry would flirt with a doorpost if he thought he'd get a reaction from it. Only Polly couldn't see it.'

'He flirted with you,' Alexi said, easily able to believe it. Maggie was attractive and had a toned body to show for all those hours of stretching and bending.

'Yeah, and I played along. It always happened in front of Polly and didn't mean anything. Well, not at first. Then Gerry made excuses to pop round here at odd times. I found myself looking forward to his visits and didn't tell Polly about them. He needed someone to talk to, he told me. Someone to confide in and I'm a good listener.'

'I'll just bet you are,' Jack muttered under his breath.

'What did he want to talk about?' Alexi asked.

'Anything and everything. His kids. His failed marriage. Polly's tendency to cling to him that he found stifling. We discovered that we had a lot in common. We're both independently minded and don't like routine.'

'But...' Alexi pointed in the direction of the yoga studio.

'I love yoga but seldom do the same thing twice in any class. I enjoy the challenge of variety and get bored with the same old. Anyway,' she added, 'things moved on and... well, use your imagination.'

'Did you tell the police all this?' Jack asked.

Maggie looked at him as though he'd suddenly sprouted a second head. 'Of course not! I couldn't do that to Polly; she's my friend!'

The hypocrisy wasn't lost on Alexi. 'But you could carry on with the man she adored behind her back.'

Maggie lowered her head and said nothing.

'How would that have affected someone with her delicate state of health once she found out? And she would have found out sooner or later,' Jack said, his voice harsh. 'You know that as well as I do.'

'And the guilt was driving both of us bonkers,' Maggie said, fresh tears streaming down her face. 'We tried to fight the attraction. As God is my witness, we tried so damned hard but when something's right, it's right. I was going to sell the business as a going concern, and we were planning a future together.'

'And yet Polly insists that Gerry had agreed to move in with her,' Alexi said, wondering if Gerry had been stringing them both along for reasons they knew nothing about. Or if he'd done so simply because he could. It would have stoked his ego and made him feel like a big man. Alexi wouldn't put it past the man she was starting to find out more about, and not liking one little bit. 'So one of you got the wrong end of the stick. Either that or he planned to ditch you both.'

'Which is why I can't go to the police. You must see that. It would destroy Polly.'

'Never mind the fact that you giving all of this up and running off with Gerry would have destroyed her even more comprehensively,' Jack said, clearly feeling as repelled by the woman's hubris as Alexi herself did.

'It would also give her a motive for murder,' Maggie added,

'and I am absolutely sure that she's incapable of killing anyone, especially not the man she adored.'

'Unless, during the course of their argument, he blurted out his relationship with you,' Alexi said. 'I can't believe she'd accept that without retaliating.'

'He wouldn't have done that.' Maggie spoke with absolute certainty. 'We were making plans quietly. I've touted the business for sale privately, but no one here knows about that. Once it was a done deal, we were going to leave.' She shook her head. 'Cowardly, I know, but I simply couldn't face Polly. How could I explain? What could I possibly say? That, if nothing else, must demonstrate the strength of feeling that Gerry engendered in me. I hated myself for what it would do to my friend but loved Gerry too much to... to care about anything or anyone else. That will play on my conscience for the rest of my days.'

'Your conscience, such as it is, doesn't concern me,' Jack said.

'Don't be so quick to jump on the moral high ground. Look what *she* did to Grace,' Maggie said, levelling an unsteady finger in Alexi's direction.

'Don't believe everything you hear. Grace and I were history long before I met Alexi.' Jack drilled her with a look. 'But this isn't about me. Polly asked for our help and we're still trying to decide whether she deserves it. So, are you absolutely sure that Polly had no idea about you screwing her guy?'

Maggie winced at Jack's harsh tone but nodded without hesitation. 'I forced myself to go round to hers last night. It would have looked odd if I hadn't and we were fine together. We both cried but only I knew that my tears weren't in sympathy for Polly.' She shook her head. 'It was torture.'

'Where did you and Gerry plan to go?' Alexi asked.

'The west country. He had something going on, he wouldn't tell me what, but he assured me we'd never have to worry about money ever again if it turned out the way he hoped.'

'You must have some idea,' Jack said forcefully.

'I don't. Really I don't.' Maggie spread her hands. 'I'd tell you if I did. God alone knows, I need to tell someone, but Gerry was adamant that I remained in the dark. For my own safety, he said.'

'It was illegal,' Alexi suggested, her doubts about Gerry's activities vindicated.

'Something to do with the runs he made into Holland, that's all I can tell you.'

'You felt comfortable riding off into the sunset with your friend's guy, unaware how he'd made the money to keep you in style?' Sarcasm dripped from Alexi's voice.

Maggie shook her head. 'I've always been contemptuous of women who get taken in by smooth-talking men and claim not to be able to help themselves. I never believed in undying love either and certainly never thought it would happen to me. I'm far too level-headed.' She lifted one slender shoulder, the innate elegance behind the gesture a testament to her day job. Alexi could see why a man would be drawn to her but was less sure why Maggie would respond when she knew that he was in a relationship with her best friend. 'As I already explained, it was a harmless flirtation to start with. Just a bit of fun. All in front of Polly, who didn't seem to mind.'

Alexi glanced at Jack and could see that he'd picked up on the lie. 'You don't really believe that?' she asked.

'Well, anyway, when I realised that I was in too deep, I tried to end it. Gerry agreed that we weren't being fair to Polly and that we should knock it on the head. At that point, we were still just fooling around. He told me Polly was hard work. He loved her but wasn't in love if that makes any sense. He said she had a load of demons that she'd never gotten over and he didn't know how to help her.'

'Playing happy families with one of her best friends probably wasn't the best way to go about it,' Alexi remarked.

Maggie scowled at Alexi. 'Yeah, well, it's easy to sit in judgement when you're not personally involved.'

'You realise that you'll have to tell Inspector Vickery what you've just told us,' Jack said.

'I can't.' Maggie bowed her head. 'It will not only crucify Polly but will also give her a stronger motive to want Gerry dead.' She lifted her head again, met Jack's gaze and held it. 'Don't you think I've already done enough to screw up her life?'

'Do you know someone called Melanie?' Alexi asked after a long, uncomfortable pause.

'Why?'

'I'd have thought Polly would have told you. The name flashed up on Gerry's screen not long before he died. It triggered the row between them that she insists ended when he agreed to move in with her.'

Maggie clutched her head in her hands and shook it from side to side. 'Melanie is the name he had me programmed in his phone under. I called him to see when he thought he could get round here but he didn't pick up.'

'Then you'll definitely have to speak with Vickery. He'll trace all the numbers in Gerry's phone and eventually get to you. I assume there are texts as well.'

'Perhaps, but he said he deleted them. He believed in being cautious.'

'Obviously not cautious enough,' Alexi said, thinking that they'd at least solved one mystery.

'Was Gerry involved somehow with James Alton?' Jack asked.

Maggie blinked. 'Who?' she asked irritably.

'The retired jockey staying at the B&B.'

She shrugged. 'No idea. Why? Is it important?'

'You never heard him mention his name, or saw them talking?' Jack persisted.

'Can't say that I did.'

'Okay, we'll leave you to contact Vickery,' Jack said, standing to indicate that he'd run out of questions. 'Do it and do it soon. Don't make us tell him for you.'

Maggie nodded.

As they left her house, Alexi noticed that she'd curled up in a foetal ball and was crying again.

'With friends like her,' Jack said, taking Alexi's hand.

'I didn't see that one coming, but something tells me you did.'

'I had my suspicions. Linda said something about Maggie lapping up Gerry's flirtation all in good fun. In my experience, flirting seldom restricts itself to fun and when Maggie hadn't shown her face, or come to us in the hope of exonerating her friend, I figured there must be something there. I didn't realise quite how deeply she and Gerry were involved, though.'

'We're thinking it gives Polly a motive, if she knew, but the same thing applies to Maggie. If Gerry did decide that he couldn't let Polly down and tried to break it off once and for all with Maggie, who is obviously smitten... Well, you know what they say about a woman scorned. She'd put her house and business up for sale for the rat and then he had a casual change of heart. It probably opened her eyes to his true character, but she still loved him and if she couldn't have him... blah, blah.'

'Yeah. It's gonna get ugly, darling. I hope Polly has the strength to withstand the revelation. It will hit her harder than Gerry's death.'

'I almost feel sorry for her.' Alexi paused. 'Scratch that, I *do* feel sorry for her, despite what she did to me. No one deserves to be shafted by a friend, not in that way.' She sighed. 'Anyway, what now?'

Jack glanced at his watch. 'Now we grab a bite to eat, pick up our security detail and go in search of an estranged son.'

9

Jack was glad that the motion of his car lulled Alexi to sleep as he drove them towards Portsmouth. He needed a moment to think through all that had occurred without worrying about her reaction to Grace's intrusion into their lives. And she would be worried about it, just as Jack was, but to her credit, Alexi hadn't mentioned her name again since the initial meeting. Maggie's revelations had temporarily driven it from her head, Jack assumed. He wished he could forget her as easily, uncomfortably aware that she arrogantly assumed she could simply force her way back into his life. His closeness to Alexi had, he reckoned, strengthened her resolve in that respect. Grace had a high opinion of her own self-worth and had never been one to accept defeat, graciously or otherwise.

Sighing, Jack joined the motorway and put his foot down, adjuring himself to concentrate on what they now knew about Gerry's life. He was playing fast and loose with Polly's affections – that much was beyond question. If Maggie was to be believed though, then Gerry had serious feelings for her. Jack suspected that he'd never been emotionally involved with a woman before. Had that been the case then he wouldn't have played the field.

He came across as a man's man and a bit of a know it all. That being the case, he would likely have been broadsided by his feelings for Maggie, if they had really existed, and probably attempted to fight them. All the evidence implied that the women fell for him, not the other way around. Previously, he'd used them either for enjoyment or personal convenience. Perhaps both in Polly's case because he'd encouraged her to open her B&B in Lambourn for reasons that Jack needed to delve deeper into.

James Alton featured high on Jack's radar and would be the next person he took a closer look at, unless this visit to Polly's son produced a more vital clue. He had to be a suspect if for no other reason than he'd been vague about his reasons for being at Polly's. There were others too whom Jack had yet to put a name to. Who had Gerry been pleading with for more time on that overheard conversation? Were there other women in his life? Given his track record, that possibility couldn't be discounted. Hopefully, Vickery would be able to throw some light on the identity of the caller once he'd been through Gerry's phone records. That might point them in the direction of the money-making scam Gerry was convinced would finance a life of luxury with Maggie. Unless that was all pie in the sky too and Gerry had encouraged Maggie to sell up so he could pocket the proceeds and scarper.

Anything was possible since the guy was a real player.

Plenty of suspects in theory, Jack thought, moving out to overtake a van hugging the central lane, but no actual evidence to back any of those theories up. Of course, the most likely suspect was still Polly and Jack wasn't convinced that she didn't do it. If Gerry had told her about him and Maggie, then he'd be surprised if she hadn't snapped. He had been involved in a case once where a person with mental illness had killed their nearest and dearest and disassociated afterwards, absolutely convinced that they hadn't done it. Vickery would doubtless be receiving advice in that regard.

Jack wasn't about to do all his work for him and make the suggestion.

Maggie was the other viable suspect. Her grief seemed genuine, but it could have been a delayed reaction. *What the hell have I done?* Perhaps Gerry had had a change of heart about the happy-ever-after scenario that Maggie had in mind. Perhaps she'd exaggerated and Gerry hadn't actually agreed to commit. That would be enough to tip a person whose emotions were involved over the edge. She couldn't have the man she loved and would have to watch him cosying up to Polly. Or perhaps he'd gotten cold feet once Maggie put her home and business on the market, unable to face a life of monogamy.

'A whole lot of speculation and absolutely nothing solid to go on,' he muttered.

Alexi jerked awake when Jack slowed to pull off the motorway.

'Sorry,' she said, yawning and stretching her arms above her head. Cosmo, asleep on her lap, woke too and took his turn to stretch.

'No problem. We're almost there.'

Jack followed the instructions issued by his satnav and turned left into a housing estate. Several turns later found them in front of a modern block of flats − all glass and stainless steel.

'Is this it?' she asked, peering through the window.

'Pettigrew House. That's the place.' Jack parked up and cut the engine. 'You're guarding the car, big guy,' he told Cosmo, cranking open a window a few inches before releasing his seat belt and opening his door.

Alexi lifted Cosmo onto the vacated driver's seat and left the vehicle. Jack didn't bother to lock it, aware that Cosmo's movement would trigger the alarm. Aware also that no one would get past their guard cat.

As they approached the communal door to the flats, someone conveniently walked out and held it open for them.

'Second floor,' Jack said, heading for the stairs. Both he and Alexi preferred stairs to lifts. Jack had got stuck in one once for hours and had avoided them wherever possible since then.

They reached the door to Michael's flat. Jack glanced at Alexi and pressed the bell. The door was opened almost immediately by a shortish guy wearing glasses, boxer shorts and not a lot else.

'Er, you're not the pizza guys, I'm guessing,' he said, waving a credit card about with an open, friendly, and somewhat sheepish smile.

'Sorry,' Jack replied. 'If I'd known you were hungry...'

'How can I help?'

'Are you Michael? Michael Pearson.'

'Michael,' the guy yelled over his shoulder. 'Someone to see you.'

A taller guy with a sweep of dark-blond hair falling over hazel eyes and the bulging muscles of a man who did physical work on a daily basis sauntered into view.

'Can I help you with something?' he asked.

Jack introduced them both.

'Hey, I know you!' The first guy pointed at Alexi and looked excited. 'I've read just about everything you wrote. It was a sad day when you left the *Sentinel*. The paper hasn't been the same since.'

'Thank you,' Alexi said, when the guy paused long enough for her to speak.

'Let them in, Michael,' he said. 'I want to pick this lady's brains. I'm Phil, by the way. Phil Smedley, Michael's much better half.' He stood back and ushered them into the flat, seemingly unconcerned by his state of undress. 'It's a pleasure to meet you both.'

He shook their hands firmly and Alexi, who seemed to have taken a liking to the guy, assured him that the feeling was mutual.

'Phil's a bank clerk with an ambition to become a novelist,' Michael said, rolling his eyes. 'You'll be lucky to get out of here this side of midnight, Alexi. Don't say you haven't been warned.'

'Warning duly noted,' she replied as she and Jack took seats in an immaculate lounge.

Phil had disappeared but came back again almost immediately with a towelling robe preserving his dignity.

'Can we offer you something to drink?' he asked.

'Not for me, thanks,' Jack said. 'We won't keep you for long. It's just that we wondered if you'd been contacted by the police, Michael?'

'The police?' Phil sent his partner a quizzical look. 'Why? What's he done that he's not told me about?'

'Nothing as far as we know.' Alexi paused. 'It's about your mother.'

'My mother.' Michael blinked. 'What about her? Is she okay? I saw her today and she was on top form.'

Alexi and Jack glanced at one another.

'Sorry,' Jack said. 'We should have explained. We're from Lambourn.'

'Ah, you mean my birth mother, Polly.' Michael's expression closed down. 'I can't think of her as my mother. The woman who brought me up earned that accolade.' He sighed and threw himself into the chair beside Phil's. Phil reached over and squeezed his hand. 'Okay then, why has she sent you to see me? I told her I didn't want to see her any more. It's too late for us to play happy families and I won't change my mind.'

'She doesn't know we're here.'

Jack went on to explain about Gerry.

'Bloody hell!' Michael looked shellshocked. 'Do you think she killed him?'

'Do you?'

'I don't know her very well. We've only met half a dozen times, so it's hard for me to give an opinion.' Michael rubbed his chin. 'I remember her from when I was little. My brother and sister were too young, but I heard it all and felt the sharp side of my dad's belt at regular intervals for no apparent reason. Mum bore the brunt of his temper though and young as I was, I started to think he'd kill her eventually.'

'They talked about it when they met,' Phil said, when Michael fell silent. 'She still insisted the abuse was all her own fault. She made him mad, wound him up, but he was always sorry afterwards.'

'A typical victim response,' Alexi said, nodding.

'Why did you meet her, as a matter of interest?' Jack asked.

'Because she tracked me, tracked all of us down, and I was curious. Besides, Phil encouraged me. He said I had to lay the demons of my childhood to rest.' He chuckled. 'He believes all that guff and I like to humour him.'

Phil grinned and blew Michael a kiss.

'You're in touch with your siblings?' Alexi shook her head. 'I'd like to think that what happened to you, your separation, wouldn't happen nowadays but I'm afraid it probably still does. That can't have been easy.'

'It was hardest for me. I wanted to protect them, a bit like I'd instinctively protected them from our dad, young as I was. Anyway, yeah we're in touch. My brother's in London and I see him occasionally. But my sister's in Australia so it's Christmas cards and not much else. We did have a family summit online when Polly surfaced. Those two were adamant that they'd moved on and didn't want to see her. I was the only one who decided to give her a chance, out of curiosity as much as anything else.' He sighed. 'Bad luck seems to follow her. Anyway, what is it you think I can help you with?'

'Gerry. I assume you met him.'

'I did, just once and didn't much like what I saw. I thought he was using Polly but that was her business.'

'Freeloading is the word he used,' Phil said. 'And he was homophobic too, which didn't help matters.'

Alexi and Jack exchanged a look. From what they'd heard about Gerry, they had no difficulty in believing it.

'Is Polly in custody?' Michael asked, his expression sombre. 'Do they think she actually did it?'

'The police always look at the family first,' Phil said. 'As a budding crime writer, I know at least that much. It's the line of least resistance.'

'And statistically, someone close to the victim is the most likely person to have done the deed,' Jack added.

'A crime of passion, perhaps.' Michael stroked his goatee in a considering fashion. 'The worm has finally turned.'

'Yeah, that's another statistic,' Phil said. 'The abusee becomes the abuser. She took all that shit from your dad and then realised it was happening again.'

'We don't know that,' Michael said quietly.

'It's a fair assumption,' Phil replied. 'You said she was besotted with the guy but if... I don't know, if he'd decided to bail on her, she probably couldn't take the rejection and snapped.'

'Why do you say that?' Jack asked.

'I'm speculating,' Phil replied without hesitation. 'If everything in their garden was rosy then she'd have no reason to harm him. So, if the police think she's the guilty party then it stands to reason that he did something to piss her off.'

Jack nodded, unable to fault Phil's logic, given that they knew Gerry had slept with her best friend and was likely planning to abandon her.

'What did you talk to Gerry about when you met him?' he asked.

Michael shrugged. 'Not much. He tried to thrust a beer on me but I'm not much of a drinker and if I do indulge then I prefer wine. He thought that made me soft, less of a man. He didn't actually say as much but his expression did all the talking for him. Then he started going on about football, which I hate, so I had nothing to contribute and frankly, I couldn't wait to get out of there.'

'So,' Alexi said, 'if you'd been considering keeping in touch with your birth mother, the type of company she kept might have deterred you.'

'No might about it,' Michael replied without hesitation. 'It did. But I really didn't want to see her again even before I met Gerry. I could tell she still had issues, and harsh as it sounds, I didn't want to bear the load. Not again. Frankly, I owed her nothing and so I walked away. End of.'

Jack nodded, well able to believe it. These guys appeared to be open and honest and on the surface, he could see no reason for Michael to have bumped off Polly's lover. Be that as it may, he would keep an open mind since he knew better than to jump to conclusions.

'Did she tell you why she'd turned hotel keeper?' Alexi asked.

'Oh yes. An insurance payout after my late and unlamented father's departure from this world. She said it was my inheritance, but I told her in no uncertain terms that I didn't want anything from her.'

'It didn't deter her, though,' Phil said. 'She wanted Michael to invest in the place and be a co-owner.' He rolled his eyes. 'Can you imagine?'

'You think she needed an investor, or could it be that she was trying to mend fences?' Jack asked, wondering if she was hurting financially. This was the first he'd heard of the need for a co-owner, other than Gerry, who Jack was pretty sure would not have been asked to make a financial contribution. 'To find a way to have you back in her life?'

'Trying to con me out of what savings I have to invest in that place was hardly the way to mend fences,' Michael replied. 'I don't like the countryside much and definitely don't like horses.' He glanced with affection at Phil. 'Not like some I could mention.'

'Okay, so I enjoy the occasional flutter. Sue me,' Phil replied easily, reaching across to touch Michael's hand. Both men laughed and the closeness between them was impossible to ignore.

'Nothing else you can think of from that one meeting that might help us?' Jack asked. 'Despite your differences with your birth mother, I don't suppose you want to see her arrested for murder if she didn't do it.'

'I have no truck with her,' Michael replied easily. 'I just didn't see the point of us pretending. That ship has well and truly sailed.'

'Well, if there's nothing else, we won't take up any more of your time,' Jack said, standing as the doorbell sounded.

'That will be the pizza guy, finally,' Phil said, standing as well and heading for the door.

'Thanks for your time,' Jack said, shaking hands with Michael and then standing back so that Alexi could do the same.

'No worries. Let me know what happens. In spite of everything, I hope she didn't do for the guy,' Michael replied. 'Not that I'm sorry he's out of her life. He was a bit of a leech, I reckon, playing on her emotions and getting free bed and board and... well, anything else that he wanted. What sort of man does that?'

Phil came back into the room, bearing two boxes. 'Sustenance,' he said grinning. He placed the boxes on a table and took his turn to shake their hands. 'Good meeting you. Come again and I'll pick your brains, Alexi.'

'It's a date,' she replied, smiling at him.

Cosmo greeted them with blithe indifference when they returned to the car.

'Glad you missed us, big guy,' Jack said as he slid behind the wheel and fired up the engine. 'What did you make of those two?' he asked, as Cosmo settled down on Alexi's lap, purring now and condescending to have his back stroked.

'I liked them,' she replied without hesitation. 'It's to Michael's credit that he's matured without hang-ups, given the nature of his upbringing. I think Phil has to take a lot of credit for that. They're obviously soulmates.'

'Huh-hum.'

'What does that mean?' Alexi demanded waspishly. 'You clearly picked up on something that I didn't. I hate it when that happens and you go all superior on me so out with it, Maddox, what did I miss?'

'Not sure,' he replied pensively. 'There was something in Phil's attitude that waved a red flag. I'm wondering if it's to do with money.'

'Polly needing an investor, you mean?' Alexi nodded. 'Yes, I wondered about her financial situation too. Do we need to ask if we can see her bank statements?'

'You know as well as I do how hard it is to keep a hotel business in Lambourn in the black.'

Alexi shuddered. 'Don't remind me.' She paused. 'Michael said he had no interest in investing, or having anything to do with his mother,' she pointed out.

'Yeah, he did say that, didn't he, but people have been known to lie to us.'

'You're thinking, I suppose, that if he wanted to meet the mother who neglected him then there has to be some enduring bond between them.'

'The thought crossed my mind,' Jack replied, easing the car onto the motorway and merging with the flow of traffic. 'Those two are doing well for themselves, I assume, given their top-end flat and good quality furniture. Suppose Michael did feel duty bound to bail his mother out, I wonder how Phil would react to a dent being made in their income? He seemed easy going but very possessive too. You saw the way he kept touching Michael?'

'Yep, but I can't see Michael entering into any financial arrangements with Polly without Phil's agreement. Besides, it was obvious that he didn't like or approve of Gerry, especially if he made homophobic comments.'

'Yeah well, we'll talk to Polly again in the morning and get her take on Michael. For the record, I don't think he or Phil came down here and bumped Gerry off but it pays to be thorough.'

'Maggie will be baring her soul about now, I imagine, if she keeps her promise and tells Polly about her and Gerry.' Alexi pulled a face. 'I hope she makes sure there are no sharp objects in the room before she 'fesses up.'

'We'll have Polly come to us in the morning,' Jack said. 'When she's away from the familiar, she's less likely to get emotional. Besides, something tells me that Maggie's revelations won't come as a complete surprise.'

'You think she knew?' Alexi blinked at Jack. 'And did nothing about it.'

'I think she had an inkling but she's the type who would have turned a blind eye, expecting the flirtation to run its course.'

'Because Gerry was a flirt and she won't believe it was anything more than that with Maggie, otherwise she would have had to confront him. And we both know that she avoided confronting Gerry as a general rule because he could do no wrong in her eyes. And because if she didn't raise her concerns then she could pretend that the problem didn't exist.'

Jack gave a grim nod. 'Welcome to paradise,' he said.

10

Alexi and Jack were back at Hopgood Hall early the following morning. So early that they caught Cheryl and Drew still at breakfast, with Verity in her highchair spreading yogurt all over its tray and squealing with laughter.

'Bed caught fire?' Drew asked, looking up from his plate of eggs and smiling.

'We're on Polly's case so there's no time for sleeping,' Alexi replied, leaning over Verity and kissing the top of her silky head.

Jack poured coffee for them both as Alexi took a seat beside Verity and helped her to eat rather than to wear her breakfast. Cosmo sniffed the air and then joined Toby in his basket, from where he watched proceedings with an indolent air.

'Are you making progress?' Drew asked. 'I can see it's wearing you down, and I'm guessing that you can't decide if Polly is actually the guilty party. If I were you, Alexi, I'd convince him that she definitely is and not lift a finger to help her. She definitely doesn't deserve having you fighting her corner.'

'I very well might do that.'

'She will not! Not unless she's absolutely sure and that's

because she's a better person that you will ever be,' Cheryl said hotly.

Drew laughed. 'No question. Okay then, what have you found out?'

Jack updated them.

'Well,' Cheryl said, fanning her face with her hand, 'if Polly did do it then she had a damned good reason, and I almost don't blame her. I mean, with friends like Maggie...'

'We'll know soon enough,' Alexi said. 'We left a message for her to meet us here at nine this morning. Vickery might have already decided to charge her and she needs to be prepared for that eventuality. He'll know about Maggie and Gerry by now because we told her she had to come clean.'

Jack nodded. 'That will give him the motive he needs but whether he thinks that's enough to secure a conviction remains to be seen.'

'It doesn't sound as though Polly's a rational person, Alexi,' Drew remarked, 'which helps to explain why she conducted a whispering campaign against you for no obvious reason.'

'To say nothing of being a woman scorned,' Cheryl added, shaking her head. 'It doesn't look good for her.'

'Yeah.' Jack sounded weary. Alexi knew he hadn't slept well and that he'd been up well before the sun, probably stressing over Grace. Not that he would ever admit it to Alexi. 'Let's hope today throws further light on matters.'

'I hear your ex is in town,' Cheryl said, glancing at Alexi. Cosmo looked up from washing his face and hissed. 'Is she planning to stay?'

'She's a friend of Polly's, apparently.' It was Alexi who answered, forcing herself to sound more casual than she actually felt. Grace seemed determined to get her claws back into Jack, but Alexi felt secure in the knowledge that she and Jack were solid and that there was nothing Grace could do to come between them. Even so, Grace's sudden appearance made her feel distinctly uneasy. She had been married to Jack and understood his character, so she must realise that he'd never take her back just because she'd decided that leaving him had been a mistake. There had to be more to it than that, some angle Alexi hadn't picked up on, and that was what worried her. 'She's here to support her friend in her hour of need.'

'Not for long,' Jack added, an edge to his voice. 'She has a job to get back to.'

'I can't help wondering why Gerry coaxed Polly into setting up shop here in Lambourn,' Alexi said in a deliberate change of subject. 'She could have gone anywhere in the country, has no links to this area and no interest in horses.'

'Not everyone in Lambourn is involved with racing,' Drew pointed out.

'Perhaps not but it's what keeps the local economy ticking over,' Jack said. 'Alexi has a point. Gerry walked on water as far as Polly was concerned. If he sneezed, she reached for the tissues. He suggested Lambourn and she bit. Now he did like the horses and then, just before Gerry was topped, James Alton, the bookie's runner and disgraced ex-jockey fetched up at Polly's. Coincidence?' Jack shook his head. 'I don't believe in them.'

'You think he had some sort of racing scam going on?' Drew asked.

'Frankly, as things stand, I don't know what to think.' Jack spread his hands. 'Let's see what Polly knew about Gerry's relationship with Maggie and take it from there.'

Cheryl and Alexi both stared at Jack.

'You think she knew?' Cheryl asked.

'I don't see how she couldn't have. Not if the affair was as intense as Maggie insists was the case. This is a small village and

Polly was infatuated. If Gerry kept going AWOL, she would want to know where he was. I wouldn't put it past her to have followed him.'

Cheryl shook her head. 'She's volatile and wouldn't have been able to keep that knowledge to herself. After all, she confronted Gerry when she saw a woman's name flash up on his phone.'

Alexi shrugged. 'I'm not so sure about that. If confronting him meant losing him, she'd have thought twice. You're right about her being suspicious of his movements, though. He didn't like going out. Well, not taking *her* out socially. He must have been on the missing list for big chunks of time if he was with Maggie, so Polly had to wonder what he was getting up to.'

'Absolutely.' Cheryl nodded resolutely.

'I've met women like Polly before,' Alexi said. 'Gerry kept coming back to her so she pretended not to know what he was up to and didn't try to clip his wings, thinking the affair would run its course.'

Cheryl twitched her nose. 'Not much self-respect. But still, I get what you're saying. If she forced him to make a choice, she might not like which way he swung.'

'We already know that she didn't have much self-confidence, her outgoing public persona notwithstanding,' Jack said. 'Think back to what she put up with in her marriage and how it tipped her over the edge mentally. She'll always be fragile and probably thinks that she isn't worth loving. And women like my ex fighting her corner will do her no favours whatsoever.'

Drew sighed, pushed himself to his feet and extracted Verity from her highchair. 'Come on, princess,' he said. 'All this talk of murder and mayhem is not for your precious ears. Let's go and have some fun.'

Cheryl stood too and cleared away their breakfast things, smiling at the retreating figure of her husband, still with the baby in his arms. He was singing a ridiculous song of his own creation to her. 'If he has to choose between us,' she said, 'I know where the suitcases are kept.'

Alexi laughed. 'Somehow, I think his heart is big enough to embrace you both.' Her smile widened. 'And the new addition.'

'It had better be!' Cheryl swiftly loaded the dishwasher, wiped the table and sink down and then also took herself off. 'The paperwork waits for no woman,' she said, rolling her eyes. 'VAT returns scare me shitless but have to be done.'

'You are a brave woman,' Alexi assured her.

Cheryl gave a mock tremble. 'Keep telling me that.'

It seemed quiet in the kitchen without the baby's laughter and the larger-than-life presence of Drew. Only Cosmo and Toby shuffling about for space in their shared basket broke the silence.

'You're worried about Grace,' Alexi eventually said softly, reaching for Jack's hand. 'Talk to me.'

'Yeah, she is on my mind but not in a good way.' He shook his head and then lowered it. 'She never does anything without a reason, but I can't for the life of me think what it is that she wants from me.'

'Modesty does not become you, Mr Maddox.'

Jack lifted his head again and blinked at her. 'What do you mean? Our relationship has been over for a while.'

'Yes, but you ended it.'

'It was already beyond resuscitation and she'd moved on to someone else anyway.'

'But that didn't work out,' Alexi reminded him. 'If he ended it then a woman who thinks as well of herself as Grace does will feel slighted to have been dumped twice in fairly rapid succession. And, as you yourself said, now that you're no longer in the police and earning a good wedge, she probably realises what she walked out on and thinks she can waltz straight back in again and carry on where you left off.' Alexi smiled at him. 'There's no great mystery.'

Jack made a *perhaps* motion with his eyes. 'Which is probably why she set Polly against you, I imagine, just to clear the path. She underestimated you and thought you'd be scared off by a bit of name-calling.'

'It wouldn't surprise me if Cassie shared Patrick's plans with Grace insofar as he'd encouraged Cassie to frighten me out of town and back into his waiting embrace in London. Grace would have told her to go for it, unaware that Cassie hoped to move in on you and pick up the pieces.' Alexi grinned. 'How does it feel to be in such demand?'

'Just so long as it's you making the demands,' he replied, taking both of her hands in one of his and giving them a squeeze, 'you can be sure of my full and exclusive attention.'

'Well, I'm glad we resolved that one.'

Alexi leaned over to kiss him, just as the door opened and Grace preceded Polly through it.

'Oh!' Grace said, stopping dead in her tracks and glowering at Alexi.

'What are you doing here?' Jack asked in a mordent tone.

Cosmo arched his back, hissed and stalked across the room towards Grace, baring his teeth. Grace gave a little shriek and backed off.

'I brought Polly over. We need to know if there's any progress,' Grace said, her eyes never leaving Cosmo, who was now circling her with vicious intent, growling every so often for good measure. Alexi didn't call him off.

'You don't need to know anything. Go back to Polly's,' Jack said wearily.

'But I thought—'

Jack stood and Cosmo immediately rubbed his big head

against Jack's shin, a harmless pussycat once again. Alexi almost smiled but had no trouble in quelling that particular impulse. Grace really was determined to intrude. Although dressed casually, Alexi could see that her designer jeans and the thin sweatshirt that clung to her curves had been carefully chosen. Grace's hair and makeup had taken more than the two minutes to perfect that Alexi only ever allowed herself in the mornings.

Polly watched the exchange but had yet to open her mouth. Alexi felt a mixture of sympathy and annoyance for a woman who didn't seem to realise that she'd been manipulated all her life. Or then again, perhaps she did but was so keen to be liked and accepted that she put up with it. Alexi could never forgive Polly for the way that she'd treated her in the past but if she'd been influenced by someone with Grace's grit and determination then she could see why she had gone down that route.

'Sit down, Polly,' Alexi said, 'and I'll get you some coffee.'

Polly glanced at Grace, then slowly pulled out a chair and sat at the table. Jack stood his ground with Cosmo beside him, who probably picked up on the tension and once again hissed a warning at Grace. Cosmo really was an excellent judge of character. Alexi was proud of her cat and made a mental note to feed him some of his favourite tinned salmon later. She was almost tempted to let him attack Grace's ankles too, which she knew he would do given the slightest provocation. Before that situation could arise, Grace wisely chose the course of least resistance.

'I'll wait for you back at yours, Polly,' she said. 'We need to talk,' she added to Jack, lowering her voice.

'Nothing to talk about,' Jack replied, closing the door behind her.

'Okay, Polly,' Jack said, letting out a long breath as he resumed his chair beside Alexi, 'how are things?'

Polly looked to be on the verge of tears. 'I think Inspector

Vickery is convinced I killed Gerry but I didn't do it! You have to believe me.'

'Okay.' Jack held up a hand in a placating gesture. Cosmo, seeming to think that his services were no longer required, fixed Polly with a warning glare and then stalked back to the basket and settled down. 'Has he been in touch again?'

Polly shook her head. 'Not yet.'

'Have you seen Maggie?' Alexi asked, cutting to the chase.

Tears leaked from the corners of Polly's eyes. 'Yeah. She came round last night. I gather you told her to but you needn't have bothered. She didn't tell me anything that I didn't already know.'

Jack fixed Alexi with an *I-told-you-so* look.

'To be clear, you were aware that Gerry was having an affair with one of your best friends?' he said. 'But you didn't think to mention it when we spoke yesterday. It seems like an important detail to omit.'

'It was hardly an affair.' Polly extracted a tissue from her bag, mopped her eyes with one hand and blew her nose with the other. 'Of course, I knew he was spending time with her. I knew whenever he strayed, but he always came back to me. Men don't understand the meaning of monogamy. I learned that much years ago. If you don't nag and don't ask questions, then they stay with you.'

'You didn't mind?' Alexi asked.

Polly couldn't meet her gaze. 'Sure, I minded.' She tugged at the hem of her sweater. 'I felt hurt that Maggie could do that to me, but I also knew just how alluring Gerry could be when he turned on the charm, so it wasn't entirely her fault.'

'Maggie thought it was more than a fling,' Jack pointed out. 'They were making plans to start a new life together in the west country. She'd put her house and business on the market for that reason.'

Polly glowered at Jack. 'No! She didn't tell me she'd done that.'

She shook her head. 'He wouldn't have encouraged her to go that far. She must have gotten the wrong end of the stick.'

'The thing is,' Alexi said, 'if Maggie told Vickery that she had then it will be easy enough for him to find out if she's marketed her property. And that, I'm afraid, will give you motive, which is the missing component from their perspective right now. You need to prepare yourself for that possibility.'

'Then it's hopeless. I've been shafted by my best friend and the man I loved.' She fell momentarily silent but quickly brightened again. 'It also gives Maggie a motive, though. I mean, if Gerry hadn't known she'd put her place up for sale, he'd have been horrified when he realised she genuinely believed they were going to ride off into the sunset. If he told her that it wasn't happening, well then...' She spread her hands and allowed her words to trail off.

'It does indeed give her motive,' Alexi said.

'At the very least, it casts doubt upon *your* motive,' Jack added.

'We went to see Michael yesterday,' Alexi told her after a brief pause.

Polly's head shot up. 'Why? I don't want him dragged into this. It has nothing to do with him.'

'He's your son and so he *is* involved.' Jack's tone was brisk, business-like. 'The police will get to him in time. Bear in mind that the money you used to purchase your business came from a life insurance payout when his father died. He might look upon it as his inheritance and saw Gerry's presence in your life as an impediment. After all, it was Gerry who encouraged you to set up shop here and I suspect that you're not doing too well, so if Michael was keeping tabs then he'd have seen his inheritance being frittered away.' Jack shifted to sit sideways on his chair and cross his legs. 'Anyway, we'll get to that later.'

'Michael doesn't want to know me and has no interest in my money, such as it is,' Polly replied with a sad little shake of her head. 'If that's what you think then you're barking up the wrong tree.'

'He tells us that Gerry didn't approve of his living arrangements,' Alexi remarked.

'Gerry held old-fashioned views about same-sex relationships. A lot of people do but I don't think it bothered Michael much. He told me that he meets prejudice every day and is used to it. It certainly wouldn't have incensed him to the point that he felt compelled to do away with Gerry. You can forget all about that. Don't drag my son into this.' For the first time, a modicum of steel entered her tone – a mother hen protecting her chick. 'I've let him down quite enough as it is.'

'Fair enough.'

Jack rested an elbow on the table as he ran the fingers of that hand absently across his lips. It was a gesture that Alexi recognised and one he employed when he was about to ask difficult questions. No surprises there. All questions in this investigation were sensitive.

Alexi had expected Polly to fall apart. Discovering that her best friend had been carrying on with the man she was fixated with on top of being suspected of murdering the man in question would be enough to floor most women, especially one with Polly's mental frailties. But she was obviously made of sterner stuff. After her initial bout of tears, she now sat upright, her eyes completely dry, her attitude determined.

'Ask me whatever you need to,' she said, breaking the heavy silence. She picked up her coffee mug for the first time and took a sip. 'I have no secrets.'

'Very well. You implied earlier that your financial situation isn't good. Care to elaborate?'

'Not much to say. Business isn't exactly brisk and, no offence, but establishments like this one don't help.'

'We're not your competitor,' Alexi replied. 'We're at different ends of the market.'

'Well, all I can tell you is that costs have shot up since the pandemic, but I can't raise my charges enough to keep up with them and still fill my rooms.'

'I'd like to see your bank records, if you don't mind,' Jack said. 'The police will look at them and I'd like to know what they know.'

'Fine. I'll send you my business and personal statements as soon as I get home.'

'Thanks. Anyway, you were saying.'

'I'd have no customers if I put my rates up high enough to cover the increased bills, but Gerry said not to worry. He was going to help me out. He intended to give up long-distance driving within a year or so, Maggie got that part right, but he wasn't going to spend his time with her. He was planning to stay with me and make the business a going concern.'

'How?' Alexi asked, aware of the scepticism underlying the one word.

'He was working on getting various horseracing syndicates together. He reckoned he could get deals with the trainers to let the syndicates into the yards to watch the horses on the gallops.'

'That's done as a matter of routine,' Alexi said. 'I don't know anything about horses, but I do know that owners come down here regularly for that reason. A lot of them stay here the night before because they have an early start on the day they plan to watch their pampered equines doing their stuff.'

'I don't know the details, but he assured me he was onto a winning idea,' Polly insisted, jutting her chin pugnaciously. 'So, you see, he couldn't possibly have been planning to take off with Maggie.'

Her instinctive belief in Gerry's half-baked ideas tugged at Alexi's heartstrings, which annoyed her when she thought of the way that Polly had treated her in the not-so-distant past. Could Polly really be that naïve or was she drumming up a counterargument to the motive that Maggie's revelation had thrown up? Alexi was unable to decide.

'Okay, so the business is in the red?' Jack asked.

'I'm running on a business overdraft right now,' Polly conceded. 'But what has that got to do with Gerry's death, other than to provide me with a compelling reason not to kill him, given that he had plans to bail me out of trouble?'

'Plans that only you knew about,' Alexi replied. 'Presumably, there was nothing in writing.'

Polly shook her head, looking dejected again, her momentary strength quickly draining away.

'Okay.' Jack smiled at her. 'You didn't kill Gerry, so who did? Who would be your prime suspect?'

'Maggie's name has to be in the frame.' Polly flapped a hand. 'I can't see her being capable of murdering anyone any more than I am, but Gerry did engender fierce emotional reactions; that much I can tell you. And we all know that the most unlikely people are capable of violent crimes of passion when sufficiently roused. You read about it every day. Other than that, I have absolutely no idea. I never met any of his work friends. Not that he really had any. Long-distance driving is a lonely business.'

'We really need a viable alternative so that it takes the heat off you,' Jack told her. 'As things stand, Maggie's admission harms you more than it does her. We know what time Gerry was killed to within an hour or so, and you were in the house. Maggie had classes at that time but could have slipped out for some reason in between them to come and see Gerry. Would she have done that without popping her head round the kitchen door and saying hello, just to make sure you were occupied and unlikely to interrupt?'

'If he'd broken things off with her then she wouldn't have wanted to see me.'

'But nor would she have gone there with the intention of killing Gerry,' Alexi said. 'She was more likely to have gone to try and reason with him so wouldn't have taken a kitchen knife with her. Besides, she wouldn't have just walked into your bedroom and stabbed him. They would have talked first, argued most likely, and you'd have heard raised voices.'

'Not necessarily. The kitchen's on the other side of the house and I always have daytime telly on in the background when I'm working.'

'Okay, so Maggie's name is in the frame.' Jack paused. 'What about James Alton? Did Gerry recommend him to the B&B?'

'Yes. They were friendly but this is the first time he'd stayed at mine. Talked a lot about horses with Gerry, he did. I think James was going to be involved in the syndicate scheme. He had a connection to a yard in Lambourn, knew his horseflesh and Gerry said something about trusting him to find decent horses for the punters to invest in.'

Alexi and Jack exchanged a glance. James had implied when they spoke to him that he didn't actually know Gerry very well.

'Okay, is he still at yours?' Jack asked.

Polly nodded. 'He wants to stay a couple more days, but I barely see him. He's out on the gallops all the time, I think.'

'And your other guests. The Grants and Mr and Mrs Sears. Are they still staying put?'

Alexi and Jack had more or less cleared the two couples of suspicion. On the face of it, they had absolutely no reason to kill Gerry but then again, they were involved with syndicates. If Gerry had tried to drag them into one of his and it had ended badly... well, that meant they couldn't be ruled out.

'Yes.' There was a bitter edge to Polly's tone. 'They seem to be enjoying the fact that they're in the middle of a murder investigation.'

'We'll have another word with them as well,' Jack said, 'just to see if they recall anything else. We've spoken to Gerry's ex-wife and are happy that she had nothing to do with his death. But there's also the question of the person he was heard arguing with on the phone. I'll try and get a look at his phone records, see if we can track his caller down. It will also be interesting to see who else he spoke with on a regular basis.' Jack stood to indicate that he'd run out of questions. 'Go home now and try not to worry. Carry on as usual if you possibly can. Let me know if Vickery calls you in again for another interview and if he does, don't say a word to him without Ben there. That's really important.'

'Okay, thanks.' She glanced at them both and seemed emotional again, as evidenced by the tears that swamped her eyes. 'Thank you,' she said, dabbing at her eyes with a crumpled tissue. 'I know I don't deserve your help, not after the way I've behaved, and I'm sorry about that. If there's anything I can do for you in return...'

'Yes. Send Grace back home,' Jack said, an edge to his voice. 'There's nothing for her to see here.'

11

'Well,' Jack said, as the door closed behind Polly, 'thoughts?'

'I have absolutely no idea.' Alexi sighed. 'I think my prejudice against her is clouding my judgement. I mean, we've gotten involved in difficult cases before. Our client has always appeared guilty, but I've never doubted their innocence. Well, not really. But with Polly, I honestly don't know. All the evidence points in her direction. It's overwhelming, and yet I feel the need to fight her corner.' She shook her head. 'I just don't get it.'

'Yeah, I hear you.' Jack stretched his arms above his head and rolled his shoulders. 'We're running thin on alternative suspects. I agree that it would have been impossible for Maggie to calmly walk into the B&B when she knew Polly was there and casually stab the man she loved. And she did love him. I think we're both agreed on that point.'

'Perhaps they were in it together,' Alexi said whimsically.

'Now that,' Jack replied, lowering his arms again and looking directly at her, 'is a distinct possibility.'

Alexi laughed. 'I wasn't serious.'

'I think Gerry bled Polly dry financially but she'll never admit it. He not only got free board and lodging but probably handouts too. That's the real reason why her business is struggling. His bank records, and hers, will make for interesting reading.'

'So he took all her cash *and* carried on with her best friend,' Alexi said, pouting. 'In her position, I'd have taken a knife to his sensitive parts instead of aiming for his heart because he clearly didn't have one.'

Jack shuddered. 'Remind me never to upset you.'

Before Alexi could respond, a tap at the door preceded Vickery putting his head round it. Alexi smiled and got up to pour coffee. DC Hogan was with him, so Alexi poured one for her as well without bothering to ask either of them if they had time for a beverage. Detectives always seemed to make time for coffee.

'Greetings,' Vickery said, seating himself and making immediate inroads into Cheryl's biscuits. 'Nice day for it.'

'For what, precisely?' Jack asked.

'Well, there's the question. Seems your Ms Pearson is up a gum tree without a paddle so to speak.'

'Looks that way,' Jack responded cheerfully, 'discounting the fact that her best friend was getting uptight and personal with the victim.'

'Excellent motive,' Hogan remarked, munching on a biscuit and nodding her thanks to Alexi when she placed a steaming mug of coffee in front of her.

'Depends who you believe,' Jack replied. 'Maggie insists that she and Gerry were planning happy ever after, but Polly says he was a serial strayer who always came back when he tired of the chase.'

'Not sure he intended to this time,' Vickery replied. 'Ms Ambrose showed us the messages between herself and the victim. They were enough to set the phone on fire.'

'On both sides?' Alexi asked.

'Well...' Vickery waggled a hand from side to side. 'I guess she made the running. She was big on future plans. He went along with her but—'

'It was almost as though he was keeping her sweet,' Hogan said. 'As the inspector says, she was the one banging on about their future together and he responded with platitudes.'

'I'd like to see those messages,' Jack said.

'Sure.' Vickery sipped at his coffee. 'I'll get a copy emailed to you.'

'Sounds to me like you have an alternative suspect, Mark,' Alexi said sweetly.

'Oh God!' Vickery scrubbed a hand down his face. 'Why can't one of them have a fit of remorse and admit to the crime?' He dunked a biscuit in his coffee. 'Murderers nowadays have no respect for the social lives of hard-working policemen.'

'Or women,' Hogan added, grinning at Alexi.

'We talked to Polly's son yesterday,' Alexi said. 'He's the only one of her three kids who wanted to know her, albeit briefly. His partner encouraged him to see her, just to lay the ghosts of his childhood to rest.'

'We'll talk to him ourselves,' Vickery replied.

Hogan made a note in her book and underlined it.

'Do you have his phone records?' Jack asked. 'The victim's, that is. I'm curious to see who he regularly talked to.'

'Yeah, I'll get them sent over to you as well. Nothing jumped out at us at a glance, but I have someone ploughing through them as we speak.'

'Thanks.'

'Any other directions you think we should take?' Vickery asked. 'All suggestions welcome.'

'Polly reckons that Gerry had big plans for early retirement from life on the road and that James Alton was involved.' Jack went on to explain about the syndicate scheme.

'Sounds a bit airy-fairy,' Vickery said, screwing up his features.

'Yeah well, Alton was going to be our next port of call, unless you'd prefer to take him yourself.'

'Can't. Have to be in court soon. Likely to be kept hanging about all day, so have a go at him and let me know how it goes.' Vickery sniffed. 'I probably wouldn't bother even if I had the time, truth to tell. Other priorities and nothing definitive to make me look beyond my existing suspects.'

'Sure.'

Vickery sighed and pushed himself to his feet. 'Adios, children. Play nice without me.'

'Well,' Jack said once the door closed behind Hogan. 'If Vickery's in court then he won't be able to bring Polly back in again today, which buys us a bit of time and is probably why he pointed out that he'd be tied up all day. He's not absolutely convinced that he's got his woman and wants us to do his work for him.'

'Can't Hogan or someone else haul her in?'

Jack shook his head. 'If that was his intention, he'd have said something. He knows I won't do his leg work for him if he keeps too much to himself.'

Alexi nodded. 'I see.'

'He won't be able to spend much manpower on such a seemingly open and shut case either; he made that much obvious. Too few resources and so he'll be under pressure to make an arrest.'

'Okay, boss, so what now?'

'Ah, that's what I like.' Jack grinned at her. 'A little respect.'

'Don't push it, Maddox!'

Cosmo looked up and mewled, presumably in agreement with Alexi, although with Cosmo, it didn't do to make assumptions.

'Hey, big guy, you're supposed to be on my side,' Jack chided. 'Us boys have to stick together.'

Cosmo treated Jack to a searing look and then turned in a circle, settling down with his back to Jack.

'He remembers who rescued him,' Alexi said, sounding proud of her taciturn cat's behaviour.

'And who feeds him, which happens to be me half the time.' Jack leaned towards her and stole a kiss. 'Anyway, I think we need to try and track James Alton down and have another word. I have a feeling about him.'

'Okay. He left us his number. You want me to try it?'

'Go for it.'

Jack watched as Alexi dialled the number. Alton answered quickly. Alexi identified herself, put the call on speaker and asked if they could have another word.

'Yeah, I guess,' James said, sounding sullen. 'But it won't do no good. I've told you everything I know.'

'We have a few more questions. I don't know where you are but if you can come to Hopgood Hall, we'll buy you a pie and a pint.'

'See you in ten,' came the immediate response.

'You know the way to a man's stomach,' Jack said, after she'd cut the call.

Alexi grinned. 'Whatever it takes.'

They left Cosmo snoozing with Toby and made their way to the bar. Alton came in not five minutes later, looking windswept and untidy. A good bath wouldn't have gone amiss either, Jack thought.

'How's it going?' he asked. 'Any idea who did for Gerry yet? Well, not that there can be much doubt about that, but I guess the law needs to be seen to be going through the motions.'

'What can I get you?' Jack asked, declining to answer his question.

'A pint and one of those pasties would hit the spot, thanks.'

Alexi stood up. 'I'll go.'

Jack sensed that she didn't want to be left alone with Alton, who insisted upon speaking to her chest, and so he let her do the honours. They made small talk until she returned with his order.

'Thanks, darlin',' he said, supping a third of his pint in one swallow. Alton clearly wasn't one to look a gift horse in the mouth. 'So, how can I help to condemn the bitch?' he asked.

'You don't like Polly Pearson?' Alexi asked.

'Didn't think much about her one way or the other, truth to tell, but I did get along with Gerry. He was a decent bloke *and* we had plans to go into business together.' Alton looked highly affronted. 'I'll have to find someone else now. Don't suppose you're interested in syndicates, by any chance?'

'You're not too hot on the truth, are you?' Jack asked.

'Dunno what you mean.'

'Yesterday, you said you only knew Gerry a bit but now you're saying you were business partners.'

Alton looked furtive, his small eyes darting from side to side as he struggled to mitigate his error.

'The early stages,' he eventually said. 'Not sure it would have gotten off the ground. Didn't seem worth mentioning since it can't have had anything to do with his death. Being stabbed with a sodding great knife in his own bed smacks of a crime of passion. Stands to reason. Even the old bill must think so. Anyway, in terms of business, I have a lot of irons in a lot of fires. Not all of them come to anything. The thing with Gerry was still very much in the planning stages.'

'Care to elaborate?' Jack asked.

Alton lifted one shoulder. 'Like I just said, horse syndicates. It's done all the time but Gerry reckoned we could get an edge, what with me being tight with Baxter and him having space in his yard.

We could do one another a favour, if you like, nothing more to it than that.'

Jack suspected that there was a great deal more and that it was anything other than legal, but he had no leverage to use in order to force the truth out of Alton.

'Gerry intended staying in Lambourn with Polly then?' he asked.

Alton sniffed. 'Yeah, I reckon, but whether he saw himself with her long term only he could have said. Seems more than likely not, given what she did to him.'

'Did Gerry have other women?' Alexi asked.

'One in every port, darlin'. Polly was the only one who didn't seem to realise it.'

'You know a lot about his habits,' Jack remarked.

'We drank together when he was here. Had to talk about something.'

'I thought Gerry didn't like going out much,' Alexi said.

'He didn't like going out and being hampered by a woman's presence.' Alton sniffed yet again. Jack somehow refrained from asking him if he needed a handkerchief. 'When he was drinking, and he did like a drink, he was a man's man. He reckoned he could go home and get what he wanted from a woman any time he liked. They didn't need to be joined at the hip twenty-four seven.'

'He sounds like a real charmer,' Alexi muttered.

'Yeah well. We'd meet up when he was in Lambourn but not in Lambourn itself, if you get my drift. This town is gossip central and we didn't need everyone knowing our business. We wanted a bit of privacy, so we'd meet at the Royal Oak on the Newbury Road more often than not. Sometimes other places but usually there.'

Jack nodded. He knew the place.

'Then you moved into the B&B, which made it easier for you both, I'm guessing.'

'Yeah, if you take away the fact that Polly never left Gerry alone. A right mother hen, so she was. The poor guy couldn't draw breath without her fussing over him.'

'I assume you were the person who'd choose the horses for your syndicates and Gerry drew the punters in,' Jack remarked.

'Yeah, we played to our strengths,' Alton replied evasively.

'Where did you intend to get the horses from?'

'The sales, if absolutely necessary, but there were easier ways.'

'Like what?' Jack asked.

'The racing world is insular and, like I say, gossip abounds. So, if an owner gets into financial do-do and needs to sell a good horse, word of mouth is still the preferred method of communication. He might get a better price at the sales, but it takes time and there's a sixty-day wait for the dosh once the horse has sold. People with their backs to the wall can't always hold out for that long. Besides, there's the not insignificant fact of having to continue stumping up training fees until the horse does sell. And those costs ain't cheap, believe you me.'

Jack nodded. 'Go on,' he said.

'At the end of the day, it's all down to breeding.' Alton wiped his nose on the back of his hand. Alexi looked repulsed and turned her head away. 'The fees that a stallion standing at stud and with a decent track record can command are staggering and beyond most people's reach. The skill comes in finding the progeny of stallions *without* the track record and who no one's talking about yet. That's where I come in.'

Alton looked meaningfully at his empty pint, but Jack was through with staking a thoroughly dislikeable person.

'Well, thanks for your time,' he said, abruptly standing. 'We won't keep you hanging about any longer. I expect you have things to do, places to be.'

'Oh, er yeah.' Alton scratched his ear. 'That's right.'

Alexi and Jack returned to the kitchen.

'I feel like I need a shower,' Alexi said. 'What a creep! It wouldn't surprise me if he and Gerry fell out over money and Alton knocked him off.'

'Me neither,' Jack replied, 'but still, at least we've learned that Gerry did go out and about.'

'He just didn't take Polly with him.' Alexi sat down, her expression severe.

'What is it?' Jack asked.

'I can't help feeling a bit sorry for Polly. Well, sorrier than I already was. Gerry not only played the field but talked Polly down to men like Alton. What a scumbag!'

'Men like him are players and know how to pick their targets.'

'Yeah, but even so...'

'Brace yourself,' Jack said, watching Cosmo get up, leap from the floor and land on her lap with a thud.

'He missed me,' she said, blowing kisses at the cat.

'I didn't buy a word of sourcing horses by word of mouth,' Jack said, sinking into the chair across from Alexi. 'I reckon Gerry had something going on the continent. I mean, he was there regular as clockwork. We know that he was a popular guy who got along with everyone and inspired loyalty.'

Alexi nodded. 'Good point. He went to Holland a lot. They breed horses there, don't they?'

'I think, and it's all supposition,' Jack said, throwing his head back and closing his eyes, 'that someone, somewhere, is pulling a scam, passing off foals from a decent stallion as not being that stallion's progeny.'

Alexi widened her eyes. 'Good God! Where did that idea come from?'

'Not sure. I might be way off the mark. It was that smug look on Alton's face when he talked about quality stallions that got me thinking. It was like he couldn't resist boasting, just a bit, assuming we wouldn't have a clue what he was inferring.'

Alexi shook her head. 'I don't buy it. Are you sure you aren't letting your dislike for the man cloud your judgement?'

'I'm not sure about anything right now but still, hear me out.' Jack paused to assimilate his thoughts. 'The horseracing world is all about betting, right?'

'With you so far.'

'Picking the outsider that can make you a fortune and those who study form look at—'

'The horse's parentage,' Alexi finished for him, nodding.

'Right. So, if a young horse was sired by an established stallion, it wouldn't be an outsider and the likes of Gerry and Alton wouldn't make a killing.'

'Okay, I hear you,' Alexi said, frowning. 'But why would the owners of an established stallion, who can charge thousands for his services, want to buck the system and risk prosecution by passing off a youngster as being *not* that stallion's baby?' She paused. 'He would have to use his own broodmares to pull off a scam like that as well. Couldn't do it with a genuine owner who'd paid an arm and a leg for the stallion's services.'

Jack grinned. 'I haven't worked that part out yet, but there could be any number of reasons. They wouldn't get away with it in this country; the regulations are too strict, but an established French stallion say...'

'I think the regulations are pretty tight there as well.' Alexi paused. 'You could possibly be onto something, but I think you've got it the wrong way round.'

'How so?'

'Just supposing that an established stallion lost... shall we say, his momentum?'

'Ah!' Jack grinned. 'It happens. I heard talk about something of that nature quite recently.'

Alexi rolled her eyes. 'There's no escaping horsy gossip in this town. Alton got that part right.'

'A famous stallion started firing blanks for no apparent reason. If several mares weren't in foal after two coverings, word would inevitably spread. That would spell disaster for the stallion's reputation. So you're saying that if that's happened then the stallion's owner could have brought in a ringer, same colour and what have you, but the foals wouldn't be top quality.'

Alexi nodded. 'Gerry gets his syndicate to purchase the foal at the price expected for that stallion's offspring, but at a discount if they commit quickly. The yearling might or might not win some races for them but either way, Gerry and Alton are ahead because they pocketed a fat profit on the purchase price.'

'It sounds plausible,' Jack said, 'but we know next to nothing about horses and don't have a hope in hell of proving it. Besides, even if we're right, who would have killed Gerry and why? That's what we're trying to discover. Breaking up illegal horsy scams is above our paygrade.'

'We're not getting paid,' Alexi pointed out.

'Yeah, there is that. Bear in mind too that if we're right then it puts Alton in the clear. The two of them needed one another. Gerry was the front man with bucketloads of charisma. He'd have got the would-be syndicate participants opening their wallets, especially if they were women.'

Alexi sighed. 'So, how about we go to that pub where Alton and Gerry had their meetings? A nosy barmaid on a quiet night might have heard something to point us in the right direction. Or seen someone hanging around Gerry. He was supposed to be a babe magnet and probably couldn't help flirting if there was a woman behind the bar, so the chances are that she took an interest in his activities. God alone knows, just about every other female we've spoken to so far appears to have done so.'

'Just so long as the bar person isn't a hairy bloke of forty,' Jack said laughing, 'but I agree, it's as good a place to start as any.'

'And it's lunchtime. Besides, we don't have any other ideas.'

'Oh, I don't know. I'll be interested to see Gerry's bank records. Not that he'd be daft enough to bank anything incriminating, I imagine, but you never know.' Jack stood up. 'Come on, you two. I'll buy you lunch at the Royal Oak.'

Cosmo leapt from Alexi's lap and was the first to reach the door.

12

Alexi again bore Cosmo's weight on her lap as Jack drove them towards the Royal Oak. Neither of them spoke. Alexi guessed that Jack would be mulling over their wild speculations, as was she, aware that it was important not to get distracted by the possibility of fraudulent horse deals. At the same time, given that Gerry and Alton were involved with drumming up syndicates, perhaps their hypothesis wasn't *that* far-fetched. There was a lot of money to be had from fraudulent racing and if Gerry had reneged, or pissed someone off badly enough, then his being murdered wasn't quite so implausible. It was another avenue to explore but as things stood, they didn't have the first idea where to start looking.

'If Gerry was killed over the syndicate business, wouldn't Alton have been more uptight?' she asked.

'You'd think so, and yet he's still hanging around.'

'So we're probably on the wrong track.' Alexi sighed. 'Bugger! I thought we were onto something.'

'We still could be. Let's see what we get at the Oak first.'

'We didn't ask if any syndicates have already been set up,' Alexi said, jolting upright and almost dislodging Cosmo, who voiced a loud growl by way of protest. 'It could be important,' she insisted, wondering why she was so hung up on the horsy angle. 'If it has already happened and the horse has disappointed, someone in the syndicate who'd been promised the moon might have taken the ultimate form of revenge.'

'A good point,' Jack agreed, 'and plausible, or would be but for the location of Gerry's death. There would be easier, less risky ways to get him alone and do the deed.'

'But no better way to point the finger of suspicion towards Polly.' Alexi closed her eyes and allowed her thoughts to wander haphazardly. 'Perhaps it's nothing to do with horses and the murderer had a score to settle with Polly.' Alexi wrinkled her brow. 'If she treats anyone she takes a dislike to in the same cavalier manner that she harassed me, then it's possible.'

Jack nodded as he paused at a red light. 'Perhaps.'

'You don't sound very sure but if we're running on the premise that Polly *didn't* do it, then you have to admit that the guilty party went to a hell of a lot of trouble.'

'I'm not discounting your theory. I've come across wilder situations in my time. If it did happen that way, then the killer was not only desperate enough to take the chance but, as you rightly point out, also bore a massive grudge against Polly. She can be a pain in the neck, but who would resort to such an elaborate murder just because she pissed them off?'

'Not even I would have tried to frame her for murder.' Alexi chuckled. 'I might have considered murdering her myself, though. In fact, it was on my to-do list.'

Jack grinned. 'We need to ask her if she's got any ongoing disputes. Dissatisfied customers. Someone with a prior claim to Gerry's affections which, given what we know about him, is entirely possible.'

'I think it's more likely to be someone Polly knew. He or she could explain their presence in the event that Polly caught them in the house.' Alexi paused. 'Maggie, for example. Now she *was* upset. We thought it was because the love of her life was dead, but it could be that she'd killed him because he'd thrown her over and we witnessed her delayed reaction.'

'Precisely. I haven't lost sight of the fact that the door was permanently unlocked.'

'Yeah, but even so...'

They reached the Royal Oak and Jack pulled his car into a half-full parking area. Cosmo decided he wasn't willing to be left behind and jumped from the vehicle the moment Jack opened his door.

'Okay,' Alexi said, 'you can come but if there are any dogs in there, you are *not* to terrorise them. Are we clear?'

Cosmo gave her an imperious look and trotted towards the door.

The bar was cosy and inviting and half full of lunchtime punters. A silence descended when Cosmo stalked through the door.

'Blimey, a black panther,' someone quipped.

Cosmo twitched his rigid tail and stalked around the bar as though he owned it. A small terrier looked up and yapped but then hid under a table. Such was Cosmo's intimidating presence that the terrier knew better than to take him on. Alexi had witnessed many similar scenes since adopting the feral feline.

Jack ordered soft drinks, a sandwich for himself and a tuna salad for Alexi which she anticipated being bullied into sharing with Cosmo. She rolled her eyes when a very pretty barmaid of perhaps thirty homed in on Jack and took her time filling his order.

'Have you seen this guy in here?' he asked, pulling up a picture of Gerry on his phone.

'Yeah,' she said, leaning over the bar and getting closer than was strictly necessary to Jack in order to study the picture. 'Isn't he the guy who got murdered? We've all been talking about it. It's terrible. He was a real character. He asked me out on a date as a matter of fact and I was tempted, I can tell you, but I think my boyfriend might have had something to say about that. Anyway, he came in quite often with a jockey, or ex-jockey.'

'This guy.' Jack showed her a picture of Alton.

'That's him.'

'Anyone else with him?'

The girl looked askance at Jack. 'You ask a lot of questions.'

'It's what I do. I'm an investigator.'

'I heard the woman he lodged with did it,' a barfly who'd been listening to their conversation remarked.

'No one's been charged,' Alexi said.

'There was someone else who joined them the last time, I think,' the girl said. 'The three of them were having a heated conversation, that's why I remember. I hadn't seen him in here before and have no idea what his name was.'

'Paul. His name was Paul,' the barfly said. 'I heard one of them call him that. I have a good memory for names.'

'A good memory for not minding your own business,' the barmaid pointed out.

Jack indicated the man's almost empty glass. The barmaid caught on and refilled it for him.

'Right civil of you,' the man said, saluting Jack with his replenished pint.

'Can you remember what Paul looked like?' Alexi asked.

The man shrugged. 'Just a bloke. Tall, gangly, black-framed glasses. Could have been anyone.'

It could indeed but Jack and Alexi shared a glance, aware that

their loquacious and observant friend had just described Paul
Seers, one of Polly's guests.

'The plot thickens, as is so often the case,' Alexi remarked as
they moved to a table close to the open fireplace. Cosmo settled
down in front of it, staking his claim. The terrier whimpered and
retreated further beneath a table. No one else batted an eyelid at
an oversized feline taking control of the bar.

'Only in this part of the world,' Jack said, laughing.

'It kinda makes sense, in some respects,' Alexi said, 'Paul Seers
meeting with Gerry, I mean. They did say that they were looking
for horses to invest in.'

'But does not explain why they felt the need to meet here, out
of the way,' Jack replied. 'They were all staying at Polly's.'

'The fact that they did increases the likelihood of Gerry being
up to no good, I suppose.'

'We'll go to Polly's once we've had our lunch and ask Mr Seers
about it,' Jack said, smiling at the barmaid as she sashayed towards
them with their food. Cosmo sat up and took an immediate
interest in proceedings.

As soon as they'd finished eating, they hit the road again and
made the relatively short journey back to Lambourn. They parked
up but this time left Cosmo in the car. Despite the fact that Polly's
door was unlocked, Jack tapped on it and waited for someone to
invite them in. Grace rather than Polly did the honours. Alexi
inwardly groaned when she turned on the smiles for Jack and
pointedly ignored her.

'Twice in one day,' she muttered, thinking of the barmaid's
fascination with Jack.

'Polly's resting,' Grace said. 'Her nerves are shot to pieces and
I'm worried about her. I don't want to wake her unless it's impor-
tant. Can I help with anything? Are you making any progress?'
Grace glowered at Alexi.

'We're not here to see Polly. Are the Seers in?'

Grace looked surprised by the question. 'Yeah, I think so.' She glanced through the window. 'That's their Volvo. They're in Room 4. Why do you want to see them?'

Jack didn't bother to respond. Instead, he took Alexi's hand and brushed past Grace, heading for the stairs. Alexi appreciated Jack's gesture, but she really didn't need her hand held, neither physically nor figuratively, just to make a point. She snatched it free, wondering why she felt so tetchy. Jack wasn't to blame for Grace's appearance, or her determination to get her claws back into him.

Get a grip!

Jack smiled at her, clearly understanding her turmoil, as he tapped at the Seers' door. It was pulled open by Michelle, who blinked up at him in obvious surprise. Her clothing was rumpled, and it was evident that that'd woken her.

'Oh hello,' she said. 'Is there news? Come in.'

She opened the door wider and they stepped into a large room, pleasantly decorated, with a picture window overlooking the downs. Paul occupied a chair in front of that window and had the *Racing Post* open in his lap. He looked up at them and Alexi could have sworn that a combination of fear and guilt filtered through his expression. Then again, perhaps her imagination was getting the better of her. Either way, it was gone again before she could draw any helpful conclusions.

'Hiya.' He folded the paper and threw it beneath his chair, as though embarrassed to be caught with it. Alexi wanted to tell him that for the majority of Lambourn residents, it was the reading material of choice. 'What gives?' He stood up and shook their hands. 'Polly's in a right state. We thought we ought to move on so that she can shut up shop, but her friend reckons she needs something other than the murder to occupy her mind.'

I'll just bet she does, Alexi thought, somehow resisting the urge to roll her eyes. But at least she knew what Grace's motivation was, she thought, glancing at Jack. She was less sure why the Seers felt the need to hang around, though. If they'd had anything to do with the murder, they would surely have taken an early opportunity to distance themselves from the enquiry. The fact that they'd stayed put implied innocence, and morbid curiosity.

'Looking after us, in other words,' Michelle added. 'It's a bit like being in the middle of a TV show, what with detectives, and scenes of crime people and what have you coming and going.' Michelle looked animated, almost as though she was enjoying being in the heart of things. 'Anyway, what can we do for you?'

'We've been following up on Gerry's movements,' Alexi said, perching her backside against the window ledge since there weren't enough chairs for them all to sit. 'We gather you met him in the Royal Oak with James Alton recently, Paul. What was that all about, if you don't mind my asking?'

'Paul?' There was accusation in Michelle's voice.

'Look, it was nothing.' Paul spread his hands, attempting to look casual, but Alexi could see that he was tightly wired. 'No biggie. Just an exploratory meeting away from walls that have ears.'

'I thought we agreed that we wouldn't...'

Michelle's words trailed off when Paul sent her a warning look.

'We're aware that Gerry and Alton were scraping syndicates together,' Jack said, 'and assumed you were interested in becoming part of one. Nothing untoward about that. It happens all the time.'

The Seers exchanged a prolonged look.

'You might as well tell them.' Michelle broke the silence, her tone loaded with innuendo. 'It looks as though they'll find out anyway and it's not as if we've done anything wrong.'

Paul sighed. 'The fact of the matter is that we're already involved. I'm the liaison between them and the syndicate. Most of its members are personal friends of mine and I persuaded them to get involved with a promising two-year-old. Or so we thought. Six outings now and not a peep. Hasn't even been up there in the chase. Nothing to get excited about and a bitter disappointment.'

'I didn't want to get so heavily involved,' Michelle said. 'We took a quarter share and it's so expensive. But Gerry convinced us that the horse was hugely promising and greatly underrated. He effectively made it seem as though it couldn't lose.'

'And I got overexcited; I'll be the first to admit that much,' Paul added. 'I fell for the hype. But after our sixth loss, even I ran out of enthusiasm. So too did my fellow syndicate members and we all wanted to cut our losses and sell up. Gerry said no way, we were contracted for two years before we could even consider selling and that we'd known there were no guarantees going in. He persuaded us to come down here and see the horse in training.'

'Where is it?' Jack asked.

Alexi suspected that she knew the answer to that one and so wasn't surprised when Paul said the horse was at Baxter's yard.

'We didn't tell you all this because it didn't seem relevant,' Paul said, a defensive edge to his voice. 'We might have been pissed off with Gerry, but we weren't going to murder him because of it.'

Perhaps not, Alexi thought, but they too now had a motive at least as compelling as Polly's: they were out of pocket.

'Why did you go to the Royal Oak to have it out with them?' Alexi asked. 'What was wrong with thrashing it out here? And why didn't you go along too, Michelle?'

'Gerry insisted that we not talk about it in front of Polly,' Paul replied. 'I got the impression that she wasn't aware of the extent of Gerry's involvement in... well, horse trading.'

'And I'm pretty sure that she financed it without being aware,' Michelle added. 'She was putty in his hands. I didn't know Paul had gone to the Oak with Gerry and James. I told him not to and that if we wanted out then we needed to do it through our solicitors. Gerry had the gift of the gab and could talk anyone out of anything.'

'How was it left?' Jack asked. 'Did you see the horse in training up at Baxter's?'

'No.' Paul shook his head. 'We were supposed to be going the day after Gerry was killed but obviously that didn't happen.'

'And I have shown our contract to our solicitor,' Michelle added.

Paul blinked. 'You have?'

'You're not the only one who can keep secrets. Unfortunately, I've had it confirmed that we have no way of getting out of it, even with Gerry dead, so we're stuck.' She let out a long breath. 'But still, at least we get to go to the races as owners, which is something. So if you think we had anything to do with Gerry's death then think again.'

'That possibility hadn't crossed our minds,' Alexi assured them.

'I assume that the syndicate owns the horse,' Jack said. 'How much did you pay for it, if you don't mind my asking?'

Paul told him and Jack let out a low whistle.

'No wonder you're disappointed if it hasn't performed but surely, if you own the horse outright, the syndicate can decide to sell.'

'We could but it has to be a unanimous decision,' Paul replied, 'and unfortunately, Gerry owned a small share. Smaller than the rest of us but he still had an equal vote. It's in the contract and none of us picked up on it. He was adamant that the horse would come good. We just needed to be patient and not lose our nerve. He insisted that some take longer to develop than others, which is true, but I honestly couldn't see Spring Venture making the grade.'

And all the while the horse was in training, Baxter could pile on the charges, Alexi knew. Presumably, Baxter was a-party to the scam and Gerry wasn't required to pay any part of the training fees. Then again, if he'd charged the others over the odds for the horse, why insist upon holding onto it if the syndicate wanted to sell and if he knew it was never likely to make the grade?

She glanced at Jack and could see that he was equally perplexed. None of this made any sense. Unless... unless the horse did have potential and was somehow being held back, literally, for bets. Horses were routinely dope-tested when they won but if a horse appeared to make an effort but was held back by a skilled jockey, or if said jockey deliberately got boxed in, would anyone notice or suspect anything untoward?

'Who is Spring Venture's sire?' Jack asked.

'That's just the thing,' Paul said, animated now. 'It's Valid Reason, one of the best stallions to stand at stud in Chantilly.'

France!

Impossible though it seemed, Alexi realised that her and Jack's speculations could well be on the money, even if they got some of the details wrong. This was potentially a bigger business than they'd realised, with more than Gerry, Alton and Baxter involved.

And yet another potential reason for Gerry's murder that had nothing to do with his womanising.

'So, what happens now?' Jack asked. 'With Gerry dead, will you be able to sell?'

'Unfeeling as it sounds, we've discussed not much else since learning of his death,' Michelle said. 'We reckon it depends upon who inherits Gerry's share. We wanted to ask Polly if he's made a will but it seemed a bit heartless. Still, I suppose we'll find out soon enough.'

'Other than Gerry's share, were all the other syndicate members known to you?'

'Yes,' Paul replied. 'I got them all involved but none of them have been down here so none of them could have knocked Gerry off.'

'One last question,' Alexi said. 'Do you think Polly killed Gerry?'

'Hard to say.' Paul lifted one shoulder in a negligent shrug. 'We don't know her very well. We only met her for the first time when we took up this booking. It was obvious that she was besotted with him but I don't think her feelings were reciprocated. If that penny finally dropped, I guess there's no saying what she might be capable of...'

13

'Phew,' Jack said when they left the Seers' room. 'The plot thickens.'

'Indeed.' Alexi flicked a strand of hair away from her eyes, still feeling a little shellshocked by Paul's revelations. 'Do you think Paul killed Gerry, though? Does he have it in him?'

'Money is a pretty powerful motive.'

'Yeah, and he was thoroughly pissed off about the horse's lacklustre performance. I got the impression that they'd overreached themselves only because Gerry sold them a lie. From what I've learned from living in this village, anyone with a love for the horses can be easily persuaded.'

'I honestly can't get a handle on Seers. He's either a practised liar or an innocent dupe. He was certainly on the spot though, so had the opportunity. I'm not writing him off as a suspect yet. Not by a long shot.'

'Right. So where to now?' Alexi asked.

'I'd like another word with James Alton and I'm betting we'll find him up at Baxter's yard.'

'Will the police already have spoken to him?'

Jack shrugged. 'If not yet then they will but Vickery didn't seem to have him down as a priority. Anyway, we can push buttons that they can't.'

Cosmo mewled, making them both smile.

'Okay.' Alexi pulled up the yard's address and punched it into the satnav on her phone, then stroked Cosmo, who'd resumed possession of her lap. Jack turned the car and followed the disembodied instructions that emanated from Alexi's phone.

'We need to find out if Gerry made a will and who benefits from his demise,' Alexi remarked.

'I expect Vickery's already on it, but yeah, we do need to know that.'

As though aware that they were talking about him, Jack's phone rang and Vickery's name appeared on the display. Jack pressed the button on his steering wheel and took the call.

'Hey, Mark,' he said. 'What gives?'

'I've got the victim's bank records. He's heavily in debt.'

'How heavily?'

'Nearly a hundred grand.'

Alexi's jaw fell open. 'Blimey,' she muttered. 'Does the debt die with him or will whoever he's left his worldly goods to assume responsibility for it?' she asked.

'Haven't found a will, so we'll leave that one for the legal people to thrash out.'

Jack told Vickery what they'd discovered about the syndicate and added their speculations about race fixing.

'Nothing would surprise me in this town,' Vickery replied in a weary tone.

'Do we know who he was in debt to?' Alexi asked.

'Nope. Not yet at any rate. I have people working on it.'

'It could be significant,' Alexi remarked.

'Not necessarily.' It was Jack who responded. 'If he borrowed from the sort of people that it would be unwise to cross then they wouldn't have killed him. It wouldn't be in their best interests because they'd never get paid if they topped him. They'd be more likely to break a few bones, just to remind Gerry of his obligations.'

'That ties in with the overheard telephone conversation,' Alexi said. 'We know he was assuring someone that they'd get paid.'

'I'm convinced that this murder was either a crime of passion—'

'Which puts your Ms Pearson firmly in the frame,' Vickery reminded them.

'He was a womaniser, Mark, carrying on with Polly's best friend. Either one of them could have done it, which is sufficient to put doubt in a jury's mind,' Jack pointed out. 'A jury will take a dim view of Gerry's behaviour, especially those who are happily married, or religious. But then, I'm not telling you something you don't already know, am I?'

Vickery's sigh echoed down the line. 'You think like a policeman,' he said.

'My money's still on Gerry's dodgy dealings with horses having led to his demise,' Jack said. 'A falling out amongst thieves, if you like, who knew enough about Gerry's habits to also know that he could get into Polly's place without having to knock, get the deed done and scarper, leaving suspicion to fall on a spurned lover.'

'Now you're being downright difficult, to say nothing of giving me a headache,' Vickery complained.

'He does that all the time, but he also has a point.' Alexi smiled as she spoke. 'You don't have enough to charge Polly and you know it. A good defence lawyer would drive a coach and horses through your theory.'

'Okay, enough. You two have made your point.' Alexi could see Vickery in her mind's eyes, throwing up his hands in defeat. 'It's worth being aware that Ms Pearson is in the red too. She has a business loan that she's struggling to repay, and she's made a lot of transfers to the deceased over the past few years, even though she couldn't afford to.'

'She was financing him,' Alexi muttered. 'We thought she might be.'

'Have you spoken to James Alton yet?' Jack asked.

'Can't find him. He appears to have gone to ground.'

'And that's not the slightest bit suspicious?' Alexi asked.

Vickery made a non-committal noise.

'If there's nothing else, we're off to Baxter's yard,' Jack told the detective. 'We'll try to find Alton and let you know what we unearth, if anything.'

'Okay, but I'm coming under pressure to charge Polly Pearson, regardless,' Vickery said. 'There is enough evidence to build a case against her, despite the anomalies you just pointed out, and she is the most likely suspect.' He paused. 'The only viable suspect, really.'

'Your lords and masters want it wrapped up quickly, I get that, but if you jump the gun then it could come back and bite you on the arse.'

'And finish up on the front pages, painting the police as the bad guys,' Alexi said sweetly: a timely reminder of both her profession and the power of the press.

'Yeah, yeah, I hear you.'

Jack laughed. 'You know she's right. Anyway, let me know if you intend to make the arrest and we'll ensure that Ben's there to hold her hand.'

'Will do.'

Vickery thanked them and cut the call.

'You look pensive,' Alexi said when they drove on in silence for several minutes. 'What are you thinking?'

'I'm thinking that Vickery isn't telling us everything,' he replied, frowning. 'Otherwise, he would have made the arrest.'

'He will already have thought about the things we pointed out. A charge doesn't necessarily mean the case will make it to court, remember, but it does make the force look good.'

'And means they'll move on to the next one without looking for anyone else.' Alexi scratched Cosmo's flat ears, eliciting a loud purr from her feline friend. 'Not sure why that makes me feel uncomfortable, given what Polly's put me through in the past, but there you have it.'

'Your reminder... make that threat about using the press will doubtless have already occurred to Vickery.'

'Good. I don't mind him charging Polly if he has solid evidence pointing to her guilt, but really, he has nothing. I still have my doubts about her innocence. I mean, the more we find out about Polly, the less stable she seems and the easier it is to imagine her committing a crime of passion in the heat of the moment, but even so...'

'If he had definitive proof of her guilt, he'd have given me a heads-up.'

'But he doesn't or, like I say, she'd be in handcuffs by now.'

Jack took his turn to sigh. 'I guess. But what I don't get is why Gerry was so hard up. If he was race fixing then he ought to have been raking it in. So where are his ill-gotten gains stashed?'

'He probably has an offshore account tucked away in some remote corner of the world where the banking regulations are looked upon as optional. That's what I'd have done in his situation.'

'Then why leave himself in debt, especially if the people he owed money to don't take kindly to being kept waiting?'

Alexi spread her hands, feeling frustrated. 'Who knows? So many dead ends.' She paused. 'Let's refresh our minds about what we do know of the victim. He was a womaniser and had both Polly and Maggie clinging tenaciously.'

'He'd made them both promises that he probably didn't intend to keep.'

'Very likely not, so why get involved with Polly's best friend? He was playing with fire, especially because he must have been aware of the fragile state of Polly's mental health. Not to mention the fact that women tend to confide in one another when it comes to affairs of the heart.' Alexi twitched her nose. 'Not that Maggie could have opened up to Polly, of course, but I bet Polly spilled the beans to Maggie, banging on about the plans that she and Gerry had for the future. Or the plans that Polly thought they had. Perhaps they were so similar to the promises that Gerry made to Maggie that she saw the light and decided to do them both a favour.'

Jack nodded. 'I think he couldn't resist the challenge. I've met men like him before, who think they're God's gift and walk on water. Irresistible.'

'Ha!'

'You think he was going to sail off into the sunset and leave them both as well as his debts behind him?' Jack pulled a face. 'If either of his ladies got wind of that fact then they probably joined forces to do away with him. Dealing with one woman scorned would be challenging enough...'

'I'd be tempted to agree with you, but for the fact that he was killed in Polly's home. She might have her issues but she isn't stupid and wouldn't do anything to turn herself into the main suspect.' Alexi shook her head. 'No, if they were in it together then one of them would have lured him to an isolated spot...'

'So, apart from his women, we have to look at his business arrangements, which is where I hope Baxter can point us in the right direction, albeit unintentionally. Race fixing is a big business, and the sport doesn't attract the passive type.'

Jack indicated and turned his BMW into the parking area outside Baxter's yard. They left Cosmo on guard duty and stepped from the car.

'It looks run down,' Alexi said, unimpressed by what she saw. A less welcoming sight it would be difficult to imagine. There was muck everywhere, the paint was peeling, and the stabling looked decidedly dilapidated.

'It does indeed. And unless half his horses are out at grass then he has a lot of spare boxes,' Jack replied, indicated a row of uninhabited stables with the doors hanging open with the wave of one arm.

A dog appeared from out of nowhere; a mean-looking mutt with a loud bark and a wagging tail.

'Mixed messages,' Alexi said, not hesitating to offer the creature her hand. The dog seemed surprised and a little afraid but submitted to a good ear scratching. The stupid animal lapped up attention that he was clearly unused to receiving. Alexi despised people who neglected their animals and so had already taken an intense dislike to Baxter. 'Not much of a guard dog,' she added, grinning up at Jack.

'Most people wouldn't have your courage.'

'Most people are wimps. This poor creature is starved of the love he deserves.'

A short man with shaggy, grey hair and an obvious attitude appeared from out of nowhere and glowered at them.

'Something I can do for you?' he asked in a gruff voice, watching his dog being fussed over and frowning. He clicked his fingers and the dog whimpered. Alexi defiantly continued to scratch his ears and the animal stayed where he was, but Alexi could feel him trembling, which made her blood boil. No dog should be afraid of its owner.

'If that's the way you greet potential new owners then I'm

hardly surprised that your yard is half full,' Alexi replied with asperity. 'In fact, I'm astonished that you have any clients at all.'

'Most prospective owners phone for an appointment.'

'Phone ringing off the hook, is it?' Jack asked, stepping forward. 'Name's Maddox. Jack Maddox, and this is Alexi Ellis. I assume you're Baxter.'

'Yeah, John Baxter. I know who you are. I also know you ain't here to employ my services so what the hell do you want? I'm busy.'

'We're here about your friend, Gerry Dawlish.'

'Yeah, I heard. Tragic.' Baxter appeared unmoved by the tragedy in question and made do with wiping the back of his hand beneath his nose. 'But we weren't friends. We just did a bit of business together.'

'What sort of business?' Alexi asked, still making a fuss of the dog.

Baxter scowled. 'Don't see what that has to do with you,' he growled. If his tone was intended to intimidate, it failed in that objective. Alexi could sense a distinct unease beneath all the bluster.

'Okay.' Jack turned away. 'We'll just tell Vickery, the inspector investigating that you've got something to hide.'

Baxter shuffled his feet, scowled at Jack and quickly lowered his gaze. 'I hear his woman got fed up and offed him.' Another sniff. 'Can't say that I'm surprised.'

'You knew her?' Alexi asked as she and Jack turned back in Baxter's direction. The dog hadn't moved but followed Alexi's progress through huge, liquid eyes that jolted her heart. She wanted to take the poor thing with her and give him all the love and kindness he so richly deserved. A mixture of German Shepard and... well, just about anyone's guess what else, she had already fallen half in love with him. What Cosmo would have to say about that situation didn't bear thinking about it, but Alexi couldn't help the way she felt. 'He brought her here?'

'Nope, but I knew of her by reputation. A bit of a clinger, by all accounts, and Gerry was a free spirit. Liked to put it about and wouldn't be nagged into being tied down so it was never gonna end well.'

'When did you last see him?' Jack asked.

'The day before he died. He often came up here, to chew the fat. We go way back. He liked the turf and came looking for tips.'

'I hear you, he and James Alton had a bit of business going on the side,' Jack remarked.

Baxter's head jerked up. 'Where did you hear that?' A modicum of fear flashed through his weathered features and his bushy eyebrows furrowed. 'It don't do no good to listen to gossip. Load of old women in horseracing, always making stuff up.'

'There's nothing illegal about syndicates,' Alexi said. 'So why are you getting your knickers in such a twist?'

Baxter planted fisted hands on his hips and glowered at Alexi. 'If I'm getting in a stew, it's 'cause I'm allergic to people like you coming round here and stirring up the muck, stopping me from getting on with my work.'

'Not much stirring necessary,' Jack remarked, glancing at an overflowing muck heap and shrugging.

A loud noise caused all three of them to glance towards Jack's car. Cosmo was bashing at the window with a paw and growling fit to burst a gut. The dog whimpered, causing Alexi and Jack burst out laughing.

'I don't think my cat likes me making a fuss of you, darling,' Alexi said, scratching the dog's ears.

Baxter snapped his fingers. 'Here, Silgo.'

The dog slunk to his belly, trembling, but didn't move. Alexi crouched down and made more of a fuss of him. 'Don't be scared, darling,' she cooed. 'I won't let the horrible man hurt you.'

'Is James Alton here?' Jack asked. 'It would be useful if we could speak to you both.'

'No, he ain't here.' Baxter's voice was gruff. Threatening. But Jack wasn't easily intimidated and stood his ground.

'Don't be an idiot,' Jack said impatiently. 'It's either us or the police poking our noses in. They might well come anyway, given that you're one of the last people to see Gerry alive.'

'Nothing I can tell them. He was alive and well when he left here. Besides, James was with him. He'll tell you.'

'Funny, he didn't mention that when we spoke to him before,' Alexi said, standing up straight again. The dog stood with her and clung to her leg.

'Tell us about the syndicates they were flogging,' Jack said. 'Any winners?'

'Not yet. These things take time. You'd know that if you know anything about horses. They're unpredictable creatures. Moodier than women, in my experience.'

'Which is undoubtedly extensive,' Alexi said derisively.

'Losers can be just as profitable, I'm guessing,' Jack remarked languidly.

Baxter's entire body went rigid. 'Here, what's that supposed to mean? There're rules against that sort of thing as could see me struck off, or worse.'

'Nothing could be much worse than this,' Alexi said, sending a scathing glance towards a sagging stable roof.

'You might as well tell us,' Jack said wearily, 'because, rest assured, we'll find out one way or another.'

'I'm telling yer, there's nothing to see here. Gerry was killed by an irrational woman. End of. Now get out of my yard and take my advice: you really don't want to be poking your noses into stuff you don't understand.' He snapped his fingers at the dog and this time, it reluctantly trailed after its owner.

'Not much guilt going on there,' Alexi said, as they turned back for the car.

'He's a worried man, that's for sure.'

'Wish we could have brought that dog away with us. The poor thing.'

'It was fed, just not given much love,' Jack said, flinging an arm around her shoulders. 'You can't rescue the entire world, darling. If I were you, I'd concentrate on appeasing one annoyed cat.'

Cosmo sprang from the car the moment Jack opened the door and stood with arched back, hissing at the spot where Alexi had made a fuss of Silgo.

'Oh, do stop posturing!' she said impatiently bending to stroke Cosmo's head. 'Poor Silgo needed a little TLC. You of all cats ought to appreciate how that feels.'

'I think,' Jack said, starting the engine and snapping his seat belt into place, 'that we should run James to ground—'

'In the local, no doubt.'

'That's my best guess. And after that, another visit to Maggie's in order. I want to know if she lent Gerry money too.'

14

Jack didn't much care for the direction that the investigation was taking. Every avenue appeared to lead to a dead end. He wasn't impressed by Baxter's threats either. The man was scared. Scared of whoever he'd gotten involved with. Scared because if Gerry had become impatient or too greedy then those same people might well have done for him.

Then again, if Gerry had spoken out of turn, or perhaps told Maggie too much about his future plans then Maggie could be in danger too. Baxter was tough and likely didn't scare easily. Maggie needed to be warned.

'You're quiet. What are you thinking?' Alexi asked as they made the return trip to the centre of Lambourn.

'I'm thinking that there's something not right about Baxter's setup,' he settled for saying, keeping his concerns for Maggie's wellbeing to himself for now. Gerry could just as easily have confided in Polly, but Jack doubted it. He'd taken an almighty risk, getting together with Maggie and still leaching off Polly. He wouldn't have wanted to face the music if Polly found out the truth.

He seemed like the type to cut and run, without bothering to leave an explanation.

'Putting aside the fact that he's cruel to dogs,' Alexi replied, curling her upper lip.

It took Jack a moment to realise that Alexi's disdain was reserved for Baxter, whilst his own thoughts dwelt upon Gerry's manipulation of the women in his life. Each were reprehensible. 'Baxter's running scared, Alexi. He tried to warn us, in his way, to keep our noses out.'

'You think Gerry got greedy, or wanted out of whatever scam they were pulling, and got bumped off because he'd become unreliable.' She paused, presumably to consider a possibility that hadn't previously occurred to her. She had disliked Baxter on sight, Jack knew without having to be told. She thoroughly disapproved of the way he treated his dog and hadn't seen beyond the posturing. It wasn't like her to get distracted, and Jack knew she would be beating herself up because of it. 'This is obviously bigger than we first thought, if we're right. Perhaps we should simply hand it over to Vickery.'

'And we will, once we know a bit more. At the moment, it's entirely speculative.'

Alexi nodded. 'Okay, you're the boss.'

Jack sent her a sideways glance and laughed. 'Since when?' he asked.

They pulled up in the car park attached to the local, but a quick search of the sparsely populated bar showed no sign of Alton. The barman said he hadn't seen him all day.

'He's running scared too, is my bet,' Jack said as they returned to his car. 'Let's see if he's holed up at Polly's. If not, we have to assume he's done a runner.'

'We could try calling him.'

'We could, but I'd prefer to catch him unawares. Besides, all my instincts tell me he's gone into hiding. But if he's still in the area, we'll run him to ground. It's a small town. Someone, somewhere will have seen him.'

'He might have been holed up at Baxter's. We didn't get to have a look around and Baxter sure as hell wouldn't have given him up.'

'True. We'll go back if we have to. Or better yet, have Vickery send in uniforms mobhanded.'

'Perhaps we should have done that anyway.'

Jack shook his head. 'If Baxter has something to hide then he'll shut the operation down and it'll be moved elsewhere.' Jack removed a hand from the steering wheel and rubbed his chin. 'This is bigger than we realised, Alexi. And Baxter isn't the mastermind.'

Alexi blew air through her lips. 'We're agreed on that point. All he's capable of is bullying innocent dogs.'

They parked outside Polly's B&B and found Grace and Polly sitting together in the kitchen, working their way through a bottle of wine. They both looked up when Jack put his head round the door. Grace's face lit up but her expression quickly faded when she observed Alexi on Jack's heels.

'Any news?' Polly asked, looking up with a combination of fear and hope competing for dominance in her expression.

She looked terrible, Jack thought. Her face was pale and drawn and there was a spiderweb of lines working their way across her cheeks. Her eyes were red and bulging, with massive pouches forming beneath them. Her hair could do with a good wash, and she looked as though she'd slept in her clothes. She had always taken a pride in her appearance, Jack knew, which made the sight of her now considerably more surprising. Or then again, perhaps not. She had suffered a double, stifling whammy of loss and betrayal, even if she was in denial, at least insofar as the betrayal part was concerned.

Jack didn't believe that she was as indifferent about Gerry's 'flirtation' with Maggie as she made out. He had seldom seen the woman in the months leading up to this disaster when she hadn't been with Maggie and Linda, stirring up rumours about Alexi's involvement in the recent spate of murders in Lambourn.

Polly was obviously easily led and loyal to her friends. But when one of the friends in question had shafted her quite so blatantly Polly had trouble handling the situation.

'Nothing yet,' Jack replied in response to Polly's question.

He pulled out a chair for Alexi before taking the one beside her, despite the fact that Grace shuffled along on the bench she occupied, presumably in the hope that he'd sit beside her. It was like being back at school, he thought, glancing at Alexi, who was clearly struggling not to roll her eyes. Cosmo, who had come in with them, hissed at Grace before jumping agilely onto Alexi's lap, eyeing Grace speculatively across the table. Jack knew that look. When Cosmo took against a person, it seldom ended well.

Polly offered them wine but they both declined.

'Is James Alton here?' Jack asked, getting straight down to business.

'No,' Polly replied, looking confused at a question that she obviously hadn't anticipated. 'He went out early this morning, as a matter of fact. Far earlier than was usual for him and said he'd be gone all day.'

'Are his things still here, in his room?' Alexi asked.

Polly shrugged. 'I assume so. To be honest, I haven't checked. Why would I?'

'What's Alton got to do with anything?' Grace asked.

'That's what we're trying to establish,' Jack said. 'Mind if we have a quick look in his room?'

Polly shrugged for a second time. Alexi and Jack, with Cosmo tagging along, made their way upstairs to the room in question. It was a tip and Jack thought at first that someone had been rifling through his possessions. The smell of unwashed clothes was almost overwhelming. Alexi nudged the window open to let in a little fresh air.

'Doesn't Polly clean the rooms?' she asked, pushing the bathroom door open and wrinkling her nose.

'I guess she's been preoccupied. Besides, I doubt if Alton would notice, given that he appears to live in a pigsty.'

'What are we looking for?'

'Not sure.' Jack rummaged through the bedside drawer with Alexi looking over his shoulder. There were credit card receipts but no helpful notes to point them in the right direction.

'There's nothing here and the smell's making me nauseous,' Alexi said after they'd conducted a methodical search.

'Yeah, but we do know that he likes a flutter,' Jack said, waving some betting slips in her face.

'I thought people did that sort of thing online nowadays.'

'Not all, apparently. I think accounts are sometimes closed if a punter gets too lucky, so he might prefer to spread his love.'

'Yuck. Don't make me feel any worse than I do already.'

Jack laughed as he closed the window. 'Okay, let's get out of here.'

'Find what you were looking for?' Grace asked as they returned to the kitchen. Cosmo responded with an arched back and another hiss.

'You lent Gerry a lot of money over the months,' Jack said, turning towards Polly and seeing no reason to sugar-coat his questions. Someone needed to nudge her out of her apathetic state. 'What was that all about?'

Polly's head shot up. 'I was helping him out short term, is all. Anyway, it's private and not relevant.'

'It's a murder enquiry and you need our help. You came to us, remember.' Jack's voice was hard, uncompromising. Grace shivered and covered Polly's hand with her own. 'If you don't tell us everything then we can't help you and we'll be out of here.'

'I just don't see how it's relevant,' Polly repeated, her voice an annoying whine.

'She'd hardly kill him if he owed her money,' Grace indignantly.

'That rather depends upon what the loans were for, especially as you couldn't afford to make them,' Alexi said, ignoring Grace and focusing her attention upon Polly.

'I've already told you about our plans.' A note of impatience had entered Polly's tone.

'Tell us again,' Jack said.

'Sorry.' Polly buried her face in her hands and let out a protracted sigh. 'All this is getting to me. I have a raging headache and can't think straight.'

'The wine won't help with the head,' Jack told her.

Polly shrugged. 'It dulls the senses.'

'We need to know what the loans were for,' Alexi said crisply. 'The police will ask you, if they haven't already.'

'Gerry was starting a business, in France. We were going to settle there, and he needed some help with the deposits and stuff.' Polly spread her hands. 'I don't know. He never gave me much information and I was happy for him to handle that side of things. I trusted him,' she added, an edge to her voice.

'I thought he was going to help you run this place,' Alexi said.

'Only until I could sell it, then we were out of here. He said to keep it going until he finished his time at Holby's, make it profitable again and therefore a going concern, then it would be all systems go.'

'Where in France did you plan to go?' Alexi asked, probably suspecting that she already knew.

'Chantilly. Why? Does it matter?'

'It could be vital,' Jack said.

'Did he take you to see it?' Alexi asked.

'No. We spoke about it several times. He showed me pictures of this lovely old house that needed renovating. It had paddocks with horses and looked idyllic. It needed work but Gerry reckoned we could turn it into a gite, doing what I do here, I suppose, but with people keeping their horses in the paddocks.'

'You put money up without even seeing the place?' Alexi couldn't keep the scepticism out of her tone.

'She did start to push Gerry about it,' Grace said. 'Polly had told me about their plans, and I made her realise she was perhaps being a tad too trusting.'

'We argued about it the day before he died, to be honest,' Polly said, tears streaming down her face. 'That's why I'm so upset. My last words on the subject were spoken to him in anger.' She shook her head. 'He kept finding excuses not to take me to France. It was never the right time. He was too busy, or I was, but Grace had made me suspicious about the delays and so I pushed him, even though I knew he didn't like being put on the spot. He said he'd had quite enough of being nagged in his married life and enjoyed being with me because I gave him space.'

'I'll just bet he did,' Alexi muttered beneath her breath.

'Gerry was always so plausible, so caring. So interested in me. I've never had that before. He could talk me round with little or no effort because... well, because I loved and trusted him to do the right thing by us both.'

'Do you have pictures or details of the place he was buying?' Jack asked.

Polly shook her head. 'He showed me on his phone but I didn't ask him to share them with me. He said he would when he'd finished negotiating but someone else was interested, pushing the price up, which is why I offered to help him.'

Alexi and Jack exchanged a look. Even after all his years in the police, some people's naivety still held the power to shock.

They continued to pepper Polly with questions, attempting to discover something, anything, that would point them in the right direction. Jack was becoming increasingly convinced that Gerry's death had something to do with his dealings in France but nothing more than instinct to guide him.

Yet.

Polly became more and more distressed by their questions and Jack knew they'd get nothing useful from her. Alexi clearly realised it too because she tipped Cosmo from her knee and stood up. Jack got up as well and patted Polly's shoulder.

'We'll be in touch,' he said. 'Let me know at once, or more to the point, let Ben know, if the police call you in again.'

Polly nodded sullenly, managed to offer a few insincere words of thanks and then picked up her wine glass again.

'Getting slaughtered won't achieve anything,' Jack said to Alexi as they left the room.

'It's probably what she needs right now. If nothing else, it'll make her sleep. Besides, Vickery can't interrogate her if she isn't sober. Perhaps she's clever enough to realise it.'

'Anything's possible.'

Jack pulled his mobile from his pocket and called Vickery.

'Mark, a quick question. You've been through Gerry's phone. Any pics of a des res in France come to light?'

'I don't think so. Hang on, I'll check.'

Jack heard Vickery calling the question to someone in the open-plan office. He came back on the line a short time later.

'Nope. Nothing like that. Why?'

'It was just a thought.'

'Very little on his phone at all, come to that, which makes me suspicious. I'm thinking he perhaps had another that we know nothing about. One that the killer took with him, or her.'

'I'll be in touch,' Jack said, cutting the call and climbing into his car.

'Curiouser and curiouser,' he remarked.

Alexi nodded. 'So it would seem.'

They headed for Maggie's yoga studio, neither of them saying anything else for the duration of the short journey.

'There's no sign of life,' Alexi remarked when Jack cut the engine. 'Looks like classes are still cancelled.'

'She'll be holed up inside, licking her wounds. I doubt whether she's gone anywhere, if that's what you're thinking. Vickery would have actively discouraged it. She's more likely keeping out of Polly's way.'

Jack rang the bell three times before they heard someone moving around inside. Maggie opened the door wearing a dressing gown, her hair tousled, eyes puffy from sleep. Or from crying.

'Oh, it's you.'

She opened the door wider and moved into her sitting room. Jack, Alexi and Cosmo followed in her wake. They could have hoped for a warmer welcome, Jack thought, especially if Maggie really wanted to know who'd murdered the love of her life, to say nothing of removing suspicion from herself.

'What news?' Maggie asked, sitting down and tossing the hair away from her face. Even in mourning, she was, Jack conceded, an attractive woman. Elegant, self-contained and far less needy, he imagined, than Polly. Jack could see why a man with Gerry's tastes and wandering eye had fallen for her.

'No news but more questions,' Jack said. 'I can see that we woke you so we won't keep you for long.' He allowed a short pause. 'How much money did you lend Gerry?'

'What?'

Alexi showed no surprise at the question. She wasn't aware that Maggie had opened her purse strings too. Nor had Jack been. He'd acted on a hunch, and it appeared that Alexi was perfectly attuned with his thought process.

'It's a simple enough question,' Jack replied amiably. 'And one the police will likely ask you as well before too long. They're going through Gerry's bank records as we speak.'

'They won't find anything leading to me.' She sighed. 'I did give him quite a bit, as a matter of fact, but I sent it to an offshore account they won't know anything about.'

'Why on earth would you do that?' Alexi couldn't keep the shock from her tone.

'To keep the taxman off his back. Obviously. Everyone does it.'

'Yeah, we all have offshore accounts on standby,' Alexi replied sarcastically.

'Tax would have been the least of Gerry's worries. He was brassic,' Jack told her.

Maggie smiled and shook her head. 'Not a bit of it. He had funds stashed away that he'd prefer the revenue not to know about. It was a fund we were building up prior to making our move.'

'Let me guess,' Alexi said. 'To France. Chantilly.'

'You found that out, did you?' Some of the animation returned to Maggie's features. 'I know what you're going to say. He spun Polly the same line. But then, everything changed. He was going to tell her that it was a no-go for them and let her down gently. Then I was going to sell up and join him. And before you ask, I'm not as daft as I look. I know where his offshore account is and have the access codes.'

Jack raised a brow but refrained from comment, not believing a word of it. 'Why tell us you were moving to the west country?' he asked.

Maggie shrugged. 'It was the first thing that came to mind. Daft, I know, but I hail from that part of the world so it would make a sort of sense if anyone delved.'

'You wanted time to reclaim your funds, I'm guessing, before anyone found out about the offshore accounts,' Jack said.

Again Maggie shrugged, her expression aggressive. 'Something like that.'

'Polly was more trusting than you,' Alexi said accusingly. 'I suppose you realise she put herself in debt to help Gerry set up the same future for her.'

Maggie looked shocked. 'No, I didn't know that. She never said a word. She could be quite secretive. Gerry certainly didn't tell me either.'

'Perhaps he hoodwinked the pair of you and was going to disappear and leave you both behind,' Jack said. 'Perhaps the two of you compared notes and did away with him when you realised that you'd been conned.' He held up a hand to cut off Maggie's protest. 'I don't think that's necessarily what happened, but you can bet your life that when the police find out he was leeching off you both, that's what they'll think.'

'They can think what they like,' Maggie replied with asperity. 'But there's the small matter of proof, which they won't find because there's none to be found.'

'They could still build a pretty circumstantial case,' Jack told her, 'which could be sufficient to see you both convicted. Women, best friends, scorned. It has all the makings of a bestseller and would certainly get the public's attention.'

Maggie folded her arms beneath her breasts. 'It's never going to happen. I can show you where those funds are. If I was the vindictive type, I'd have cleared that account out already and disappeared.'

'Which, without wishing to repeat myself, you could well be in the process of doing,' Jack pointed out. 'But you can't leave here yet without putting a target on your back.'

'Look, I didn't know Gerry had tapped Polly for handouts. I swear that on my life, and I'd have had a word or two to say on the subject if I had known. Never doubt it. I'm not proud of the fact that I went behind my friend's back, but Gerry convinced me that their relationship was on life support.' She let out a prolonged sigh. 'Perhaps I believed it because I wanted it to be true. Anyway, he promised me that he'd square it with Polly and all would be well.'

'Do you think he tried to tell her, and she responded by killing him?' Alexi asked. 'When the police hear what you just told us, that's what they will think.'

Maggie shook her head. 'I honestly don't know. I would never have said she was capable of violence but we none of us know how we might react under such circumstances, do we? If I thought that Gerry intended to run out on me then I might well have killed him myself. He generated that sort of passion in me. And in Polly too; I'm absolutely sure of it.'

'That's kinda my point,' Jack said. 'And, as I say, the police will likely be thinking along the same lines.'

'How is your relationship with Polly now?' Alexi asked.

Maggie sent Alexi a wry glance. 'How do you think? She's in denial about Gerry's interest in me and... well, I've avoided her since that awkward conversation we had. I can hardly help her through her grief while I'm grieving for the same man myself.'

'You haven't told her about the overseas account?'

Maggie shook her head.

'I'm increasingly inclined to think that you're waiting for the dust to settle so that you can clear it out and scarper.' Jack spoke in a conversational tone.

'Well, I can't stay here but I won't touch that money, if that's what you're thinking. I can't. I know where it is and what the access codes are, but any withdrawals I make require Gerry's input. In other words, he could have withdrawn any amount he liked on his own, but I can only do so if he backs up the request with his own code.'

'So much for trusting you,' Alexi said, a wry twist to her lips.

'He insisted it was for my own protection.'

'Good heavens!' Jack pretended surprise that he didn't actually feel. Gerry had either intended to disappear with the funds or was worried about Maggie being targeted by his partners in crime. Partners whom Jack was becoming increasingly convinced he'd somehow shafted. Their visit to Baxter had gone a fair way to convincing him that Gerry's death had to do with his nefarious activities in the horsy world and wasn't actually a crime of passion. 'We were right about the lack of trust. What sort of basis is that for a loving relationship? I don't suppose you ever asked yourself that question.'

'Look, I know you don't have a high opinion of me, or of Gerry.' A spark of defiance shot through Maggie's dull eyes. 'I can't say I blame you. Looking at the situation as an impassive observer, I'd feel the exact same way. But these things happen. I didn't intend to fall in love and certainly wouldn't have acted upon my feelings for Gerry if he hadn't come on to me with all guns blazing. Not to speak ill of the dead and all that, but it takes two.'

'Okay,' Jack said, holding up a hand in a placating gesture. 'We're not here to judge.'

Maggie tossed her head. 'Of course you're not. But if it's any consolation, in your position, I wouldn't be too impressed by what I saw either. Still, I'm the architect of my own downfall and will have to leave Lambourn, even though I now have nowhere to go.' She shook her head. 'I can't stay here. Polly will have to accept the truth eventually and then her spite will know no bounds.' She glanced at Alexi. 'I don't need to tell you that.'

'What we see doesn't signify,' Jack replied. 'It's what the police think they can prove that matters.'

'You don't think I did it and I'm pretty sure you can't see Polly doing it either.'

'You're wrong.' Alexi sat a little taller. 'You both have a case to answer for but there are other aspects of Gerry's life that interest us. What do you know about his involvement in horse racing syndicates?'

'Bugger all.' She threw up her hands. 'Sorry, but it's the truth. I do know that our move to France was involved with that business but that's all I know. You must bear in mind that our time together was limited. And precious. We didn't waste a lot of it talking about detail. Suffice it to say that I trusted him.'

'You didn't once ask how you were going to support yourselves in France?' Alexi asked with an expression of wide-eyed disbelief.

'Sure, we talked about it but only in abstract terms. Gerry had a place in mind where I could open a residential yoga retreat and he was going to invest in a horse stud nearby.'

'Do you have an address for this idyllic location? Did he take you to see it? Show you pictures?' Jack reeled off the questions, but Maggie shook her head in response to all of them.

'He was going to,' she said quietly, so quietly that they barely caught the words. 'He was talking about taking a trip next month.' A small sob escaped her lips. 'Now we never will.'

Jack glanced at Alexi and stood up. She pushed herself to her feet as well, aware that they had gotten as much out of Maggie in her current state of grief as they were ever likely to.

'You need to tell Inspector Vickery about that account,' Jack told her as he turned to face her from the open doorway. 'It could be significant and if you don't, you could be arrested for withholding information from a murder enquiry.'

Maggie gave a brief nod, the only indication that she had heard him. With his hand still on the door, Jack retraced his steps.

'Actually, let's have a quick look at that account,' he said.

'Why?' Maggie became defensive. 'What will that achieve?'

'Indulge me.'

Maggie got up and flounced across the room to fetch her mobile. She returned and clicked on an app, tapping her fingers as she waited for a connection. She keyed in a series of passwords and codes and the account finally came into view.

'What the hell...' She covered her mouth with her hand.

Alexi and Jack peered over her shoulder. The account balance was zero.

15

'What did you make of that?' Alexi asked as they waited for Cosmo to re-emerge from a bush that he'd crawled beneath in pursuit of some hapless rodent.

'What indeed? Phew!'

'I think Maggie and Polly have both told us what they believed to be the truth. Gerry kept them both dangling, making extravagant promises he had no intention of keeping whilst he extracted all the cash that he could from them both. Polly's went straight into his pocket, but Maggie was less of a pushover. So he gave her access to his offshore account, she saw her funds going into it and was hooked. I don't think he had any intention of riding off into the sunset with Polly, but Maggie...' She paused and waggled one hand from side to side. 'The jury's still out on that one. I might have veered towards him sticking with her but for the fact that someone has wiped those accounts clean and done it since his death.' She tapped her fingers on her thigh. 'Who the hell could have done that?'

'Another woman?'

'Blimey! I'm struggling to keep up with his romantic conquests. Where did he get the energy?'

Jack smiled. 'I wouldn't be so quick to write Polly off.' He raised an amused brow when Cosmo emerged from the bush with leaves adhering to his ears, looking annoyed. 'Beneath that fragile exterior, she has a backbone. I can't believe she didn't have her doubts about Gerry, but she wanted him badly enough to let herself be fooled.' He allowed a significant pause. 'To a degree. Everyone has their limits. A breaking point.'

'A scumbag of his ilk would know exactly how to play her.' Alexi wrinkled her nose disdainfully. 'Anyway, she believed what she wanted to believe, but I don't think that his involvement with another woman came as that much of a shock to her. She just didn't want to think he'd gone behind her back with one of her best friends, so she blocked the possibility from her mind.'

'You could well be right. Tunnel vision, in other words. Want something badly enough and through a combination of tenacity and determination, you'll eventually make it happen.'

'Hmm.' Alexi sighed. 'I don't think we're going be much help to Polly. I mean, she asked us for our help but seems to be holding out on us too and gets shirty when we ask questions she doesn't want to answer. How's that supposed to help her? The police won't give up because she gets upset.'

'We can let it drop, if you're feeling uncomfortable. No one would blame you if you did.'

'No.' Alexi shook her head. 'We've come this far so let's carry on for now. Let's do a bit more delving before we reach a decision.' She let out a protracted sigh. 'So, who took the money from the offshore account?'

'You noticed that it was cleared out the same day that Gerry died?'

'Of course I did. So, either Maggie has the funds and is fronting it out or, as you suggested a moment or two ago, someone else had access to that account. That seems more likely.'

'I don't think Maggie took it.' Jack paused at a junction and signalled to turn left in the direction of Hopgood Hall. 'Her reaction was genuine. She seemed pretty upset, to say nothing of mystified.'

'Given how much she told us she'd passed over to Gerry, that's hardly to be wondered at. All her savings have gone. Will you tell Vickery?' Alexi asked.

'Not yet. Let her break it to him. If she doesn't then we will have a genuine reason to suspect her.'

'Fair enough.'

As they pulled up to the hotel, Jack's phone rang. The number that flashed up was unknown to him. Sharing a glance with Alexi, he took the call.

'Maddox.'

'Mr Maddox?' A quiet voice whispered his name.

'Sorry, you'll have to speak up,' Jack said, putting the call on speaker so Alexi could listen in. 'There's a lot of background noise your end.'

'Sounds like a pub,' Alexi said quietly.

'It's James Alton.' The voice was louder now. 'I hear you're looking for me.'

Jack again glanced at Alexi. They could both hear how afraid he sounded.

'I was. Where are you? We need to talk.'

'I'm in Newbury.'

He gave the name of a pub that Alexi could see Jack had heard of but probably not frequented.

'I know where it is,' Jack said. 'We'll come over now.'

'Make sure no one follows you.'

Jack seemed sceptical but agreed to Alton's terms.

'We'll be there in half an hour,' he said, doing a U-turn in the car park.

'The man's delusional,' Alexi said. 'Who on earth would want to follow us?'

'No one has been but it's interesting that Alton thinks they might be. He's running scared,' Jack replied, getting clear of the village and putting his foot down. 'He wouldn't be seeking our help otherwise. People like him tend to fix their own problems.'

'I wonder what he thinks we can do for him, if that's the case.'

'Only one way to find out.' Jack paused. 'That pub he's in is a real dive. A villains' hangout that law enforcement tends to give a wide berth to.'

'He should feel comfortable then,' Alexi replied disdainfully.

'Might be better if I see him alone.'

'Don't go all caveman on me, Jack. I can take care of myself. Besides, we have our security detail.' Cosmo was again installed on her lap. Alexi stroked the cat's back, and he purred his appreciation. 'See, he's ready to spring into action at a moment's notice.'

'How reassuring.'

The light moment helped to settle Alexi's nerves. She had no idea why she felt quite so edgy, but she was damned if she'd let on to Jack, otherwise he would try to protect her. She told herself she had nothing to fear. For once, the enquiry didn't centre around Hopgood Hall and no one was trying to accuse her of anything. Jack was right to say that they had no obligation to investigate but she knew that she couldn't walk away now. Her journalistic nose was twitching and she wanted answers.

'This is it.' Jack found a parking spot in a dingy side street full of run-down, terraced houses.

'You sure it's safe to leave the car here?'

'I'll risk it.'

'Let's leave Cosmo on duty in the car then. I'm sure we can manage without him.'

Cosmo mewled, jumped into the back seat and sat alert, watching out the window, ready to terrify anyone who came too close.

'How the hell does he do that?' Jack asked, scratching his head.

'How many times do I have to tell you? He's highly intuitive and likes to earn his keep.'

'Obviously. Keep a keen eye out, big guy,' Jack said, reaching across to scratch the cat's ears.

Alexi and Jack left the car in Cosmo's capable paws and headed towards the pub, dodging litter, a tumbling pile of empty bottles that the landlord hadn't bothered to stack properly and a gaggle of youths hanging around on the corner.

'I can see why this type of establishment doesn't often get a visit from your ex-colleagues.'

'Too much paperwork for little or no reward,' Jack replied. 'Budget cuts forced us to prioritise. We could have arrested kids like that lot,' he added, jerking a thumb in the direction of the sullen youths, 'for all manner of misdemeanours, but there's no point. They all know their rights nowadays and would be out again in no time flat with nothing more than a slap on the wrist to deter them from reoffending. Not worth the paperwork.'

'So this den of iniquity, free from the not so long arm of the law, would make an ideal bolthole for Alton, who is doubtless seeking sanctuary within its grimy walls as we speak.'

'Spot on,' Jack replied as he opened the door for her. 'Keep your criminals in one place. Makes it easier to find them.'

'I'll bear that in mind the next time I'm on the run.'

A hush fell over the half-full bar as they walked in. The lights were dim, no doubt deliberately so in order to hide the grime on the floor. It was obviously there though because their feet stuck to the wooden boards, making a sucking sound as they walked. A rumble of discontent echoed through the room, presumably because Jack still wore all the signs of his old profession. A game of pool, taking place at the far end, was temporarily halted and a general air of suspicion fuelled the atmosphere as a burly individual sporting a man bun and wild beard took hold of his cue like a weapon, flexing it between his hands.

'We come in peace,' Jack said, wincing at his corny choice of words.

'Easy guys, they're with me.' Alton's head, complete with flat cap still in place, popped up from a corner booth.

'Buy a drink.'

The barman's words were not a suggestion and Jack duly complied, purchasing soft drinks for them both and a pint for Alton.

Alexi hesitated when it came time to slip into the booth across from Alton. The plastic seat was as sticky as the floor. She preferred not to dwell upon the possible source of the stickiness in question, aware that her clothes would all go in the wash the moment she got home. To make matters worse, the smell of stale cigarette smoke and spilled beer permeated. Clearly the smoking ban had passed this establishment by.

'Much obliged,' Alton said, taking the pint that Jack passed to him in an unsteady hand and downing a third of it in one swallow, just as he had once before.

'Why all the cloak and dagger stuff?' Jack asked, no doubt aware that spending time in that particular pub wouldn't be good for their health. Their presence was being tolerated but it was obvious that the patience of those in control was not limitless. Several very large individuals lolled on the bar, arms bulging with muscles crossed over huge chests as they eyed them with open suspicion.

'The old bill are sniffing around Baxter's place. Think we had something to do with offing Gerry.'

'We think they could be right,' Alexi said without prevarication.

'They'll protect you if you tell them what you know.' Jack probably knew he was wasting his breath, as evidenced by his wry expression.

Alton threw back his head and laughed. 'Get real!'

'Let's save time. We have no desire to linger,' Jack said, 'so we'll tell you what we know. Or suspect.'

Alton nodded.

'Gerry was stringing Polly and Maggie along, making wild promises about happy ever after and simultaneously extracting money from them both.'

Alton raised a brow, clearly surprised.

'You didn't know about Maggie?' Alexi asked.

He shook his head, a half-smile playing about his cracked lips. 'Have to hand it to the guy, he liked to put it about a bit.' He brightened considerably. 'That gives both of them a motive for offing him, as well as opportunity. We're off the hook.'

'You wouldn't be wetting yourself, or talking to us, if you believed that,' Jack said.

'I wouldn't be so sure about that anyway,' Alexi added. 'We were called in to try and help Polly, so that means we have to find others with a reason for wanting Gerry out of the way.'

'So far, we haven't had to delve very deeply.'

'Don't look at me.' Alton warded off Jack's words by pushing both grubby hands towards him, palms first. 'I needed him alive and breathing.'

'Because you had a race-fixing scam going on,' Alexi said. 'Something about passing off foals as the prodigy of famous stallions, getting people heavily involved and then having the horses fail.' She sent Alton a withering look. 'Nice.'

Alton couldn't hide his shock. 'What makes you say that?'

'You'd make a lousy poker player,' Jack said, taking a sip of his drink. 'It's written all over your face.'

'And,' Alexi added, 'you think, or probably know, that a falling out between thieves was the real reason for Gerry's murder. What's more, you're terrified that you might be next because, and I'm guessing here, you were the go-between for him and Baxter. No one thinks twice about seeing a failed jockey hanging around horses but someone like Gerry would stand out.'

'Even supposing you're right,' Alton said, leaning his arms on the grimy table, 'Gerry weren't the brains. There's someone else, and don't ask me who because I don't know and don't want to know. But I can tell you that he's a ruthless individual. Something happened between him and Gerry quite recently. A disagreement of some sort. I don't know what it was about and that's the way I want it to stay, so there's no point asking me.'

'You don't seem to know very much,' Alexi remarked.

'It's healthier that way, darlin', believe me. All I can tell you is that Gerry had something on his mind. Wanted me close by and asked me to move into the B&B for a while. Squared it with Polly so I got a room. Then, two days later, before we could talk proper like, he was dead and I was warned off from sticking my nose in.'

'Warned off how?' Jack asked.

'A phone call telling me to keep my head down and me trap shut.'

'Who from?'

Alton sent Jack a *what-the-hell* look. 'No idea.'

'So why talk to us?' Jack asked. 'Isn't that going against orders?'

'Look, I'm just a gofer, low down the food chain, and that makes me dispensable. Whether I talk to you or not, I'm in the firing line because I spent two nights under the same roof as Gerry and whoever offed him probably thinks I know what he knew. But I don't, and that's the God's honest truth.'

'Did you see or hear Gerry talking to anyone while you were at Polly's?' Jack asked. 'Anyone whose voice you recognised.'

Alton shook his head. 'He was holed up with Polly for the most part. I was at Baxter's working with a new colt for a lot of the time. That's why we hadn't had a chance to talk. I wish now that we had, then I'd know what I was running from.'

'Well, whoever did for Gerry obviously thinks that you *do* know something.'

'Thanks a bunch.' Alton stared morosely at the bottom of his empty glass.

Jack and Alexi both fell silent, mulling over what they'd been told and, in Jack's case, wondering what Alton had left out.

'What's the man from Holland, Hank or Henry, got to do with the horses?' Alexi asked. 'We've heard his name in connection with Gerry's various dealings.'

'Nothing as far as I'm aware.' Alton vigorously scratched his chin. 'I think Gerry had something going with him on the side. He said something once about bringing fresh flowers in and avoiding the duty. It's the sort of thing he'd do. Gerry was never slow to earn an extra bob or two.'

Probably more than just flowers, given their source, Jack reasoned, but saw no point in expressing that view. Even if Alton knew he'd smuggled drugs into the country, he'd never say so. Honour amongst thieves still thrived, even when the thief in question was dead.

'Okay, so leaving the Dutch side of things out of it, we're talking a horse scam centred around Chantilly.'

Alton grunted, which Jack took to be an affirmative.

'The young horses go to Baxter and then what?' Jack asked. 'Where do you fit in?'

'I break 'em in. Get them ready to sell on. Despite what you see, I'm still a decent horseman and treat young horses with the patience and respect they deserve as I prepare them for the track.'

He sounded proud and sat a little straighter. Jack believed him, at least insofar as his part in things was concerned.

'You make out you're a bookie's tout, just to cover your real activities?' he suggested.

'Yep, and no one suspects a thing.' He looked smug. 'That's what comes of being a has-been. No one takes you seriously.'

'Gerry was intending to set himself up in Chantilly, but presumably you already knew that,' Alexi remarked.

'Is that how he got the women onside?' Alton laughed and shook his head. 'I just knew he had to be stringing them along. He never would have done it.'

'You think he wasn't planning to purchase a property in Chantilly?' Jack asked, sensing that Alton knew for a fact that he wasn't.

'Why would he when he's already got one?' he asked. 'Along with a wife and two kids keeping it running for him?'

16

Alexi's jaw fell open. 'You have got to be joking,' she said.

She glanced at Jack, who looked equally shellshocked.

'How can you be so sure?' he asked.

'I met Celeste and her kids, well, kid, she only had one at the time, when Gerry approached me about the idea. I was sceptical like and wanted to see the setup for meself before I made a commitment.'

'When was that?' Alexi asked.

'Getting on for three years now. This is our third season.'

'Tell us everything, from the beginning,' Jack said, leaning forward.

'Baxter and I go way back. He told me he had a mate who could put us on to a sweet little earner. Was I interested?' He sniffed. 'I knew at once that it'd be dodgy, but I was willing to at least listen. We're talking off the record, by the way. I ain't repeating any of this to the old bill.'

'Get on with it, Alton,' Jack said impatiently. 'You need our help, which you won't get if I think you're holding anything back.'

'We don't care what you've been getting up to,' Alexi added.

'We just want to find out who killed your friend. I'd have thought that would have been your main priority too, especially given that you're running scared.'

'Yeah, okay.' He rubbed the side of his hand beneath his nose. 'It just don't come natural, talking about this stuff.'

'Nothing natural about murder,' Jack said. 'Just spit it out.'

'Okay, so Baxter introduced me to Gerry. I knew at once that he was a punter. His knowledge of the gee-gees would have given the Tote a run for its money. He was a long-distance driver... Had a regular route into Holland and France, contacts there. Said he knew this woman who'd inherited her father's stud farm, along with a pile of debts. Inheritance taxation is crippling in France apparently, and she was struggling to make ends meet. She had a famous stallion standing, Sound Advice, the one valuable asset her father had left her with but... well, he was shooting blanks all of a sudden, which sounded the death knell for her business. She was gonna have to sell up.'

'But Gerry saw an answer?'

'Yeah. A ringer. I mean, it was pretty foolproof because Sound Advice was hers and his reputation was solid. She didn't want to go along with Gerry's suggestion to begin with but was also determined to hold onto her home, so she had no choice. Besides, I could see at once that she and Gerry were getting pretty friendly. Can't say as I blame him. She's a right good-looker, but hard as nails beneath that pretty exterior. Once she got persuaded to involve herself in the scam, she became the driving force and woe betide anyone who underestimated her.'

'So why did Gerry not live in France?' Alexi asked. 'He had you and Baxter this end. Can't see that his presence was required.'

'No idea and I didn't ask.' He sniffed. 'I call tell you that the operation is big and he ain't the one in charge. Like I already said, I don't know who is and I don't wanna know.'

'You don't seem to know very much about anything,' Alexi remarked.

'Safer that way, darlin', like I already said.'

'What's your take on all this?' Jack asked. 'Do you think someone involved with the horse scam killed Gerry?'

Alton shrugged. 'I didn't think so, not at first. I was convinced Polly lost her rag, and I don't blame her for that. Gerry led her a right song and dance and I think even she eventually became disillusioned. But now I got that call, I guess there was something else going on and Gerry got too greedy or somefing. It's been known.'

'I don't see what we can do to help you if that's all you have to go on,' Jack said.

'Do you have an address of the property in France?' Alexi asked. 'I'm guessing that no one's told Gerry's wife about his death, given that no one knew she existed.'

Alton reeled off the name of a stud farm in Chantilly. Alexi Googled it on her phone. It brought up a shiny online brochure, extolling the services of Sound Advice amongst other, presumably lesser stallions.

'This it?' she asked, showing Alton the pictures.

'Yep, but it ain't that posh. Them pictures must have been photoshopped, or whatever it is that they do to 'em nowadays.'

'So,' Jack said, leaning an elbow on the sticky table, thinking better of it and sitting upright again, 'what is it that you think we can do for you? Why did you have us come here for that matter? It's all a bit cloak and dagger.'

Alton shrugged and looked furtive.

'You guessed that we were onto your scam,' Alexi said slowly, 'so wanted to find out how much we know. You told us what little you say you know in the hope that we'll find out who did kill Gerry before he bumps you off too. That implies you don't think Polly did it and it's her name we're trying to clear. No offence, but we don't know you and have no reason to fight your corner, given that you're involved in very illegal stuff, ripping off honest people for personal gain.' Alexi tutted. 'I'm not impressed.'

'I don't know whether Polly did it or not.' Alton threw up his hands. 'I thought she did, and I'd still put money on her being the guilty party, iffing Gerry gave her the old heave-ho.'

'Any reason to suppose he did?' Jack asked.

'Nothing specific. Just a feeling I got from one or two throwaway comments he made. He seemed to think we'd pushed our luck with the Sound Advice foal business and that someone would catch on eventually. I think someone from the BHA had been sniffing around. Not sure, but I know Gerry had got the wobbles.'

'So, if he chucked it in, he'd likely have gone to Chantilly?' Alexi suggested.

'Reckon so. Celeste will likely pack it all in now once she hears what's happened to Gerry and that will bring a very profitable sideline to a halt. No one involved wanted that to happen, other than Gerry, and I can't be sure that he actually did. Anyway, even if he did have his differences with whoever else is involved, I can't see that person doing away with him. But then, what do I know?'

'Then why the warning phone call?'

Another negligent shrug. 'Your poking your noses in, stirring things up, will have shaken a few trees, I expect. I'm being warned to keep me trap shut if you talk to me.'

'But you've done just the opposite,' Alexi said impatiently, 'and approached us.' She shook her head. 'I just don't get it.'

'I got you here because I *do* want you to find the culprit, and quickly,' Alton replied, his eyes now wide and wary. 'Then I'm out of here. I didn't sign up to get involved with murder investigations. But if I cut and run now, either the old bill will feel me collar or, if Gerry was done by the mystery figure behind the scam, then he'll have me in his sights too.'

'If the killing is connected to the scam then it will all come out, including your part in it,' Jack pointed out.

'I know.' Alton looked resigned. 'But better that than looking over me shoulder for the rest of me days.'

'Okay, I think we're about done here.' Jack stood up and Alexi followed suit. 'I'll have to tell Inspector Vickery about Celeste. Someone will have to inform her of Gerry's death. She's presumably his next of kin.'

And probably the person who cleared out that overseas account, Alexi thought but did not say.

'She knows.'

'How?' Jack and Alexi asked together.

'She called me today. She was worried because she couldn't get hold of Gerry. I had to tell her. She was devastated.'

'I don't suppose you told her to contact the police,' Jack said in a resigned tone.

'Nah, she wouldn't do that even if I had.'

'She will have to eventually. We're obliged to tell them about her,' Jack said, 'but I'm guessing you knew that much when you told us about her.'

'Yeah, but she obviously wants some answers first. She's on her way over. I... er, told her to ask for you at Hopgood Hall.'

* * *

A crowd of youths had gathered close to Jack's car when they returned to it, but Cosmo had prevented them from laying so much as a finger on it.

'He's enjoying himself,' Jack said, laughing as he pointed towards Cosmo hissing at the kids from his backseat perch. 'After-noon, lads,' he added, opening the door for Alexi. 'It was unlocked,' he added, watching their jaws drop. 'Nothing to stop you nicking it. You missed an opportunity there. Not afraid of a cute pussy cat, are you?'

The kids shuffled their feet, shouted a few insults and scattered.

'Good boy!' Alexi said, as she slid into the car and leaned across to scratch Cosmo's ears. 'God, I feel filthy! That place. How can anyone frequent it?'

'The plot thickens though,' Jack replied as he started the engine and headed for Hopgood Hall. 'A wife in the wings. Even I didn't see that one coming.'

'If Polly and Maggie somehow found out about her then it gives them an even stronger motive to band together and do away with Gerry.'

'It gives the wife an equally strong motive if she found out that he'd got two women here on the hook. She could have had her suspicions if she had access to the overseas account and saw the deposits from Maggie.'

Alexi conceded the point with a nod. 'It does make you wonder why she's coming over here, given the nature of her crimes. She's involved in the scam up to her ears and Alton did suggest that she's a tough cookie.'

'Probably wants to square things with the mystery leader.'

'Okay, I get that, but why come to us specifically?'

'She'll be fishing, I dare say. Wants to know how much we know, how much the police know and, more to the point, she'll want to find out who killed the love of her life. All without revealing the nature of the scam.'

Alexi tapped her fingers restlessly against the dashboard. 'Who on earth is the brains behind this operation? It sure as hell isn't Baxter or Alton, and Alton is definitely running scared. Who could it possibly be?'

'We might never find out,' Jack said, sympathy in his tone, 'and

I know that will infuriate the journalist in you. But facts have to be faced.'

Alexi scowled. She knew Jack had got it right but wasn't ready to accept defeat. She hated unsolved mysteries. 'What about Jane and Derek Grant, Polly's other guests? We've pretty much dismissed them. The Seers too, for that matter.'

'We will have to look closer at them. I already have Danny, our new guy, doing some digging, but my instincts tell me they're in the clear.'

'Then who the hell is he?'

'It may not be a man. Women being the deadlier species and all that.'

'True and don't you forget it, buster!'

They both laughed but Alexi's expression quickly sobered.

'What are you thinking?' Jack asked.

'Well...' She looked up at him, unable to decide if she should voice her thoughts, even more unsure why said thoughts had lodged themselves in her brain. 'I can't say why my suspicions are veering in this particular direction. Probably because I dislike her so much, but still...' She spread her hands and allowed her words to trail off, thinking she'd come across as jealous and petty if she said anything more.

'Let me help you out. You're wondering if Grace is the mastermind.'

'Actually, yes.' Alexi should have known that Jack would be attuned to her thoughts. 'Why did she persuade Polly to conduct a vendetta against me? She only did so *after* we solved Natalie Parker's murder. I thought she was jealous of our relationship, but I don't think she actually wants you back; she's just using that as an excuse. She worked with Gerry and came down here the moment he was murdered, showing no immediate desire to leave again. The faithful friend holding Polly's hand in her hour of need, and

conveniently inserting herself in the centre of the investigation.'
Alexi sent Jack a worried look. 'I know it's not what you want to
hear but...'

'I'd been thinking along the same lines,' Jack replied. 'There is
nothing that Grace wouldn't do to earn herself a bit of extra cash.'

'And we know that she introduced Gerry and Polly.' Alexi let
out a slow breath. 'Does she know much about horses?'

Jack shrugged. 'A bit. It's all a tad tenuous though and I definitely can't see her stabbing a grown man, even if they did have a
falling out. Besides, she wasn't actually in Lambourn when he was
killed. At least not as far as we know. I'll get Danny to see if he can
pick her car up anywhere around here at the time of the murder.'

'I hope it isn't her,' Alexi said, meaning it.

'Are you sorry we got involved?' Jack removed a hand from the
wheel and covered one of her own with it. 'We can knock it on the
head any time you say.'

'Not a chance! We're in too deep now.'

'It's getting dangerous.'

'Yeah, I know. The mystery man behind the horse scam is obviously a threat, but not against us. But anyway, let's see what the
fragrant Celeste has to say for herself and then regroup.'

Jack smiled at her. 'Whatever you say.'

'You ought to tell Vickery about the French wife.'

'I will when we get back to the hotel.'

But Jack didn't get the chance. He knew the moment he walked
into the entrance foyer and saw an elegant woman with blonde
hair rippling down her shoulders in deep discussion with Cheryl
that their uninvited guest had already arrived.

17

'Game on,' Alexi muttered.

'Evidently,' Jack replied, squaring his shoulders.

Cosmo stalked ahead of them. He assessed the woman and clearly didn't like what he saw, expressing his feelings through an arched back and equally vicious hiss. That settled matters from Alexi's perspective. She'd been prepared to give Celeste the benefit of the doubt, but Cosmo's judgement was ordinarily spot on and if he'd taken against the woman then Alexi already didn't trust her.

'Here they are,' Cheryl said, sending Alexi a curious look. 'There's a lady here, asking to see you both.'

The woman turned and Alexi withheld a gasp. She was truly beautiful. Tall, elegant, with impossibly long legs and features to inspire the most irascible of artists. She knew it as well, Alexi decided, noticing the subtle changes in her attitude as her gaze locked onto Jack and remained fixed there. Alexi might as well not have existed. If Celeste even noticed one very pissed off cat flexing his vocal chords then she gave no sign.

'Oh. You are Mr Maddox.' Celeste's gaze roamed over Jack's body as she spoke. 'I did not expect you to be—'

'Hello.' Jack held out his hand, cutting off whatever she'd been about to say. 'I don't think I've had the pleasure. Is there something we can do for you?'

'Is there somewhere we can talk?' Celeste asked in almost faultless English.

'Who are you?'

Jack was obviously playing dumb.

'Celeste. Celeste Beauchamp. I am... I was a friend of Gerry Dawlish.' She swallowed, the first sign of grief and probably the only one that such a focused woman would allow herself, Alexi imagined. She felt none of the sympathy she would ordinarily reserve for a grieving widow. Celeste was on a damage-control mission, she sensed. She had spoken exclusively to Jack and clearly thought she could use her femininity to manipulate him, just as Alexi had predicted would be the case. Why wouldn't she? Alexi doubted whether that tactic usually failed but almost laughed aloud at the thought of Jack falling for such an obvious ploy.

'Please,' Celeste added, when Jack maintained his silence. 'I have come a long way.'

'The police are dealing with the case,' he said. 'I don't know why you imagine we can help. You'd be better advised to go to them.'

'I can't.' Celeste shook her head, sending hair spiralling over her shoulders. A deliberate ploy, Alexi suspected, that somehow managed to make her seem vulnerable. She was good at playing a part, Alexi already knew, and so she wouldn't make the mistake of underestimating her. 'At least not yet.'

'This is Alexi Ellis, my partner,' Jack said. 'If you want to talk to me, you talk to us both.'

'Of course.'

Celeste finally recalled her manners and offered Alexi her hand, but it was a perfunctory gesture, and she didn't once look

Alexi in the eye. She really didn't like women, that much was already apparent. There was also a ruthless air about her, hidden behind a thin veil of helplessness that certainly didn't fool Alexi and probably failed to impress Jack as well.

'Use the kitchen,' Cheryl said, having observed the exchange and clearly bursting with curiosity. 'You won't be disturbed there.'

'Thanks,' Alexi said, rolling her eyes at Cheryl behind Celeste's back.

Jack led the way into the kitchen. Celeste clung to his side, leaving Alexi and Cosmo to bring up the rear. Was she for real? Alexi wondered, feeling a combination of irritation and amusement as she watched the woman attempting to make an impression upon Jack and failing to elicit the response she'd probably come to expect from any man she set her sights on as a matter of course.

'Take a seat,' Jack said, indicating the scrubbed, pine table that dominated the kitchen.

He waited for her to do so, then turned to Alexi, smiled and pulled out a chair for her across from Celeste. He didn't offer their guest coffee and instead got straight down to business as he sat down next to Alexi.

'Now, what's this about?' he asked. 'How did you know Gerry?'

'He is my husband.' She stared at them both as she responded, a note of defiance underlying both her words and her expression, no doubt expecting a plethora of surprise that didn't materialise.

'I see,' Jack said calmly.

Celeste blinked.

'Our condolences,' Jack added, his tone all business.

'*Merci.*'

Jack said nothing more. Alexi knew he was making the silence work for him. People were seldom comfortable with silences and usually felt the need to break them. Celeste proved to be no exception.

'I want to know who killed him,' she said, sounding truculent, like a child deprived of a promised treat.

'In that case, I fail to see why you haven't gone straight to the police,' Alexi said.

Celeste didn't even look at Alexi.

'You're French,' Alexi persisted.

'Yes.'

'And you came over from France when you heard of Gerry's death.' Jack fixed her with a steely stare. 'How did you hear about it?'

'How?' She looked bemused. 'I tried to call him. When he didn't answer for over a day, I got worried. I called a friend and he told me the tragic news.'

'What friend?' Jack asked.

She spread her hands. 'Does it matter?'

'I wouldn't ask if it didn't.' Jack sighed, pushed his chair back and stood up. 'There's nothing we can do to help you, especially if you're unwilling to be honest. Go to the police. They will want to talk to you.'

'No, no! Please, listen to me!'

Jack perched his backside against the work surface and folded his arms. 'Go on.'

'Gerry and I, it's complicated. We are legally married and have two small children, but he still worked driving his lorry while I restored my late father's stud farm to its former glory.'

'With you so far. Why is that complicated and why the secrecy?'

'The business in France with the horses... My late father didn't manage it well. There were debts, crippling death duties. The business was in crisis.'

'We know about the stud,' Jack said, his voice silk on steel, 'and we know that the enterprise is fraudulent.'

'*Mon dieu!*'

'And that is why you are reluctant to speak with the police,' Alexi added, feeling absolutely no sympathy for the woman. 'You are worried that you'll be detained. You're also worried that whoever killed Gerry might come after you if they think you've opened your mouth, so I can quite see why you're in a bit of a spin. What I fail to understand is why you came. Surely you'd have been better off staying in France.'

'It was never supposed to go this far.' Celeste hung her head and the curtain of hair that fell over it prevented Alexi from reading her expression – deliberately, she had no doubt. 'No one was supposed to get hurt.'

'Leaving aside the people who got involved with fraudulent syndicates,' Jack replied without an ounce of sympathy in his tone.

'It is true,' she conceded, clearly struggling to sound contrite. Alexi suspected that she didn't lose any sleep over the plight of the people she'd conned. 'I should have conceded defeat and closed the stud but it was my family's work for generations. I love horses; they are in my blood. Then Gerry and I met, fell in love and he saw a way out.'

'We understand that there's a sinister mastermind behind the entire operation,' Jack said. 'A name would be useful.'

'Gerry's death has nothing to do with that.' She waved the suggestion aside. 'Besides, I don't know who Gerry dealt with in this country and that's the God's honest truth. He kept me out of that side of things, and I was happy not to know. Anyway, it's my understanding that he was killed by the woman he lived with here in England.'

'If that's what you believe then why come to us?' Alexi asked.

'You are aware that he was romantically involved with the lady in question, and with another too,' Jack said.

Celeste gave a negligent shrug. 'You have to understand that Gerry was attempting to build a life for us, his family. I knew what he did and how he went about it. I didn't mind. It was necessary and meant nothing to him. I knew it was me that he loved and that he was doing what he did for our sake.'

'Very new age,' Alexi remarked scathingly.

'I would not expect *you* to understand.'

'Good. That means you will not be disappointed.' Alexi, unable to keep still in the presence of such a selfish woman whom she actively disliked, stood to join Jack at the counter. 'Of course, your casual acceptance of Gerry's infidelity could be a smokescreen. Perhaps you are not quite as understanding as you make yourself out to be. You found out about his other women and overcome with jealousy, you came to England to confront them. But instead of finding Polly, you found Gerry sound asleep in her bed, leaving you in no doubt about what they'd just done. It tipped you over the edge, you lost your temper and killed him yourself.'

Celeste stood and flung her arms in the air. 'But that is ridiculous!'

'Is it?' Jack asked. 'From what we've been able to find out, Gerry generated extremes of passion in all the women he consorted with. I doubt whether you're the exception and I'm equally sure that you weren't quite as accepting of his methods as you'd have us believe.'

'Killing Gerry in Polly's bed would be a very good way to assuage your wounded pride *and* place the blame on your rival,' Alexi added, tag-teaming Jack and starting to enjoy herself. This was not the type of reception that Celeste had expected, and it was obvious that she didn't know how to handle their accusations.

'I have not left France for months,' she said, tossing her head, 'and a simple check on my passport will prove it. Gerry was the love of my life.' She dashed at her eyes with the back of her hand, but Alexi couldn't see any actual tears disturbing her annoyingly beautiful face. 'The other women meant nothing to him. They were simply a means to an end.'

'For someone who has lost their soulmate, you don't seem very distraught,' Alexi remarked.

'I have to keep myself together for the sake of my children.'

'Let's talk about the offshore account that Gerry opened, the one in which he stashed the funds he extracted from another lady, as well as goodness knows what other scams.'

'What about it?' Celeste couldn't meet Jack's eye.

'You emptied it yesterday.'

She stared back at him but remained silent. Clearly, Jack's knowledge had wrongfooted her. This interview wasn't going the way she'd hoped, and she didn't seem to know how to get it back on track. Alexi enjoyed watching her discomfort, wondering if she could actually be the brains behind the entire syndicate scheme. She certainly appeared to be hard-headed enough, but if that was the case, would she have killed Gerry or ordered him to be killed?

And if so, why?

For the reasons that Alexi had already suggested, perhaps. The oldest motive known to man.

Jealousy.

'Yes, I took the money as soon as I heard about Gerry's death. I didn't want it to be misappropriated.'

Alexi and Jack exchanged an astounded look.

'That would never do,' Alexi said, her tone tinged with renewed sarcasm.

'Which implies that you knew about Gerry's murder way before you suggested was the case,' Jack said. 'You really aren't helping yourself by lying but you are wasting our time.' He pulled his mobile from his pocket.

'What are you doing?'

'Calling Inspector Vickery. It's him you should be speaking to, not us.'

'No, please!'

Jack straightened himself up. 'So, we come back to my original question. What do you want with us? What is it that you think we can do for you?'

'I want to meet Polly,' she said without prevarication. 'I want to ask her why?'

Alexi's jaw dropped open. 'Are you for real?' she asked.

'Why not knock on her door in that case?' Jack asked, looking as shellshocked by the woman's audacity as Alexi herself felt.

Celeste shook her head but said nothing.

'You want a referee,' Alexi said, wondering if her opinion of this woman could possibly sink any lower.

Jack shot Celeste a look. 'Give us a moment,' he said.

Without waiting for a response, Jack took Alexi's arm and led her to the other end of the kitchen. Cosmo, who'd curled up with Toby in his basket, extracted himself and stalked over to Celeste with malicious feline intent, instinctively standing guard over an unwelcome infiltrator.

'We can't possibly,' Alexi said, speaking in a whisper. 'I simply can't believe what she's asking and anyway, I don't trust her motives.'

'She's scared and hiding behind us because she wants to find out who *did* kill Gerry. More to the point, she needs to know if she's next in line. She won't get any of that information if she goes to Vickery but has been told, presumably by Baxter or Alton, that we're in the know *and* in Polly's corner.'

'I don't have a high opinion of Polly. God alone knows, I have no reason to, but her grief is at least genuine. Celeste appears to be thinking only of herself. Polly on the other hand is fragile and doesn't deserve to have Gerry's nightmare of a wife thrust upon her without warning.'

'I tend to agree, but she's going to find out about her sooner or later. Besides, if we observe their first meeting, I'm betting we'll be able to tell if either one of them is the guilty party.'

'Maggie could be.'

'Yeah, I know. One step at a time. Do you agree that we should ask Polly to come over but not tell her why?'

Alexi shrugged. 'Why not? We've got sod all else to do moving forward and little chance as things stand of uncovering the murderer's identity. I'll tell you one thing for nothing, though: Celeste has an agenda that she's not sharing with us.'

'Of course she has.' Jack grinned at Alexi. 'No one ever tells the truth in situations like this one, so we'll just have to get creative.'

Jack winked as he pulled his phone from his pocket.

'Hey, Grace,' he said. 'Wanna bring Polly over to the hotel? There have been developments.'

'What developments?' Alexi heard Grace asked.

'Just bring her over.'

'You want Grace here?' Alexi asked when Jack cut the call.

'Oh yes.' He looked grim, determined. 'Don't ask me why, but I think her presence is vital.'

The answer to that question became obvious when Grace pushed the kitchen door open a short time later and stopped dead in her tracks.

'Celeste,' she said. 'What the hell?'

18

Jack glanced at Alexi, his suspicions confirmed.

'I see no introductions are necessary,' he said, a scathing edge to his voice.

Polly looked confused. Alexi stood and guided her to a chair, on the other side of the table from Celeste. It was probably just as well that she did since Polly's legs seemed weak and Alexi worried that she might actually keel over.

'Perhaps you'd care to tell us how you two know one another,' Jack said, sharing a glower between Grace and Celeste. He clenched his fists at his sides, wondering what the hell game Grace was playing. He hadn't seriously suspected her of being involved in the syndicate scheme but had gone along with the possibility when Alexi suggested it mainly so that Alexi wouldn't think he was defending his former wife. 'And more to the point, why you didn't think it worth mentioning Celeste's existence to me, or to the police? Withholding information in a police investigation could see you charged with obstruction.'

'Who is this person?' Polly asked, finding her voice, her expression wary.

'Well, Grace?' Jack folded his arms across his torso. 'Aren't you going to enlighten your friend?'

'Jack, we need to discuss this.' Grace's glance darted frantically from side to side. 'It's not what it seems. I tried to talk to you about it.'

'Nothing is ever your fault,' Jack replied venomously.

'I could never get you alone.' Grace's voice had developed an irritating whine. 'The time was never right. I didn't know what to say. How to explain.'

The flow of words tripped over one another: a sure sign that Grace was rattled.

'As far as I can see, there's nothing to discuss. You've been playing both sides against the middle, that much is evident, but your deceit has caught up with you.'

Grace's mouth fell open. 'I might not have told you stuff but you can't possibly imagine that I had anything to do with Gerry's murder!'

'Grace?' Polly's voice sounded pathetically small. Alexi, standing behind her, placed a hand gently on her shoulder. She glanced at Jack, wondering if the revelations would be too much for Polly's fragile state of mind. Jack's shrug implied that it had to be done.

'This person is Celeste Beauchamp,' Alexi said, taking control, 'and, sorry if this comes as a shock, Polly, but she lives in France and claims to be Gerry's wife.'

'Wife?' Polly blinked at Celeste then let out a long sigh of relief together with a smile. 'No. There's been some sort of misunderstanding. That isn't possible,' she said, shaking her head. 'My Gerry wasn't married. This... this woman...' she pointed a shaking finger at Celeste. 'She's playing some sort of sick joke.'

'It's no joke, I'm afraid, Polly,' Jack said. 'Celeste owns and lives in the house in France that Gerry claimed you would be moving into with him. Ask your *friend*, Grace, if you doubt my word. It appears that she has known about it all along.'

'I don't... that is to say...'

Jack had never seen Grace lost for words before. Her face paled, her hands were unsteady, and she almost fell into a chair. Polly instinctively moved away from her and shook off her hand when she tried to touch Polly's arm.

'Look, Polly, this isn't what you think,' Grace said, glancing at Celeste, who appeared to be ignoring her. But Jack could see that she was taking an avid interest in proceedings and appeared to be enjoying Polly's distress. Vindictive didn't come close to describing Celeste's character and Jack knew she'd be capable of every dirty trick in the book. He didn't trust her an inch and was extremely suspicious about her sudden appearance. Her story simply didn't add up. She and Grace were in communication so if Gerry had gone missing then the first person Celeste would have called would have been Grace.

None of it made sense.

Yet.

'Is it true?' Polly asked. 'Is this woman married to Gerry?'

Grace allowed a significant pause and then reluctantly nodded. 'Yes,' she said. 'I'm sorry.'

'*You knew*... you knew about her and never warned me.' Tears of disillusionment streamed down Polly's face. 'Why would you do that?' She shook her head. 'What did I ever do to you to deserve such treatment? I thought you were my friend?'

The atmosphere crackled with suppressed tension. With guilt and pain and unspoken accusations.

'I *am* your friend,' Grace said.

Jack wondered if she realised how facile that statement must sound to Polly. To everyone in the room. It was obvious that Grace *was* heavily involved with Gerry's machinations and had been playing a dangerous game.

'I couldn't tell you, Polly. What would have been the point? You wouldn't have believed me, much as you didn't believe Gerry was carrying on with Maggie, when you knew in your heart that it must be true. I knew he'd leave eventually and break your heart. I just couldn't be the one to tell you. All I could do was be your friend.' When no one spoke, Grace plucked at the fabric of her skirt. 'What would you have done in my place?'

'Don't turn this back on Polly,' Alexi growled. 'None of this is her fault.'

'It would be useful to know how involved with Gerry's business you were,' Jack said briskly, sending his former wife a scathing look. 'And the truth would be useful too.'

'Ah well.' Grace folded her hands on the tabletop and focused her gaze on them. Toby whined and curled up closer to Cosmo, as though sensing the tension. 'We worked together at Holby's... well, you know that much, but what you don't know is that we had a fling. It didn't last long and was over well before he met either of you.' Grace encompassed Celeste and Polly with a sweep of her eyes. 'He was a keen exponent of the turf, could quote chapter and verse on just about every decent horse in training's pedigree. His knowledge was encyclopaedic.'

'You really are something else.' Jack shook his head in disgust. 'How involved are you in the syndicate scheme?'

'I don't know anything about it!' Grace cried hotly.

'Try again.' Jack's voice was flintlike. 'You obviously know Celeste and presumably her kids too. You're up to your grubby neck in this.'

'Kids,' Polly said weakly.

'Gerry asked me to keep an eye on Polly. He cared about you,' Grace added, speaking directly to Polly.

'More likely he didn't want her to find out about his relation-ship with Maggie, or with Celeste either,' Alexi said, disgust drip-ping from her tone.

Celeste, who had yet to speak, had been examining Polly with a critical eye, clearly not imagining her to be any sort of competition for Gerry's affections, even beyond the grave. Polly was a decade or more older than Celeste and couldn't hold a candle to her when it came to looks and style, but despite her frailties, there was a quiet dignity about her that Jack admired. She had been used by ruth-less people for their own ends and was broken by the revelations she'd just endured.

Broken but not, Jack suspected, beyond repair. Life had disap-pointed her, and she'd learned to roll with the punches. She was a survivor.

'You seem like intelligent women,' Alexi said. 'What was so fascinating about such a rat of a man? I'd love to know because, frankly, I'm not seeing it myself.'

'You had to be there,' Grace replied curtly.

'In which case, I'm glad I missed that particular bus.'

'So, ladies,' Jack said, 'who do we think did away with Gerry? You all knew him well. You must have some idea. Frankly, Alexi and I are stumped. The more we delve, the more suspects with compelling motives crawl out the woodwork. A woman scorned is my best bet and right now, there are three of you in this room, with Maggie waiting in the wings.'

The ladies looked at one another and simultaneously shook their heads.

'We all loved him, in our different ways,' Grace said. 'None of us wanted him dead.'

'Someone clearly did,' Alexi said, sounding all out of patience.

'Right then. Your stud farm antics,' Jack said, turning to

Celeste. 'Who was the brains behind it and think carefully before you deny all knowledge because it won't wash.'

'Baxter was the contact here in Lambourn,' she replied with asperity. 'That's all I know.'

Alexi rolled her eyes. 'Try again,' she said, tutting impatiently.

'It is true what I told you about meeting Gerry in France. He'd stopped in Chantilly on the way back to England. We got talking about horses, he came to the stud, and I found myself confiding in him about Sound Advice's inability to perform. He said he thought there might be a solution and that's how it all started. I met James Alton once or twice but no one else.'

'You met Grace,' Polly said, looking up at Celeste with hatred and disillusionment reflected in her features.

'She came to Chantilly with Gerry one time early on. He told me she would be able to help us.'

'By setting Polly up in a B&B in Lambourn, presumably,' Alexi replied, 'thereby giving Gerry a bolthole. A legitimate reason to come and go without it being remarked upon. With friends like you...'

Alexi's words were met with a deafening silence.

'So, none of you are going to tell us who ran the operation.' Jack rolled his eyes as he spoke. 'Which leaves us to draw our own conclusions. Of course, the police will be all over it and I dare say they'll turn something up.'

'No! You cannot...'

Jack glowered at Celeste. 'I think you'll find that I can and will. You are my first choice,' he added, pointing an accusatory finger at her. 'You have the strength and determination to see it through and the most to lose if it fails. You're also ruthless, accustomed to getting your own way and I suspect that living on the bread line wouldn't match up to the lifestyle you've grown accustomed to.'

'Me?' She pointed at her own chest. 'I don't have any contacts here in England and haven't been over here for ages. Sure, I went along with Gerry's idea, but he was the one who made it happen.'

'Blame the dead guy.' Alexi rolled her eyes. 'That's convenient.'

Jack shook his head. 'Don't play me for a fool, Celeste. It's your neck on the line here because all this *will* come out so you might as well try and help yourself.'

Celeste threw up her hands. 'I cannot tell you what I don't know.'

'Gerry was planning to leave England, presumably to settle with you, Celeste,' Alexi said, 'and someone went to extreme lengths to prevent him, always supposing he was killed for that reason and not by some other scorned female we know nothing about. However, if it was his business activities that got him murdered, then it implies someone involved with the syndicate fixing didn't want him to quit. That's why the identity of the person at the top is so vital, and why Inspector Vickery needs to be made aware of what we now know.'

'No!' Celeste held up a hand. 'Please.' She looked terrified. 'This is more dangerous than you can possibly know.'

'Why?' Jack asked.

'I cannot say. Believe me, if I could then I would. All I can tell you is that none of us will be safe if the police start taking a serious look. Let me have a day, just to see if I can make people see reason.'

'No more than that,' Jack said. 'You are Gerry's next of kin and the police *will* want to talk to you.'

'Yes, of course.'

Jack glanced at Alexi, hoping she'd catch on. To her credit, she didn't hesitate.

'Take a room here at the hotel. It will make things easier if we know where you are.'

'Thank you.'

'Are you all right, Polly?' Alexi asked. 'Silly question, of course you're not. It's a lot for you to take in.'

'I want you gone,' she said to Grace, bitterness in her tone. 'I believed you when you said that Alexi had come between a reconciliation with you and Jack, which is why I persecuted her. But all the time, you were taking advantage of Jack's presence here as an excuse to stay in close touch with me. You used me, just like people have used me my entire life.' She shuddered. 'Do I have doormat tattooed across my forehead?'

'Polly, no! I'm so sorry. It was never supposed to come to this. It all just ran out of control. I couldn't tell you. There never seemed to be a right time.'

'Go home, Grace,' Jack said. 'You're not needed here. But let's be clear about one thing. If you are profiting from Celeste's scheme, then I won't have your back. You're on your own.'

Grace glanced at Jack, then Alexi and Polly but got nothing back from their stony expressions. With a sigh and without saying a word, she turned on her heel and left the room.

'Do you want to stay here with us for now, Polly?' Alexi surprised herself by asking.

'Thanks, but no.' Polly threw back her head and closed her eyes, breathing deeply. 'I'm stronger than I look, and I'll get through this. I've had a lot of practice at dealing with disappointment. Anyway, despite everything, at least it looks less likely that I'll be accused of murdering Gerry. Although, if I'd known what I now know about him then I might have been severely tempted.' She shook her head. 'How could I have been so comprehensively taken in by him?'

'You certainly weren't the only one.'

'I didn't believe Maggie, but I think a part of me always suspected that Gerry wasn't the real deal. I just didn't want to face reality.' She smiled at Alexi. 'I'm really sorry about the way I behaved before. It was juvenile and unfair.'

'Don't give it another thought,' Alexi replied. 'Stay and have some tea with Jack. It will give Grace time to clear her stuff out from yours. I don't suppose you want to see her again right now. If ever.'

'Thanks, I will.'

'Celeste, come with me,' Alexi said curtly, not looking at the Frenchwoman. 'I'll find you a room.'

Alexi consulted Cheryl regarding room availability and, promising to fill her in later, showed Celeste up to a small room at the back of the hotel.

'Thanks,' she said.

'I'm not doing it for you,' Alexi replied, leaving the room and closing the door softly behind her. She couldn't trust herself alone with the woman without giving way to the temptation to throttle her. There was something inherently flawed about a female who used her looks to get what she wanted. From what she knew of Gerry, they sounded like a match made in hell.

She returned to the kitchen to find Jack and Polly deep in conversation.

'Polly's going to call on Maggie,' Jack said, smiling up at Alexi. 'I've said I think that's a good idea.'

'Is it a good idea?' Alexi asked, once they'd seen Polly off the premises. 'One of them could well have killed Gerry.'

'I don't think any of the ladies killed him,' Jack replied, 'but I do think that Celeste knows a damned sight more about the brains behind the syndicate scheme than she's letting on. That's why she showed her face. She's running scared.'

'And, let me guess, that's why you haven't picked up the phone to Vickery yet.'

'Clever girl! She's going to lead us to Mister Big. Talking of which, excuse me for a moment.'

Alexi wasn't left alone with Cosmo and Toby for long since Jack returned very quickly.

'I've put a tracker on her hire car,' he said. 'Give me your phone.'

Alexi handed it over and watched Jack as he downloaded an app and keyed in a code.

'We'll be able to see where she goes, and when,' he said.

'Is that even legal?'

Jack grinned. 'Not remotely.'

'Okay, James Bond. So what do we do in the meantime?'

'We wait. It won't be for long. She knows I have to tell Vickery about her, so she'll have to act fast.'

'My money's on her heading for Baxter's,' Alexi said.

'Yeah, perhaps.' Jack waggled a hand from side to side.

'You don't think so.'

'I don't think the brains behind the operation will show his or her hand quite that blatantly, but I could be wrong.'

'You? Wrong?' Alexi grinned. 'Never!'

Jack laughed. 'It has been known, I won't lie, but not often.'

Alexi's expression sobered. 'I never thought the day would dawn when I felt sorry for Polly. But the fact of the matter is, she's been manipulated by controlling people all her life. I was proud of the way she reacted to Celeste's presence and feel that we could maybe be friends once the dust settles. Polly and me that is, not Celeste.'

'Yeah, I noticed.' Jack rubbed his jaw. 'Celeste and Grace have been in contact after Gerry's murder; that much is undeniable. Celeste's first action was to clear out that overseas account and stash the funds somewhere else. But the murder would have scared her rigid and she needed to come over here. That's why she contacted Alton. She needed him to tell us about her. She could hardly ask Grace to do the honours.'

'Because Vickery would have found out about her sooner or later?'

'And because, I'm guessing here, there's been a falling out amongst thieves, to coin a phrase.'

'You don't think Gerry was killed because he wanted to pull out?'

Jack shook his head emphatically. 'It doesn't add up. If he was going off to France to live with Celeste then there was no reason why the scheme couldn't have carried on. No, Gerry crossed a line and Celeste is worrying that she'll meet the same fate. That's why she came over and didn't go to the police.'

'She didn't need to come to us either.'

'Perhaps not, but she needed to find out how much we know and, more to the point, what the police know.'

'I still think you should tell Vickery.' Alexi frowned. 'He won't be best pleased when he finds out we took matters into our own hands.'

'Tomorrow. I promise we'll talk to him tomorrow. Hopefully, Celeste will lead us to the horse's mouth, so to speak, before then. Vickery can't use illegal bugs, so he'll have to play it by the book and if he goes into Baxter's yard, he won't find anything there that's incriminating.'

'Neglected dogs notwithstanding,' Alexi said, sniffing. 'You think Celeste will lead us somewhere else?' She frowned. 'But how will that help? We're not going to confront a cold-blooded murderer, are we?'

Jack winked at her. 'Not a chance but it would be nice to identify him or her, wouldn't it, and then let Vickery take over.'

'You're enjoying this, aren't you?' Alexi cried accusingly.

'The only part I'm enjoying is not being tied down by the limitations placed on a serving police officer. It's nice to be able to think outside the box.'

'I guess.' But Alexi wasn't convinced his plan would work. 'I'm sorry that Grace is mixed up in it all.'

'It couldn't matter less. Come on, let's get ourselves home. There's not much more we can do today and if Celeste goes anywhere, we'll know.' Jack tapped his phone for emphasis. 'Let's have some time for ourselves.'

19

Celeste's car didn't leave Hopgood Hall's parking area all evening. A call to Drew confirmed that the woman herself hadn't left her room. She'd had a meal delivered and not shown her face in the public areas which begged the question, what was she doing? Who was she talking to?

Jack wished he could have access to her mobile and see who she'd called, wondering for the thousandth time where Gerry's burner phone had got to. Presumably, the killer had taken it, casting more doubt on Polly being the guilty party. She most likely wasn't even aware that Gerry *had* a second phone. And even if she did know, Jack very much doubted whether she could have calmly stabbed the love of her life and then rifled through his things, looking for a rogue phone. She wouldn't have realised its significance.

Would she?

Jack tried to relax over dinner and a bottle of wine, but his mind was racing with increasingly unlikely scenarios. What if he had got it wrong? Would his arrogant assumption that he could bring a desperate murderer to book without the help of Berkshire's finest prove to be his downfall? Or worse, see someone else done away with. God forbid that Alexi got caught in the crossfire! She had taken Polly's case to heart and would, Jack knew, do anything, take whatever risk necessary, to prove her innocence.

But what if Polly wasn't innocent?

Jack hadn't lost sight of the capabilities of women who'd been used and then callously discarded, so remained to be convinced in that respect.

He wondered if he'd done the right thing in sending Grace packing. If she could cause problems, out of a sense of spite or whatever, then she would. Even so, he knew her well enough to feel satisfied that she was a very small peripheral cog in a sophisticated enterprise and that she'd have the sense to keep her head down, at least until the dust settled. His unlamented former nearest-and-dearest would run home to lick her wounds in solitude. He was positive that she wouldn't cause any problems and, as a bonus, would now steer well clear of him and Alexi.

Every cloud, and all that.

'What are you thinking?' Alexi was curled up in the corner of the settee they shared with a wine glass in her hand and her feet resting in Jack's lap.

'That I've probably missed a dozen things,' he replied with a wry smile.

'There is such a thing as overthinking, you know.' She yawned and stretched one arm above her head. 'Anyway, my money's on Celeste being the mastermind.'

'Hmm.' Jack waggled a hand from side to side. 'Possibly.'

'We've considered just about everyone else and none of them seem capable, but Celeste is as hard as nails beneath that pretty exterior and, by her own admission, would do just about anything to keep her family business solvent.'

'I should have mentioned, I heard back from Danny. He's done a deep delve into the Seers and the Grants. Their backgrounds are squeaky clean. I don't think Polly's other guests are anything other than what they appear to be. They've got caught up in this through a combination of greed and bad judgement.'

Alexi twitched her nose. 'Which doesn't leave many other candidates. Not that I seriously suspected any of them, but still...'

'Whoever's behind the scam, if it isn't Celeste then that person isn't known to us and will keep a low profile if they have the sense they were born with. I mean, they'd be safe enough going about their legitimate daily business because if Celeste or Baxter know their identity then they'll never squeal.' Jack let out a long breath. 'I can't help feeling that we've been one step behind the mastermind all the time. That person is probably watching us chasing our tails and laughing.'

'Frustrating for you,' Alexi said, smiling.

'You have *no* idea!'

Alexi glanced at the clock, opened her mouth to speak and clearly changed her mind about what she'd intended to say. 'Come on,' she said, putting her empty glass aside. 'Let's hit the sack and come at this fresh tomorrow.'

Jack knew she was right but part of him now regretted not involving Vickery. They could have had someone on Celeste the entire night. The chances were, if she intended to meet anyone, she'd do it in the early hours. Ah well, it was too late now so he'd just have to roll with the punches.

'Come on then.'

He stood and pulled Alexi to her feet. The cat flap rattled, and Cosmo joined them with tail rigid, leading the way up the stairs. The cat's instincts had long since ceased to amaze Jack, who simply laughed.

'Our chaperone is ready to retire, it seems,' he said.

'He takes his duties very seriously.'

* * *

Jack slept badly and woke before dawn. He slipped quietly from bed, trying not to disturb Alexi, and made his way downstairs. He checked his phone and was relieved to learn that Celeste hadn't moved all night – at least not by car. He doubted whether she'd called a taxi or met anyone on foot but if she had then Jack had missed an opportunity.

Definitely should have involved Vickery.

'What are you up to, Celeste?' he muttered aloud, tapping his fingers in agitation, convinced that he'd been played.

His phone rang before Alexi emerged from the shower.

'Hey, Cassie, what's up?' he asked when his partner's name flashed up on the screen.

'Sorry, Jack. I know you've got a lot going on down there right now, but you're needed here. You've got a breakfast meeting with Houghton. I thought you might have forgotten.'

He had. Jack swore beneath his breath. It was a fraud case he'd been asked to delve into, a big contract and so far, he'd made frustratingly little progress with it. The perpetrator had got him stumped. 'Can't Danny take it?' he asked impatiently.

'No, Jack. Houghton's paying top dollar. He wants to see you and you've already cancelled twice. It won't take long.'

'Okay.' Jack did a quick calculation. It was only seven in the morning. He could make it to Newbury, see his client and be back within two hours. 'Tell him I'll be there.'

'Will do.'

Alexi emerged from the bathroom, drying her hair on a towel. 'What was that about?' she asked. 'Has Celeste moved?'

'Nothing on Celeste.' He explained about the meeting.

'Then go.' Alexi made shooing motions. 'I'll take my car to the hotel and let you know if Celeste moves a muscle. I'll check in on her as well just in case she's scarpered and left her car behind. I wouldn't put it past the conniving madam.'

'Be careful. I don't trust her an inch.'

'You worry too much.' Alexi stood on her toes and kissed Jack's cheek. 'The last thing she'll do is draw attention to herself with rash behaviour. She knows we're working with the police, so she won't harm me. Besides, I have my security detail.'

On cue, Cosmo wrapped himself around Alexi's legs and mewled.

'That makes me feel much better.'

Jack grabbed his wallet and keys, threw his trusty leather jacket over one shoulder and headed for the door.

'See you in a bit,' he said, blowing her a kiss.

* * *

Alexi felt uncomfortable watching Jack leave but resisted the urge to call him back. It wasn't like her to be needy. There was just something about the ruthless nature of the investigation they'd been thrust into that made her feel distinctly uneasy. Common sense told her that only a fool would draw attention to themselves by doing anything reckless at this point, but that realisation did little to settle her skittish nerves.

'Come on,' she said to Cosmo. 'We'll have breakfast at the hotel. There's safety in numbers.'

Cosmo preceded Alexi to the door and leapt into her Mini the moment she unlocked it.

The drive to Hopgood Hall took just a few minutes. Alexi found Cheryl and Drew in their kitchen. Baby Verity was, as usual, spreading her breakfast around her highchair tray and laughing. Always laughing. The baby was a delight and Alexi loved every tiny piece of her. Toby sat immediately below Verity's perch in the hope of catching anything that fell to the floor but transferred his attention to Cosmo with a joyful yap the moment the cat put a paw through the door.

'You're early,' Cheryl said.

'Couldn't sleep.' She bent to kiss Verity's head. 'Jack got called to a meeting, so I thought I'd update you. First off though, what's Celeste been up to?'

'She hasn't moved from her room. She ordered breakfast and it was just taken up to her so we know she's still there.'

'Right. I won't check on her then. I feel no pressing need to look at her disgustingly pretty face any time soon.' Alexi poured coffee for herself and fed Cosmo a pouch of dry food.

'Come on then,' Drew said. 'What gives? We're dying of curiosity here.'

Alexi helped herself to toast and gave her friends a brief rundown of events.

'Blimey!' Drew scratched his head. 'Life is never dull around you two, is it?'

'I wouldn't mind a bit of dull right now,' Alexi replied. 'Dull has a lot going for it.'

'You need to hand it over to Vickery,' Cheryl said, looking worried. 'You don't get paid to take risks with homicidal maniacs on the loose. You don't get paid at all, come to that. I can see that Polly was manipulated but she did make your life very difficult for months. You don't owe her anything.'

'I know, and Jack has promised that he will tell Vickery everything once he gets back from his meeting. He gave Celeste one day and if she hasn't made a move by this morning then her time will have run out.'

'She could have spoken to just about anyone,' Drew pointed out.

'I'm sure she has.'

Drew pushed himself to his feet and extracted a very sticky Verity from her highchair. He wiped her fingers and mouth with a damp cloth and then swung her in the air, making her giggle. 'Come along then, princess,' he said. 'Let's get you cleaned up properly. You stay here with Alexi and keep her company, love,' he added, addressing Cheryl. 'You've got to start taking it easier.'

Cheryl patted her extended stomach. 'I felt the baby move this morning,' she said, beaming. 'This one's a boy, judging by the strength of his kick.'

Alexi grinned at her friend. 'Boys are supposed to be less trouble.'

They chatted until Cheryl was called away to deal with an emergency in the bar. Alexi tapped her fingers but was unable to settle to anything. She kept checking the app on her phone every two minutes, just to be sure that she hadn't missed Celeste slipping away. Ordinarily, she'd have had a dozen things to do at any one time and was never idle but today, her concentration was shot.

She stood up, stretched and then stashed her breakfast plate in the dishwasher. She followed the activity in the courtyard as the gardeners did their thing, cutting back and getting the area ready for the onset of summer. It made her think of Faye, the lady that she and Jack had met during the investigation into her daughter's murder. Faye had green fingers and now lived in the village. It was beyond time that Alexi gave her a call and arranged to meet up. She picked up her phone with the intention of doing so and gaped when she noticed that Celeste's car had moved. She had been so taken up with watching for the movement in question that she'd missed it when it actually happened.

Without hesitation, she grabbed her bag and called to Cosmo. He was snoozing with Toby in their shared basket but was instantly alert, tail aloft, ready to accompany her. She had to follow Celeste; she had no choice. They hadn't come this far to give up now. Her journalistic instinct wouldn't permit her to wimp out anyway. The tracker meant that she could keep well back and there was an outside chance that she'd catch a glimpse of whoever she met with. There was no danger, she told herself repeatedly. Besides, she had Cosmo to keep her safe.

She ran to her car, fired up the engine and followed the direction that Celeste had taken. Cosmo sat in the passenger seat, fully alert, peering through the windscreen. She resisted the urge to close in on Celeste and stayed several cars behind. Pressing the button on her steering wheel, she rang Jack.

'Bugger!' she muttered when it went straight to voicemail.

She left a brief message, telling him what she was doing, secure in the knowledge that he would be able to track Celeste's progress on his app too. There really was no danger, she told herself repeatedly, wondering if that was actually the case why she felt inexplicably anxious. She had no patience with members of either sex who threw themselves recklessly into dangerous situations with no form of backup. With that thought in mind, she considered calling Vickery but dismissed the idea before it could take hold. The explanation was simply too complicated. She'd just see where Celeste went and then drive straight on.

She absolutely would!

'Baxter's yard, I knew it,' she said to Cosmo when Celeste's car turned off in that direction.

That created a problem because the track was narrow, and secluded. There was no possibility of her being able to see who Celeste met with – and she was betting it wouldn't be Baxter. Baxter might not even be there. What to do? She reduced her speed and drummed her fingers on the steering wheel, thinking matters through. The isolation could work in her favour insofar as whoever met with Celeste would have to drive there. She could take a picture of any vehicles that looked out of place, or any vehicles at all come to that, and let Vickery take it from there.

With a plan, of sorts, that she could live with, Alexi took a deep breath and drove on. There was an old Range Rover rusting away in the parking area, along with a couple of ancient cars that probably belonged to grooms. Celeste's hire car was there too, the engine clicking as it cooled down. Alexi's eye was drawn to a pickup truck that looked new and didn't have a scrap of mud adhering to it.

Alexi's heart rate accelerated as she took a picture of the number plate. Okay, she'd done what she came to do so it was time to scarper. Even as the thought percolated through her brain, she opened the door and climbed out the car. Cosmo followed her and she pushed the door closed again quietly, keen not to draw attention to herself. If Baxter and Celeste were in the tack room then Alexi ought to be able to peep over the windowsill and see if she could identify the driver of the pickup.

He could be a horse owner, of course, but Alexi doubted it. The driver might not, she reasoned, be the same person as the owner. Either way, if she got a look at him, she'd either know him or at least know what he looked like. That could be the vital lead and she had no intention of letting the guilty party escape because she was too scared to act without Jack at her shoulder.

She fished her phone from her bag, put it on vibrate, and slipped it into the back pocket of her jeans, within easy reach should she need to call for the cavalry. An illegal spray can of Mace went into the other pocket.

'Stay close,' she muttered to Cosmo, who didn't need to be told. The reassuring pressure of his body against her shin gave her the courage to plough on. There would never be a better opportunity to crack this case, she told herself, thinking that she would enjoy writing the inside story.

Ever the journalist!

Alexi walked towards the tack room as though she had every reason in the world to be there. In the event that she was challenged, it would seem less suspicious if she wasn't caught creeping about. She glanced towards the stables, wondering where the owners of the two old cars were. Fortunately, they were nowhere near her location, at least not at present.

She almost turned and ran on several occasions, but Cosmo had gone into stalking mode and wouldn't be easily called off now. She had done more dangerous things during her journalistic career, she reminded herself. Even if Gerry's killer was in that tack room, he'd hardly bump her off here in broad daylight. Would he? Alexi had absolutely no idea how desperate he actually was but remained determined not to give in to irrational fear.

Just one peep and if the person was known to her then it would perhaps make sense of a senseless situation.

Hold that thought!

She reached the tack room window, which was grimy and covered with cobwebs on the inside. She could barely see through the glass and struggled to withhold a sneeze when she breathed in dust. She could hear the voices coming from inside clearly enough. She recognised Celeste's and also Baxter's nasal whine. Recognition of the third voice caused a combination of shock and fear to trickle down her spine.

What the hell!

The sound of a voice coming from the nearby loose boxes caused her to start violently, and to knock over a pitchfork that had been leaning against the wall. It fell to the concrete with a loud clatter. Alexi froze when the voices inside immediately stopped.

'What was that?'

The door was thrust open and a man's muscular form filled the aperture.

'You!' he said in a threatening tone, glowering at Alexi. 'You just can't keep your nose out of other people's business,' he added, sneering. 'You journalists are all alike.'

* * *

If Jack had told his client once that he'd found no evidence of fraud within his organisation then he must have told him a dozen times during this one breakfast meeting alone. But Houghton was having none of it. He kept insisting that Jack continue his search, going over and over his reasons. Jack listened with half an ear, even though he knew the results would be the same. Houghton was the type who saw shadows on a cloudy day.

He'd put his phone on vibrate as a matter of courtesy but made a poor job of trying to appear dedicated to his client's cause. It took over an hour to wrap up what should have been a simple meeting and by the end of it, Jack was frantic. His phone had buzzed several times, and his every instinct told him that Alexi had got herself into trouble. That instinct proved on the money when he waved Houghton off and checked the tracker. Celeste was on the move, and he knew without having to be told that Alexi would have followed her.

'Damn!'

He jumped in his car, fired up the engine and left the café where he'd breakfasted with Houghton with his foot almost to the floor, sending up a shower of gravel in his wake. He glanced at the display and could see that Celeste was heading in Baxter's direction. He played his messages and Alexi's voice confirmed that she'd followed. He tried ringing her back but his call went straight to voicemail.

Jack called himself all sorts of an arrogant sod for not having updated Vickery the night before. He was a bit long in the tooth to cover himself in glory and his ego could well have landed the woman he loved in mortal danger. He called Vickery now. Better late than never. His ex-colleague picked up and, to his credit, didn't waste time berating Jack when he succinctly explained the situation.

'I'll get someone up to the yard right away,' he said briskly.

'No lights or sirens,' Jack warned. 'We don't know what we're dealing with.'

'You might have thought about that *before* putting trackers on cars.'

'Point taken.' Jack winced. 'I'm probably closer than your guys anyway,' he added, aware that patrol cars didn't make a habit of lurking in country lanes and whoever Vickery sent would have to come from perhaps as far away as Reading. 'I'm on my way back from Newbury and the yard's on my route. Just needed you to be aware.'

Jack cut the connection and concentrated on driving the narrow lanes once he'd pulled off the A4. He was held up twice by strings of racehorses and, more frustratingly, by a tractor that seemed to think ten miles an hour was pushing it. Finally clear of the hazards, he pulled into Baxter's yard and was confronted by Alexi's Mini.

The first thing he heard was her scream.

* * *

Alexi simply gaped at Polly's son, Michael.

'You,' she repeated.

'You should have kept your nose out,' Michael reiterated, 'so only have yourself to blame for what happens next.'

The friendly tone of their previous meeting had been replaced by a threatening rumble that made Alexi's skin crawl. His expression was hard, flat and totally without mercy. She was confronting a cold-blooded killer who wouldn't know how to spell the word 'empathy'. They had finally discovered the identity of the man who'd killed Gerry and would kill again without hesitation. Cosmo arched his back and growled. Michael laughed when the cat launched himself at his ankles. Michael kicked him away without taking his gaze off Alexi, who was more concerned for Cosmo. She need not have been, she realised. Cosmo was too smart for Michael, had anticipated the kick and avoided it. But he might not be so lucky next time. Alexi wasn't sure she would be able to prevent Cosmo attacking for a second time in his defence of her and the thought of him being injured filled her with ungovernable rage.

'Deal with her,' Michael said dismissively to Baxter when he and Celeste spilled from the tack room.

'Me?' Baxter looked terrified. 'What do you want me to do to her?'

'Oh, for the love of God, I'm surrounded by idiots!' Michael threw up his hands. 'Must I do everything myself? Use your sense. She came here alone. Detain her while Celeste and I finish our conversation somewhere more private.'

'I didn't sign up for no violence,' Baxter said, looking at Michael with a combination of fear and aggression in his expression.

'You take the spoils, you deal with the fallout.' Michael's voice was a threatening rumble as he strode towards his pickup, assuming that his instructions would be obeyed to the letter.

Alexi glanced at Cosmo, who fortunately hadn't followed Michael. Instead, he remained at Alexi's side, hissing and growling at Baxter, keeping him pinned to the spot.

Celeste sent Alexi a look that could have been anything from sympathy to spite as she ran to her own vehicle.

'It doesn't have to be this way,' Alexi said to Baxter, breaking the ensuing silence. 'You got in above your head, didn't you, but we can help you now we know who's behind it all.'

'You'll never prove it.' Baxter sniffed. 'Sorry,' he added, clicking his fingers for Silgo and backing away from Cosmo. 'Get her, boy!'

Silgo slunk forward with obvious reluctance, saw Cosmo and froze. Cosmo pushed home his advantage by hissing at the dog and reaching out a paw to scratch his nose. Silgo yelped. Alexi could sense Baxter's fear, grasped the opportunity that Cosmo had created and followed her instincts. Crouching down, she called to Silgo whilst Cosmo held Baxter off. Silgo appeared to recognise her and wagged his tail as he stepped forward and licked her fingers.

'Bloody useless creature!'

Baxter picked up a baseball bat and raised it above his head, but whether to clout her, Cosmo or the dog was a matter of opinion. Not that it mattered who his intended target was since Alexi had no intention of letting any of them get injured. She felt for her Mace, but the situation was snatched from her control when Silgo found his courage and attacked.

But it quickly became clear that she wasn't his intended victim.

She could only watch in stupefaction as a growl rumbled in his throat. He then leapt towards Baxter and sank his fangs into the fleshy part of the lower leg of the man who had brutalised him for so long. Cosmo looked almost smug as he watched, appearing to know that his services were now surplus to requirements.

20

Jack heard a commotion, barking and shouting, and approached the tack room at a run. He stopped dead in his tracks when he encountered Baxter having his leg mangled by his own dog. The man was turning the air blue with his language as he yelled at Silgo to let him go. But Silgo appeared to be enjoying his revenge and didn't loosen a molar. If Alexi had the ability to call the creature off, she was taking her time about it. But Jack didn't care. All he was worried about was finding Alexi alive and unharmed. Her penchant for confronting dangerous criminals had already cost him ten years of his life.

'Ah, Jack, there you are.' She sent him a sunny smile but he could see that she was severely rattled. 'You missed all the drama. I think that will do, Silgo,' she added, and the dog obediently released Baxter's leg. 'Well done,' she added, patting the creature's matted head.

'What the hell...' Jack scratched his chin, unable to decide which question to ask first.

'It's Michael. Polly's son. He's the one behind it all,' Alexi said breathlessly.

'Michael?' Jack blinked. 'Seriously? Are you absolutely sure about that?'

'It took me by surprise too, but there's no mistake. He was a very different person to the amiable man we met: definitely a Jekyll and Hyde character. Anyway, he just took off with Celeste. We need to find him before he goes to ground.'

'Vickery's men are on the way.'

The sound of a patrol car screeching to a halt made further explanation unnecessary. Jack had a quick word with the uniforms, left them to deal with Baxter and turned towards his car.

'Leave yours here,' he said. 'We'll go together in mine.'

'Okay, but Silgo comes too,' she insisted. 'He's earned the right and I'm not leaving him here to be carted off to a kennel, or whatever.'

'Sure, but Cosmo...'

Jack glanced at Cosmo, aware that he was both very protective and disinclined to share Alexi. It had taken Jack a while to be accepted. On this occasion though, other than issuing a warning hiss to the much larger dog, Cosmo seemed happy with the arrangement. Jack simply shook his head. Cosmo had long since lost the ability to surprise him.

'I'm worried about Polly,' he said, once they were all loaded into his car, with Silgo occupying the entire back seat, wagging his tail and apparently realising that his fortunes had just taken a turn for the better. 'Michael obviously has hang-ups that hark back to his fractured childhood and holds Polly responsible for whatever trauma he endured. He hid them well when we talked, I'll give him that.'

'I agree,' Alexi said tersely, stroking Cosmo, who occupied her knee, seemingly unperturbed to have had his services usurped by a mere dog. 'But it would be madness for him to go anywhere near

Polly now. He's aware that I saw him and that it'll be the first place I look.'

'He thinks Baxter has you under lock and key. Everyone appears to be petrified of Michael and no one dares defy him. Be that as it may, the man himself must realise that the game's up. If he's got half as many hang-ups about Polly and his difficult childhood as appears to be the case, then he won't make himself scarce before he confronts her because that's what all this has been about. Laying the demons of his childhood by ruining Polly's life.'

'Which is why he killed Gerry and made it appear as though she was to blame.'

'Right.' Jack gave a terse nod. 'But why kill Gerry when their scam was running so smoothly? If Michael was head honcho, then he would have been benefiting the most. Think of his upmarket living arrangements. That ought to have been a red flag but I was completely taken in by the man.' He let out a frustrated breath. 'None of it makes sense.'

'We're not dealing with a rational person. I think he inherited his mother's mental health issues—'

'Then like I already said, he was damned good at hiding them. He had me fooled.' He bashed the steering wheel with the heel of his hand. 'I dismissed him as a suspect immediately after we spoke to him. I must be losing my edge. Anyway, my guess, and I'm no medical expect, is that Michael's suffering from some sort of split personality disorder. When we called at his flat, we saw the easy-going guy who'd put his past behind him and was getting on with his life.'

'He expected someone to come knocking because he knew Gerry was dead, so he had time to get into character, if you like.'

'Right. The side we didn't see until today is the resentful guy who'd never gotten past being caught in the middle of his warring parents' dramas. The kid who'd witnessed his mother getting beaten on a regular basis and doing nothing to protect herself or her family. Trauma causes compartmentalisation, in my experience. Some just push the bad old memories to the back of their minds, leave them there and get on with life. Others get professional help to work through it. But the Michaels of this world allow their resentments to simmer away until one day, it all comes out in a dramatic burst of revenge.'

Alexi nodded. 'You could well be right. Such situations are not uncommon. It's always the kids who suffer but most of them don't turn murderous.' Alexi paused. 'Why did Michael leave Baxter to deal with me? I could see that Baxter didn't have the stomach for violence so surely Michael could see it too.'

'He didn't want you dead, darling. He has no reason to fight with you. He just wanted to buy himself some time so that he could confront Polly.' Jack put his foot down. 'Let's hope we're not too late.'

Nothing more was said until they reached Polly's B&B.

'What if the other guests are in there?' Alexi asked. 'Michael can't afford to wait. He knows he's on borrowed time.'

'There are no cars here, other than Michael's pickup,' Jack replied, pointing to the vehicle in question parked at an angle over Polly's drive.

He pulled his phone out of his pocket and had a terse conversation with Vickery.

'Keep the troops out of sight until I give you the word,' he said. 'This guy has nothing left to lose and clearly wants to have it out with his mother.'

'Wait for us to get there. We're five minutes out.'

'No time.'

Jack cut the call and squared his shoulders. 'No point telling you to wait here, I suppose,' he said, sighing.

'None whatsoever.'

'I had to try.' Jack rolled his eyes. 'Come on then. We can't afford to hang about.'

They approached the side door that led to the kitchen. Jack thought it unlikely that Michael would confront his mother in the kitchen so took the chance, hoping that he wouldn't spook an unstable man. It was the only point of entry that they could approach without being seen from one of the windows. Cosmo and Silgo both came with them, remaining unnaturally quiet, as though they understood the situation and what was required of them. Cosmo undoubtedly did and Silgo was obviously a fast study.

The kitchen door squeaked as Jack pushed it open. It sounded like a bomb exploding but the raised voices coming from the lounge covered the sound. Jack and Alexi exchanged a look and crept into the hallway on silent feet.

'Michael, I just don't understand.' Polly's voice sounded weak, hesitant. 'You killed Gerry and wanted me to get the blame. Why? I wasn't aware that you even knew him beyond that one meeting here.'

'My God, but you're dense!'

'I can't claim to have been mother of the year, but why would you do that to me, or to him?'

'You really don't get it, do you?' Years' worth of pent-up emotion manifested itself in a wild shrieking. 'But then you always were self-centred and weak. Everyone's favourite doormat. A born victim who never stopped to think about the effect that had on others. You're pathetic!' Michael's voice abruptly turned soft, persuasive, and he sounded entirely rational again. 'Still not to worry, Mother, you can join your beloved Gerry now and finally have him all to yourself.'

Jack moved towards the door. He'd thought Michael would want to explain himself, but it seemed he was a man in a hurry.

Jack would have to challenge him and fully intended to do so but Alexi's hand on his arm held him back.

'Wait!' she said.

Jack peered through the gap in the door between the kitchen and the lounge. Michael stood with legs splayed, towering over his terrified mother, who cowered in a chair. He had no weapon that Jack could see, other than his fists, and if he tried to use those on her then Jack would intercede in a heartbeat. Meanwhile, Alexi was right to advice caution. He'd wait and see if Michael actually condemned himself with his own words since he hadn't actually admitted to killing Gerry.

'I tried to protect you,' Polly wailed, 'really I did, but I could barely look out for myself. When your father got mad, he was like a wild animal and I thought... well, I thought that if he took it out on me then he'd leave the three of you alone.'

'Sounds like Michael takes after his father,' Alexi whispered.

'Do you have any idea what happened to me?' Michael yelled. 'The living hell I barely survived. He thumped you from time to time but I would have welcomed that sort of attention.'

'No!' Polly sounded dazed, disorientated. 'He had his faults, God alone knows he had those. But all the time he hit me, he wasn't taking the belt to you and your brother and sister.'

'You just don't get it.' Michael's voice was vicious, heavily laced with sarcasm. 'You were so wrapped up in yourself that you had no idea what he did to all three of us.'

'Michael, I had no idea. Oh my God!' She sobbed aloud. Jack peered round the door again and she was now keening, clutching her face in her hands. 'What have I done?'

'She didn't do anything,' Alexi muttered.

'I think that's Michael's point,' Jack whispered back.

'We got taken into care and everything went downhill from there on in.'

'I tried to get you back, but I was ill. They wouldn't let me see you. They said I was unfit.'

'They got that bit right.'

Polly sobbed. 'I'm so very sorry. But you've got your life together now. You can look forward.'

Alexi looked at Jack askance. 'He murdered Polly's nearest and dearest, and she seems to think he can just walk away.'

'Shush, listen.'

'I'll say that I killed Gerry. They think I did anyway and now that I know he was married and carrying on with my best friend, I have enough motives to convince any jury.' She half rose from her chair and reached out to him. 'I'll make it up to you. You can get on with your life.'

Michael sneered and slapped her hand away. 'Too little, too late.'

'No, really.' Polly fell to her knees, tears streaming down her face. 'I can't change the past, much as I might want to, but I can shape your future. And that I *do* want to do.'

'Gerry used to laugh at your neediness, do you know that?'

'Laugh. Why would he laugh?'

'Because you were so pathetically grateful for the scraps from his table. I told him you would be when I put him onto you.'

'You?' Polly sat up and pointed at her son. 'You told Gerry about me?' She shook her head. 'Why? I don't understand.'

Jack did, but he ground his jaw and said nothing, waiting for the other shoe to fall.

'Your friend Grace introduced us. I did some landscaping work on her garden and got chatting to her. Gerry was a greedy bastard, already involved with Celeste and desperate for a way to make the stud farm profitable again. I worked it all out and made a small fortune. That'll come to an end now, of course, like all good things do, but we'll be okay, Phil and me.'

'Why did you kill Gerry?' Polly asked in a tiny voice. 'It was me you had issues with, not him.'

Michael chuckled. 'Don't kill the person you hate. Take away the thing they care about the most instead and watch them suffer.'

Polly blinked back tears and simply stared at her son.

'Hurts, doesn't it,' he said, but he appeared to take little comfort from Polly's distress. 'But still, not everything's about you and if Gerry had been a good boy, I might have let him live. He got greedy though, squirreling away funds offshore that ought to have been mine and assuming I wouldn't notice.' Michael threw back his head and roared, sounding as deranged as he obviously was. 'When will people stop trying to treat me like a mug?'

'You killed Gerry because he stole from you?' Polly now looked totally bemused. Jack wondered how much more her fragile psyche could take and seriously considered breaking up the family reunion. But once again, Alexi's hand held him back.

'She's stronger than she looks,' she whispered, 'and needs to hear this.'

Jack knew they couldn't stay where they were for much longer before Michael sensed their presence. More to the point, Vickery would arrive at any time and break up the reunion. Jack wanted to hear what else Michael had to say before that situation arose. He had pushed to one side his anger regarding Grace's duplicity, aware that she'd likely been motivated by a combination of greed and the desire to get up close and personal with Jack again. She didn't really want him back and yet couldn't stand the thought of him being happy with someone else. Jack shook his head, wondering how he could ever have fallen for such a shallow, selfish person.

'Get on with it!' he muttered impatiently.

'Not just because he stole from me, but because he wanted to pack it all in. He kept bleating on about pushing our luck.' Michael snorted. 'The wimp! It was over when I said it was and not before so yeah, he'd become a liability. Maggie was getting suspicious when he didn't deliver on his promises and the fool placated her by giving her access to his offshore account. He crossed a line and had to be dealt with.'

Jack glanced at Alexi, who nodded, and the two of them stepped through the door. Michael turned and looked momentarily shocked. Then he grinned, grabbed Polly by the arm and pulled her in front of him, circling her throat with a forearm roped with muscles. The man was a landscape gardener, Jack reminded himself, toned from hours of hard physical work. He could, and probably would, crush Polly's windpipe without breaking a sweat.

'Go on then,' Jack said amiably. 'Break her neck. It's what you came here to do. Or was it that you simply wanted to brag? To let her know how clever you are. I mean, no one suspected easy-going Michael of killing anything more significant than a buddleia. It must have given you a real buzz to know that you'd fooled everyone.'

That clearly wasn't the reaction that Michael had expected. He eased the pressure fractionally on Polly's throat and, spluttering for breath, she struggled to speak.

'I killed Gerry!' she said. 'It was me all along. I'll tell the inspector everything. Michael had nothing to do with it.'

'Don't, Polly,' Alexi said gently. 'None of what happened is your fault. You were a victim too.'

'No, really... I knew about him and Maggie. You have to understand, I couldn't take it any more. We argued. I told you that, right? I gave him an ultimatum. Her or me. He laughed in my face and said he'd prefer to carry on having us both. I lost it and grabbed a knife from the kitchen and... well, you know the rest.'

'We heard it all, Polly,' Jack said.

'Well, good for you,' Michael said scornfully. 'Aren't we the clever little bunnies.'

Alexi glanced at Jack, undoubtedly thinking along the same lines as him. Michael was severely deranged. And unpredictable. Making it impossible to guess how he'd react to being challenged.

'You should have just legged it from Baxter's yard and made a run for it,' Jack said, feeling no pressing need to placate the guy. Never be predictable, he reminded himself. 'There's a chance you might have got away. But now, you're looking at spending the rest of your days behind bars, never seeing Phil again. He'll find someone else, move on with his life and forget all about you.' Jack knew he'd hit upon Michael's Achilles heel when he scowled.

'Leave Phil out of this,' he growled. 'He knows nothing.'

'He will when your name is splashed across all the headlines. You've done enough harm. Give it up. If you hurt your mother, they'll throw away the key.'

'Why *did* you come back here?' Alexi asked. 'It was taking one hell of a risk and Jack's right; you won't get away.'

'Unfinished business,' Michael replied. 'I didn't want to kill Gerry because he was still useful.'

'Running the scam?' Jack suggested.

Michael waved the possibility aside. 'He was cleaning Polly out, bit by bit. I wanted her left with nothing other than a pile of debts, but he couldn't even get that right.'

He really was vindictive. 'Never mind,' Jack said. 'We can't have it all. You've made your point but time's up.'

'Seems I've got nothing to lose, in that case.'

Jack could see the intent in his eyes and sprang forward a split second before he tightened his hold on Polly. At the same time, Alexi squirted Michael's eyes with the can of Mace she'd concealed in her jeans pocket.

Michael howled, released Polly and took a swing at Jack. But Jack had anticipated that and had got in a hefty blow to Michael's midriff first. It was like smashing his knuckles into a brick wall but

Michael obviously felt it. He topped backwards, knocking over a table as he fell to the floor, clawing at his eyes as expletives tumbled from his lips.

Jack stood over him, ready to subdue him if he attempted anything stupid, as did Cosmo and Silgo. He had the sense not to and simply remained where he was, grinning up inanely at Jack.

'I had you fooled, didn't I?' he asked.

Alexi went straight to Polly, who was now weeping uncontrollably. She held her in her arms and made soothing sounds, almost as though she was placating a child.

'This is all my fault!' she wailed.

'It'll be okay,' Alexi said, but Jack failed to see how. Polly would need professional help to make sense of what had happened to her.

A squeal of tyres heralded the arrival of Vickery and uniformed backup. Jack gave him a brief account of proceedings and watched Michael as he was led away in handcuffs, still laughing to himself.

'I heard the commotion.'

Maggie put her head round the door, looking wary as her gaze focused on Polly. Everyone waited to see what Polly would do. Jack wasn't surprised when she pushed herself to her feet, crossed the room to join her friend and they fell into one another's arms. Two women who had fallen for the same man's toxic charm, comforting one another as they mourned his loss.

'Look after her,' Jack said, as he led Alexi from the room.

21

Alexi and Jack sat with Cheryl and Drew in Hopgood Hall's gardens a couple of days later, enjoy the spring sunshine as they watched Verity tumbling about on the lawns. Cosmo washed his face and pretended to take no interest. Silgo, now washed and groomed and already filling out after just a few days of being fed properly, joined in with Verity's game with unbridled enthusiasm.

'I find it astonishing that Cosmo has allowed Silgo to join the family,' Drew said, throwing a rubber toy for the dog and watching him lope after it with an ungainly gait, barking and wagging at the same time. Alexi thought his leg might have been broken at some point. Nothing would surprise her about Baxter's lacklustre care for his animals. She wondered how he had ever gained a trainer's licence and was very glad that his establishment would soon be shut down, the few horses he had in training moved to better establishments.

'Cosmo recognises a badly treated animal when he sees one,' Alexi said, pride in her tone. 'He was one himself once and is willing to give Silgo an opportunity to prove himself.'

'Just so long as Silgo understands Cosmo's the boss, which he appears to,' Jack added, grinning.

'Do you intend to keep him?' Cheryl asked.

'Well, Baxter won't be free to claim him back any time soon,' Alexi said, 'and I don't think Silgo would return to him even if that situation arose and so, I guess...'

She glanced at Jack, who shook his head and smiled at the same time. 'Of course he stays.'

Alexi leaned over and kissed his cheek.

'What will happen to Polly's son?' Cheryl asked.

'He's being assessed to see if he's fit to stand trial,' Jack replied, 'but my guess is that he'll deemed to be not of sound mind. It's sad really. He tried to be mother and father to his siblings because Polly was incapable of looking out for them, and he took the brunt of his father's temper when it wasn't directed at Polly. Apparently, there are still marks on his body from where he was thrashed.'

'It makes me so mad!' Alexi added. 'Then he got passed around the care system, separated from his brother and sister, who both fared better in that particular lottery than he did. Michael was largely neglected; the other two were more fortunate. They were too young to remember much about their parents,' Alexi explained, 'and have gone on to make decent lives for themselves without being fettered by any of Michael's hang-ups. They had no interest in reconnecting with Polly.'

'But Michael couldn't let the past go,' Jack added. 'He felt the injustice at the way he'd been... well, an irrelevance, I suppose, and it simmered away beneath the surface. Then Grace managed to stir it all up again.'

'She really is a piece of work,' Cheryl said, patting the back of Jack's hand.

'Yeah.' Jack threw his head back and closed his eyes. 'That about sums her up.'

'Why did she do it?' Drew asked. 'What did she hope to gain from it?'

'Money, obviously,' Jack replied. 'It's always been her god.' He sighed. 'She left me for a guy twenty years her senior, with grown kids, who didn't have to worry about her expensive tastes. She kept her part-time job at Holby's to make it seem like she was independent, which she absolutely wasn't. Then Barry's investments went sour. He'd been taking risks, apparently. Gambling on a falling stock market, which never ends well. Anyway, he lost almost everything, had to cut his cloth and Grace—'

'Moved on,' Alexi finished for him. 'For reasons that escape me, she appears to still love Jack and... well, manipulated Michael and Gerry by introducing them, then standing back and watching the show.'

'Will she be charged with anything?' Cheryl asked. 'It sounds to me as though she ought to be.'

'Doubt it,' Jack replied. 'She wasn't actively involved with the stud farm scam. The racing authorities on both sides of the channel are all over it and Celeste, Baxter and Alton will have their collars felt in the not too distant future.'

'The lengths people go to in order to assuage their past,' Drew said, sighing. 'It never fails to surprise me.'

'Michael should have had professional help years back,' Alexi said. 'If he'd been in a stable, loving household, he undoubtedly would have. But then again, if he'd been in that situation, he probably wouldn't have needed it. We are, after all, the product of our upbringing. He hadn't known love and affection until he met Phil. Then he felt he had something to prove to the man he loved, whose talents were apparently not properly rewarded by his employers. He wanted to throw in the day job in order to concentrate on writing a novel and Michael wanted to be in a position to make that happen for him, and to keep him in style.'

'He wanted to impress Phil, in other words, when no impression was necessary,' Jack explained. 'Phil adores him and was devastated when he learned what he'd done. He's insisting that he'll stand by him, get him the help he needs, but who knows?'

'I almost feel sorry for him,' Cheryl said. 'Even so, I'll reserve my sympathy for Polly. She's lost the man she adored but who didn't deserve her adoration.'

'No one deserves to be murdered,' Jack said, 'but Gerry sailed close to the wind, played fast and loose with the affections of the women in his life *and* got greedy. A toxic combination that was never going to end well.'

'Well, at least this time, there's no bad publicity for this establishment to worry about,' Cheryl said. 'We must be grateful for small mercies.'

'Will you write the inside story?' Drew asked, addressing the question to Alexi.

'Oh, I think so, if Polly wants me to. It might help her to recover if she sees her life sympathetically portrayed. She and Maggie are helping one another right now. There's talk of taking a cruise, to get away and lick their wounds. I shall encourage them to do it.'

'Well, all's well that ends well,' Drew said, stretching his arms above his head before leaping from his chair and sweeping Verity up before she tumbled headlong into a fountain.

'How do you really feel about Grace?' Alexi asked Jack once Cheryl and Drew had taken themselves back inside.

'Honest truth?'

'Always.'

'I think she's a conniving madam and that I'm well shot of her. If evidence does come to light to prove that she profited from Gerry's scheme, then I won't be lifting a finger to get her out the mire.' Jack firmed his jaw. 'She's on her own.'

'I just wish our exes would leave us alone to enjoy what we do.' Alexi grinned. 'Whatever that is.'

'True, but at least Patrick has kept his head down this time,' Jack said, referring to the editor of the *Sunday Sentinel* and Alexi's former, very persistent lover.

'Don't jinx things by mentioning his name. I happen to know he's overseas right now but the moment he hears about this murder, he'll use the excuse to get onto me, asking for an exclusive.'

'A holiday doesn't sound like a bad idea to me,' Jack said, leaning back in his chair. 'Polly and Maggie have got that one right.'

Alexi smiled at Toby, who was rushing round the grounds, attempting to match Silgo's speed. Poor Silgo had spent much of his time chained up at Baxter's yard and was just starting to enjoy his newfound freedom. Toby, with his short legs, didn't have a prayer of keeping pace with the much larger dog, but that didn't prevent him from trying.

'Just so long as we can find a dog and cat friendly hotel.'

Jack rolled his eyes. 'Of course,' he said, leaning over to kiss Alexi.

ACKNOWLEDGEMENTS

My thanks to all the wonderful Boldwood team and in particular to my talented and very patient editor, Emily Ruston.

ABOUT THE AUTHOR

E.V. Hunter has written a great many successful regency romances as Wendy Soliman and revenge thrillers as Evie Hunter. She is now redirecting her talents to produce cosy murder mysteries. For the past twenty years she has lived the life of a nomad, roaming the world on interesting forms of transport, but has now settled back in the UK.

Sign up to E.V. Hunter's mailing list here for news, competitions and updates on future books.

Follow E.V. Hunter on social media:

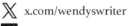 x.com/wendyswriter

 facebook.com/wendy.soliman.author

bookbub.com/authors/wendy-soliman

ALSO BY E.V. HUNTER

The Hopgood Hall Murder Mysteries

A Date To Die For

A Contest To Kill For

A Marriage To Murder For

A Story to Strangle For

A Deadly Affair

Revenge Thrillers

The Sting

The Trap

The Chase

The Scam

The Kill

The Alibi

Poison
& Pens

POISON & PENS IS THE HOME OF
COZY MYSTERIES SO POUR YOURSELF
A CUP OF TEA & GET SLEUTHING!

DISCOVER PAGE-TURNING NOVELS FROM
YOUR FAVOURITE AUTHORS &
MEET NEW FRIENDS

JOIN OUR
FACEBOOK GROUP

BIT.LYPOISONANDPENSFB

SIGN UP TO OUR
NEWSLETTER

BIT.LY/POISONANDPENSNEWS

Boldw**oo**d

Boldwood Books is an award-winning fiction publishing company seeking out the best stories from around the world.

Find out more at www.boldwoodbooks.com

Join our reader community for brilliant books, competitions and offers!

Follow us
@BoldwoodBooks
@TheBoldBookClub

Sign up to our weekly
deals newsletter

https://bit.ly/BoldwoodBNewsletter

Printed in Great Britain
by Amazon

46120257R00145